The Man Who didn't Exist

When a long-distance erotic relationship got out of hand

The Man Who didn't Exist

When a long-distance erotic relationship got out of hand

MEREO
Cirencester

Mereo Books

1A The Wool Market Dyer Street Cirencester Gloucestershire GL7 2PR
An imprint of Memoirs Publishing www.mereobooks.com

The Man Who Didn't Exist: 978-1-86151-794-4

First published in Great Britain in 2017
by Mereo Books, an imprint of Memoirs Publishing

The address for Memoirs Publishing Group Limited can be found at
www.memoirspublishing.com

The Memoirs Publishing Group Ltd Reg. No. 7834348

The Memoirs Publishing Group supports both The Forest Stewardship Council® (FSC®) and the PEFC® leading international forest-certification organisations. Our books carrying both the FSC label and the PEFC® and are printed on FSC®-certified paper. FSC® is the only forest-certification scheme supported by the leading environmental organisations including Greenpeace. Our paper procurement policy can be found at www.memoirspublishing.com/environment

Typeset in 10/15pt Century Schoolbook
by Wiltshire Associates Publisher Services Ltd. Printed and bound in Great Britain by Printondemand-Worldwide, Peterborough PE2 6XD

INTRODUCTION

During the time I have been sitting editing these emails, I have realised that life is all about people and the stories they tell, about their experiences during their lives, good and bad, and how these experiences have shaped them. Well this is my experience, my story; the story that shaped me. This is the story of how I fell in love with a man who was dominant and became his slave girl. It is a collection of email conversations that we had over a period of two separate years. The story of a poor, working-class woman and a man who claimed to be one of the most powerful men on the planet; the chairman of the Bilderberg Committee, one of the top Freemasons-rank 33, equal to the Duke of Kent, and a man who mixed with royalty and heads of state, yet he was 'The Man Who Didn't Exist;' you won't find him on the Internet or listed anywhere. But how can he *not* exist if no one knows?

Years have gone by since this exchange, the last entry on September 2010, when he was killed in Pakistan; I only found this out a year after his death, so I thought he had lied and abandoned me, when things were getting too serious. It happened the week before we were supposed to meet at last. He still haunts me; I cry whenever I think of him. I am marked by him mentally and have physically marked myself with a tattoo; I refuse to let his memory die. I find myself relating my tale to anyone who will listen, but their blank stares and disbelief just make me feel they are looking upon me as a psychotic female, one who has been scammed online by a man with a huge imagination. I know this is not true; I have found two men who confirmed his existence, though both are probably dead now. This is partly the reason why I have felt the need to publish this selection of our emails. I cannot move on. How could I form another relationship? I am, and will always be, his slave girl. He owns me heart, mind, body, spirit and soul, and I am destined to be alone until I die and join him.

Our exchange is extremely personal and mostly erotic fantasy, so why am I doing this? I have my own family whom I love, and a job I enjoy; I am content, but I miss him and cannot replace him. He promised me everything and left me with nothing, and I want some of what was promised. I want a beautiful villa in Corfu, a place he loved, and an income to keep me comfortable for the rest of my life and enable me to support my family. If I have to live without him, then I deserve to live as he intended – he owes me that much, and this book could accomplish that for me; this was also a suggestion of his within our conversations, that I write a book, so in a way I have his permission. If MI6 do still have me under observation, under protection, then I hope they will understand and let me live out the rest of my life quietly and comfortably and protect me from the people who would have me killed, the people who are erasing all traces of Him.

So here it is, mostly cut and pasted, with some of the photos I sent, starting with our profiles on the dating site Love@Lycos in 2007, when we emailed through their message system until I finally got him to give me his personal email address.

He stopped emailing me near the end of 2007. I never found out why and it hit me hard, but after two years of searching for another man to take his place, I realised that it was always going to be with him that my heart belonged, so I tried once more at Christmas 2009 and amazingly he replied, starting our exchange off again.

To begin with I cut and pasted together every individual email, complete with the date it was written, but this was confusing and I had too many words for a viable book; the signatures and kisses at the bottom of every email had to be cut too. Some emails were written within each other and sometimes we started off three or four different conversations a day, which were answered separately a week later, muddling everything up, so I have aimed to keep in the start dates of each conversation to give some idea of the time they were written.

A few emails I missed out accidentally, which has annoyed me immensely. I feel I want to ring him up and ask him if he remembers what he wrote, and that's the funny thing, I feel as if I was there with him and he did say these things to me in person; I see how women get scammed by clever men on the Internet, but he only ever wanted my company; I was there for his amusement in his stressful world, he never asked for money (he was a millionaire after all). This is what hurts me the most. I never heard him speak, I never got to hold him, to breathe in his scent, feel his body beneath his shirt, to meet his children, to walk on the beach with him, to sit in a café with him looking out over the ocean or hear him play the guitar, but most of all I never got to stand before him, look into his eyes and see my soul reflected there. Our destinies were entwined, but never joined.

I am lost.

HIS PROFILE

geordie_armani 39
Area: Norfolk
I'm really here... To make new friends
Last signed in 15/05/07
Points: 9.4
Votes: 9
"I'm not actually a Geordie..."

Description
...nor am I 'boyfriend' material. Not if I'm honest. What I am is a recently widowed father of three kids, the youngest of which is 15 months old.

If you're still reading, I am 5'10", fit & healthy, blonde hair and blue eyes. I have a sense of humour which often gets me in all sorts of trouble. I'm pretty intelligent – I took a Doctorate in Criminal Law a couple of years ago. I'm solvent (no mortgage) and, according to my kids, I'm 'pretty cool for a dad' and 'pretty smart' to boot. I wonder what they're after...

I doubt very much that Cupid logs onto this website – but if I could find some halfway decent 'adult' company (as opposed to my kids) then that would be great. Either gender is good for me, I'm not too proud to talk to anyone. Gentle, harmless flirting is good – disgustingly graphic detail is bad. I'd love to fall in love again – but I have baggage (not my phraseology; that's the label applied to my children by some of the more narrow-minded people I've met).

Before you ask, YES that is a recent picture, and YES it is me (what would be the point in putting someone else's picture on? Think about it) oh, and by the way, I have succumbed to public demand and done the Voting thing (hot or not, or whatever it's called). So go ahead – do your worst! I'm game for a laugh.

In short, I'm a genuine guy, looking to spend time with genuine people. Clear enough?

Love to you all.

These light my fire:
1. My kids.
2. Travelling.
3. Ladies who appreciate a gentleman.
4. Adult company for a change.

These leave me cold:
1. Not having any social contact
2. with people over the age of
3. fifteen!

Quick personality

Everyday occupation: Look after my family

- I'm really here...: To make new friends
- Marital status: Widowed
- Sexuality: Straight
- Children – I have: My own, hope you do too
- I smoke: Never. Smoking is fatal
- My hair colour: Blond
- Height: 5'8 – 5'10

More about me

- I am: A nice bloke
- I dress: Casual
- With the last of my money: I buy things for my kids
- Leisure/interest: Sport & health
- A perfect night is: A romantic dinner
- Holiday type: On an exotic adventure
- Music: All sorts

I dream of: peace on earth

MY PROFILE

Lavendula 45
Area: Hampshire
I'm really here... To see what happens
Last signed in 15/05/07 14.30
Points: 10
Votes 3
"INSOLENT: To fall off the Isle of Wight ferry."

Description
Hello Lycos addicts :-)
Let's expand on the categories to the right.
I'm really here: Yes I'd like to find the perfect man to fit my complicated life and family, with a fast car and lots of money, so I can stay at home cook, clean, garden and tie myself to the bed naked, ready for when he comes home from work, but it's not going to happen.

So a guy with his own life who might come around once a month would do, but would that be fair on a bloke who needs 'it' more, so I'm here to chat on and off. I don't do dates...Too much small print...Although you never know and it is a woman's prerogative to change her mind!

Marital Status – Divorced. My ex ran off with a woman he worked with when my youngest was 5 months old. He was at fault, because, he was selfish and immature. (We haven't heard from him since Jan 2002). I was at fault, because I was a good mother and had no time for anything else. (You try getting up 6 times a night in a 7 hour period, breastfeeding every 2 hours day and night for 4 months, then see if you feel like having sex!) Oh and don't forget my youngest didn't sleep through the night until he was 6.

Children I Have: Girl 16, Boy 14, Boy 12, a cat and 7 Guinea Piggies. I always wanted six kids, but that was before I found out what little sh**s they could be!!! I'd still like another baby, but it's a bit late now.

Hair Colour: Other. Dark, honey blonde, with a touch of auburn and a few bits of white.

I am: Beautiful, slim-ish, intelligent, stupid, funny, conscientious, punctual, tidy, sexy, stressed out, worried, happy, sad, practical.

I dream of: My dream prince/girl: Definitely the Prince, I'm not into girls! Also I have very violent dreams, like the one when I am beating my ex over the head with a brick!

This was what my children put on my homemade mother's day card:

M: Magical
O: Organised
T: Trustworthy

H: Helpful
E: Excellent
R: Responsible

These light my fire:
1. Wild weather on a stony beach.
2. Walks in a shady wood on a hot day.
3. Eroticism.
4. Peace and quiet.
5. Dark Cupboards with a chocolate supply.

These leave me cold:
1. The kids leaving the front door open.
2. Getting old and getting nowhere.
3. The balance of life unbalanced.
4. Leaky wellie boots.
5. The insane idea of finding love on Lycos

Quick personality
Everyday occupation: Look after my family
I'm really here...: To see what happens
Marital status: Divorced
Sexuality: Straight
Children – I have: My own, hope you do too
I smoke: Never. Smoking is fatal
My hair colour: Other
Height: 5'5 – 5'7
More about me
I am: A cool girl
I dress: Casual
With the last of my money: I buy things for my kids

Leisure/interest: Environment & the outdoors
A perfect night is: A cosy night at home
Holiday type: On an exotic adventure
Music: Rock
I dream of: My dream prince/girl

THE EMAILS

17/04/07

ME
Hi, I popped in and gave you a ten, how's it going? ('it' meaning life, as a single parent).

HIM
It's going pretty well, for a recently bereaved single dad of two teenagers and a toddler! Sorry, but little 'un started crying at 2am today and spent the rest of the night in my bed, head-butting and kicking Dad. So I'm feeling a bit frazzled and a bit sorry for myself today! How are you?

18/04/07

Don't talk to me about teenagers!!! My daughter is so...***!#**#**@><#... There, got that off my chest! I sympathize with the 2am thing. None of my children slept the night; the youngest didn't go through completely until he was 6 years old. My ex went off when the youngest was 5 months old, so most of the time he slept in my bed, but he wouldn't just lie and sleep he had to have his cheek right up against mine! I could tell loads of stories about sleepless nights and walking around like a zombie every day... No wonder my ex left!

19/04/07

My sons are learning English as a second language. They currently speak fluent 'teenager'; a raw, basic language, consisting purely of grunts and monosyllables, with the notable exception of 'wot-evaaa'. As for little 'un, it's been another sleepless night. She's had me awake since 4:30 this time!

We should meet for coffee; I bet we could talk for hours about our kids!

My middle son has his own language too; he's hyperactive and has to know what everyone else is doing. He usually has some kind of phrase that he will repeat to everyone, kind of like a passing comment. At the moment it's 'Suck your mum' which I find offensive and tell him to please stop saying it, but I will have to wait until he picks up on something else before he'll stop. It's hard to explain to other people without them getting the wrong idea.

20/04/07

My boys seem to be labouring under a misapprehension that they are black! They call each other "blood", "homeboy" (whatever that means! I have yet to discover), they add "you get me" to the end of sentences, and worship Doctor Dre, 50 Cent, and 'sing' rap lyrics about guns, knives, drugs, hoes, and how they live in the ghetto.

How they live in the ghetto! I bought our home for £950,000 years ago, and we have a home abroad. We live in a leafy, quiet part of the fine city of Norwich. Some ghetto!

I know that kids listen to music and the parents hate it. My mother liked the Beatles & Cliff Richard, my grandparents hated it. I liked AC/DC and Metallica, my mother hated that. But this stuff? The songs have such hideous subject matter, I can't see the pleasure it brings in its' enjoyment.

We haven't had "suck your mum" yet, but we have, upon occasion, had "f*ck my mother!" used in exclamation. Particularly distasteful when, in all honesty, we all mourn her passing. She was taken from us Christmas 2005 and the children still cry out for her in the night.

Cheery stuff, eh? Hope I haven't spoilt your Friday. Enjoy the sunshine!

I lost my mother in 2001 and still haven't accepted her death. I don't think it's something that can be 'healed with time', nor does it make any difference whether it's a child who has lost a parent or an adult.

I actually do like a lot of the music my son listens to and

prefer it to my daughter's, I will happily sing along to 'Let the bodies hit the floor 'and I bought a 'System of a Down' CD because I like 'Sugar'. My son calls every one 'blood' too and although I wouldn't describe where I live as a 'Ghetto' we do unfortunately live in a tiny two bed terraced house, which is the root of a lot of our problems having no space to separate.

23/04/07

Where are you? I've been bored all weekend, the kids have been difficult, everything is apparently my fault, my car went to be serviced and hasn't come back because a part is not available until tomorrow and my daughter has just told me I'm typing too loud! My only bit of sanity is talking to you... but I shall have to make do with looking at your picture of your cock! Well it's better than nothing... I guess! Happy birthday!

27/04/07

Thank you! My goodness, you've sent me a lot of messages. Do I reply to them all individually, or one, or run screaming? If you've got so much time to spare – get over here and lend me a hand! :O)

Oh, I just thought if I noticed your birthday, then I must be looking at you every day, which makes me out to be a stalker!... Oh well no worries, I couldn't afford the petrol to

Norwich, let alone enough to stalk you, although email stalking is different, but then you can block me.

Actually there are only a few men on here that I feel comfortable talking to, the rest are just... weird! I seem to get talking, then, if they start to get serious I back off... Everything else gets in the way, kids etc. or they just don't float my boat! Mind you I'm not really talking to you because...YOU DON'T COME ON LINE!!!!

Ah, now, you're not REALLY a stalker – what are 12 messages between friends? :O) I'm not on here every day (as you can tell by now). My three kids need me, I'm also working on a few legal texts, and that's when I'm not sleeping, eating, running, swimming, or doing anything else. I come on here the way some people just flip the telly on to catch up with the latest news and then flip it off again.

I'm glad you feel comfortable talking to me though – I think you now hold the record for the longest string of messages where neither my salary nor my sexual proclivities have been mentioned!

I didn't send 12, did I?

Oh well as I never meet anyone I'm practically celibate anyway, talking about sex is a waste of time when nothing is going to come of it and if necessary I have a glass dildo.

I'm not looking for a salary either, of course if I met someone suitable money would help, because I would want to stay at home and keep house, but it's communication I feel is more important, whether it's love, understanding, patience, frustration or lust etc. I'm attracted to you because you are in a similar situation with the three kids, single parent, sleepless nights etc. Although you look reasonably good looking in the photo, I bet if you sent another one you would look completely different... I mean you only look about 22 in that pic; I'm a bit old for you!

01/05/07

I think you sent 12 - you've just sent another eight on top of those. Goodness, I get more messages from you than I get from the postman! O)

I'd probably have run screaming by now! Move to Southampton and I'll come and give you a hand.

We live in Norwich, and are considering a move to Southwold in Suffolk. We've got a holiday home in Tuscany (OK, I would) like one in Corfu as well. So what's in Southampton?

Me... and, erm... me!!! Oh and a few nice parks, good shops, a load of boats and the New Forest. Sunday has been a good day. My son's team won a cup match, and we had a team barbecue, as it was our last game. I've been drinking wine to celebrate this afternoon and now all I need is a good man... None of those around unfortunately, so looks like more wine instead! How was your weekend, day, night etc?

I gave him my name here for the first time.

05/05/07

I've changed my message picture so you can see what I look like in shorts. The trouble is Lycos will only allow 30kb, so by the time I've re-sized I've almost disappeared...Well at least you can't see the bad bits, clearly that's one advantage!

My sons laugh at me and call me 'chav' whenever I'm about to go for a run in tracksuit trousers.

Heh heh. Just getting an image there of you running in tracksuit trousers... I hope it's not a shell suit!

No chance of that! And no Lycra cycling shorts either (unless I'm cycling of course).

Oh, I have to have a photo of you in Lycra cycling shorts.

There is no Lycra shorts picture! To be honest, I rarely wear them now; I don't actually race bikes any more nor participate in triathlons. I tend to wear those baggy cycling shorts with loads of pockets in when cycling, and pretty much anything (running shorts, football shorts, Bermuda's) when running. Too busy being Dad...

I used to compete when I was at University, I won time trials and criteriums (that's races around town centres) before I went for longer distances (100 miles, and 12 hour races) and cycle-cross before I just got bored with it. I still cycle when I'm abroad though – or sometimes a moped if I'm lazy.

This is a picture of me after I've seen you in Bermuda shorts! Well you won't send one, so I have to use my imagination! Although thinking about Bermuda shorts, they would give easy access. Mmmm. No I have to go to work, I can't daydream about you today!

08/05/07

A lot has happened today and since I last messaged, but most of it today. Youngest has been really bad with earache, so I haven't had much sleep. On the way back from telling school he was still ill, I found an injured pigeon. Of course I had to bring it home and ended up taking it to the RSPCA after the trip to the doctors. The male guinea pig is ill too, so I had to go to the vets in the afternoon. Then as if I hadn't done enough running around my daughter got me to take her and her friend out so they could get a pizza each and also announced that she is swimming with another friend tonight and I have to pick her up at 10.30pm!

How old are your boys? Have they got to the 'I'm independent, but need a taxi' stage?

Ok, I'll leave you in peace for a bit, Bye Bermuda Shorts! Well it's that until you tell me your name!

Captain's Log: Star Date 10/05/07

Still no sign of Captain Bermuda Shorts and his crew on the lost ship Armani. This is my ninth transmission in the hope that the Armani will be contacted and a reply will be forthcoming, but as I drift in deep space the chances of finding him are becoming slim. The crew however have agreed to keep on trying and a rescue could be imminent. Doctor Deep Throat is on standby with all her resuscitation equipment in perfect order in case Captain Bermuda Shorts needs treatment immediately and Nurse Whip can attend to any other needs he may have. My ship is now heading off for another day of searching in the great unknown.

10/05/07

No sooner do I log into this site then I find I am needed elsewhere. I'll reply to your library of messages as soon as I can, OK? Although I anticipate dozens more by then...

I suppose it will have to be ok, but it won't stop me sulking for the rest of the afternoon.

11/05/07

Still sulking?

Yes…You come on line and I have to go to work.

You need a job like mine then! I'm doing my work on the PC as we speak. Okay, it's somewhat dull - a document pertaining to European Employment Law with regards to international exchange rates and minimum wage rates in member countries, if you must know - but, I'm able to do it at anytime, anywhere.

Earlier this week I had to take the train to London - so I

put the document on my PDA mobile phone, and worked there! A shame I can't get Lycos on it though. The Internet Explorer on it isn't as good as a PC. When are you off? How long do we have?

I'm supposed to start at 9.30 am, but usually the house I clean is empty, so I please myself. It only takes about 3 minutes to drive there. Next week I'm tied up for two weeks as eldest son is on work experience and I have to take him; it means I'm going backwards and forwards practically all day. Shame it's not up and down.

That's good that you can do it anytime anywhere! Of course if you gave me your mobile number/email address I could freak you out all the time!

Which is why I'm not passing it on to you – I'm sparing you a 'Bridget Jones II' moment... So you'll be tied up for two weeks, wishing you were going up and down. You're on the wrong website, lady! Perhaps www.alt.com is more your thing!

What's a 'Bridget Jones II' moment? I'm surprised you even know about 'those' web sites! I'm shocked! A young, blue-eyed, blonde innocent looking guy like you! They say the quiet ones are the worst! And where are my replies to the other messages? I'm still waiting to know what your name is... or at least give me a clue so I can guess it. P.S. Did I tell you that I'm actually a shy and quiet person (when I'm not pestering you)? VERY quiet! ;-)

You'd have to watch the movie to see what a Bridget Jones II moment is, but imagine making a complete idiot of yourself, in front of your intended, and his entire group of colleagues, dignitaries from other countries, the TV cameras...

Innocent looking? You'd be amazed/shocked by the pictures that get sent to my Lycos email. Actually, wouldn't it be fun if I could keep all the bits I like and make a girlfriend out of that, in a totally non-creepy, nothing-like-Bride-Of-Frankenstein kind of way. You? Shy and quiet? And I thought only lawyers told whoppers...

But I still don't get it? Unless of course I rang you and you put me on speaker phone or I emailed naughty pictures and you showed your friends, who then meet me (when we start going out together... ha ha) and look at me and say "Hmmmmmm... Well we all know what she's really like!)

Ahhh! You just gave it away... I forgot. Of course everyone on L@L gets a Lycos email address, so yours would be Geordie_Armani@lycos.co.uk! I don't use mine because I can't receive it through my Incredimail programme and anyway I don't have any naughty pics except for a tasteful picture of my nipple in pink done with Adobe Photoshop to make an Incredimail letter background for the group I belong to... ... If you ask nicely (and I have the address right) I might send it to you!

15/05/07

What do you mean when you say you belong to a group?

I have an email programme which is free for basic use… 'Incredimail.com.' You can set it up to receive your emails. I belong to two adult yahoo groups, Dominant-And-Submissive-Incredimail, where you get some good erotic stats (stationary) and another closed group which is a mixture of everything you could imagine being sent in, from porn to recipes and photos of space!

I popped in to give you a ten… Look at the message I just got!!!
Email: sexygirl1… 52
Have to say, looking at you makes me feel so, so naughty, come chat. Jane.

I get some very graphic messages with step-by-step details (as if I've never done anything with my clothes off before and I don't know what's being spoken of) which might do something for the writer but it just makes me giggle.

Well you'll have to forward them on to me. It's been so long I've completely forgotten what to do!

If you need 'reminders' from these sea monsters… well, let's just say that the enjoyment would seem to be one-sided somewhat. As indeed would be the discomfort!

'Sea Monsters'… I've not heard that as a description of women before!

My boys come out with them all the time. Amongst other non-complimentary terms for the fairer sex, we have:

Ditch pigs

Five-to-two women (the club closes in five minutes, grab what you can, lads!)

Spunk dustbin (a lady of low self-esteem)

Arm-chewer (you wake up next to her the next morning, desire to do a runner, and you'd rather chew your own arm off than risk waking her) and my favourite... aeroplane blonde, which is to say, one equipped with a black box!

It seems then that this type of language is a product of the present generation of teenagers, no matter how or where they are educated!

I read your guest book over lunch... Well there wasn't much else to do. No wonder you're not letting out any personal details those women are all crackers!!!

While I'm at it, get rid of all the help and I'll come and live in with you. I can cook, clean, garden, put up shelves, paint, entertain, read bedtime stories, clean football boots, get rid of stains, unblock sinks, change washers, put oil and water in your car, deal with vomit and take care of all your dreams and desires... The list is endless... Only drawback though is that you get another three kids to pay for a cat and seven guinea pigs. Damn, I think I just blew it! And I was doing so well... I had you hooked then didn't I?

A tempting offer – but I already have a cleaner and a gardener (two in summer), someone who maintains the pool, and I love to cook (although I get bored doing 'kids' food' which you know is just going to get swamped in

ketchup...). My cars are regularly maintained and valeted, and I've pretty much got everything else covered thank-you very much. Except for the 'dreams and desires' bit... A cat & SEVEN guinea pigs? Ooooo-er...

I know! I was referring to the woman in your guest book 'Interpol'. Stupid! Men! They never listen!

Ah, Interpol. Or was it Polly? Or Heidi? One woman, three profiles, and a whole stack of lies, threats, and general nastiness. Apparently, she messaged everyone who had signed my Guestbook up until that point and each of my visitors. Strange woman.

Oh yes; and speaking as a man, we'll listen to you, just as soon as your lot has something worth listening to. And I'm not stupid.

You just brought to mind the scenes from 'A Fish Called Wanda' where the thief takes offence at being called stupid. He also seduces Wanda by speaking to her in a foreign language when they have sex, something I also find very erotic.

Allora sia preparato per me per scrivere il messaggio dispari in italiano.

Now how did I know that you would do that to me too! That's it! You've asked for it! I'm coming round on my broom!! Actually I read about your ability to speak Italian in your guestbook. See, I'm not stupid, like you!

Δε&
#957; εβ&
#955;έί
δα&
#964;όν
το&
#957; ερ&
#967;ομ
ό εν
#973;τ&#959

Ooooooh I love it when you get angry!

Actually, I wrote a message in MS Word, in Greek (being a bit of a smartarse) and pasted it here. Damn Lycos and their Hellenicaphobic shortsightedness!

Serves you right then for trying to be too clever...and its smart white arse!

Smart, white, in-need-of-a-good-wax, arse.

Now you've put me off my dinner!

Good.

Do you have a hairy chest?

My wife always said I looked best smooth. I guess some

things are sort of hard to give up. With a nice sun tan and the right muscle definition, she always said I looked like I was carved out of wood. I don't wax my own bum; there are salons which cater for such needs...

Oh yes I'm sure the girls at the salon just fall over themselves to wax your arse, which is fine if you're a rich, six pack, thong boy and even if I did have the money I still wouldn't have it done with wax... childbirth was bad enough!

Does the term 'back, sack and crack' mean anything to you?

Urgh!!! Don't tell me you have a hairy back? Chests I like, but backs no!

It's not hairy if it gets waxed, is it?

Seriously though, I did think about advertising for a 'marriage of convenience'. I'd find a gentleman who needed a wife and wanted ready-made children. He would pay for everything and I would run the house etc. It would probably be cheaper than employing people to do the work, but I want love, not money... if it exists at all!

You'd have to sell it a lot better than that! Remind me what the benefit is to the man again? Somewhere between being perpetually broke and "You can't tell me what to do! You're not my dad!"

You made me laugh and cry with that answer. Laugh, because it's funny and too true. Cry, because I'm pre-menstrual and my kids would love to have a father. The boys could really do with a male influence, someone to take them out to kick a ball round the park. Although my ex pays maintenance and the endowment, it's the physical and mental support that I really need. Saying that, he was useless, even when they did see him, so I'm better off without him, but it's the fact that he is living well somewhere while his children are crammed in a two-bed house that really bugs me.

The benefits, of course, would be numerous. Sex whenever you want it... the slushy, someone to love and adore you... The practical, not having to do everything on your own anymore and the satisfaction of shaping young lives for the future! Now it sounds like an advert for teachers... I'm rambling, so I'm stopping!

Are your parents still alive?

Mum is still alive. I don't know about Dad, he hasn't been a part of my life since I was five so I don't bother.

Something else we have in common then, or rather you have in common with my kids. My ex had an affair when I was pregnant with our second child; I had to have an amniocentesis, as my blood test showed that he could have Downs Syndrome. While I was pregnant ex slept downstairs, so I could get to the hospital when I went into labour, then he left to move into his own flat, with his girlfriend, when my son was six days old. I remember after the amnio his mum said to me that now my ex knew I was having a boy that maybe he would stay! I was devastated at the time. I found out about the affair by accident. I went to surprise him at work and someone asked how we were enjoying our holiday! He'd been going off to work as normal, but seeing her instead. The story gets worse, but it won't fit in one email.

I'll look out for the rest.

Life Saga, Part Two. After six months ex decided he missed me and wanted to start again and be like we used to be when we first met. It took about a year to get back to trusting him again and him making more effort round the house. We decided to have a third child. Surprise, surprise, as I was naturally giving all my attention to the children, two of which woke throughout the night, he felt left out being so selfish and within six weeks of the birth he had already started another affair at work. Eventually he left me when the youngest was five months old to live with this woman and as far as I know they are still together. She actually left her own two boys to be with him. Her family didn't speak to her for a year.

Gracious me.

I just re-sized a set of photos that I took of myself to give you Lycos blokes some idea of how I'm feeling, so this is my 'Oh my god you're not really going to leave the house in Bermuda shorts, are you?' face. Or it could be my 'Ooops did I really just ask you how big your willy was!' Or how about 'Oh my god did I really just say that!'

If that's your "You're wearing Bermuda shorts!" face, I'd better not tell you that I wore a thong in Jamaica a while ago then, had I? What a laugh! Some highly paid, respectable lawyer in a thong on a public beach! BUT I can get away with it. And there are not many men my age (hell, not many men full stop) that can do it. 39 and still with a six pack? Not bad, I'd say... Okay, get up off the floor now, and just try to breathe... in, out, in, out...

Ok now I'm really laughing!!! Didn't you just tell me in another message that lawyers told whoppers!!! If you want me to believe that I will definitely need photographic evidence!

I'd have to top up the tan first! It doesn't look so good with a white bum...

Oh there you go again, more excuses!

If I take a picture now, my bottom would look like white dough with a rubber band around it! Far better when I'm tanned and toned.

Who said I wanted the rear view?

Anyway... Thongs on beaches are gross, especially on men! You won't even get me in a bikini; I'm the wrong shape. Look what you have done!!! I've been thinking about you in a thong all day!!! As if it isn't bad enough that you won't send me a normal photo (Apart from your profile one) or tell me your name... Now all I can see is a six pack and a thong walking along a beach when I close my eyes!!! God and it isn't even bedtime yet!!! You're such a tease!!!

Yes, I know! ;O) I've been smiling inwardly for the last 24 hours, knowing what's been on your mind!

18/05/07

It's raining.

No it isn't. Coming for a swim?

No, if you think I'm stripping down and putting on my swimsuit in front of six-pack thong boy then you must be kidding.

I've still got the winter covers over the pool right now – it's like a collapsible greenhouse I have erected so the pool's still useable all year round. Won't be long until the covers are down though, then its tanning/swimming/barbeque time!

So you have an erection in the garden...

I do, but it only goes up once a year, and I need help to get it up. It must be my age...
So you make your own adult arty pictures and share them with others in the group to use as their own desktop backgrounds?

Not as desktop backgrounds, you incorporate them in your emails, so the writing appears over a picture. Animations and signatures can be added too, called tags, but you have to have Incredimail loaded to fully appreciate them otherwise in other email programs they just appear as cut up pictures and not the whole stat.

So what kind of pictures have you made?

I've actually only done about five stats. It takes ages to get the measurements right. I just save the ones other people send, however I've included my nipple picture for your viewing, which I tiled on a stat and it came out looking fairly good with the effect.

And a lovely nipple it is too. Pert. Have you only got the one then?

No they come in pairs, but that was my best side!

You have a 'best angle' to view your nipples from? How is viewing it/them from one side better than the other? Do you have one inny and one outy or something?

No of course not I was joking... Stupid!

21/05/07

Yes, that's right. I'm stupid. And you've got one bright red nipple.

It's pink not red and I had to work on it to get it to stick out for the camera.

Yeah, right. YOU had to work on it. Selfish beast.

Well I suppose if you are good... VERY good... I might let you come over and help next time. ;-)

23/05/07

You've got two, haven't you? We could do one each!

Ahhhh... Now I would say 'So you like to watch women play with themselves! But then we will be regressing to the level of what you have received from other women, so I won't say it.

It did make sense, and yes. And for the record, that level seems to feel OK with you. ;O)

Oh now there's an offer I can't refuse... Talking dirty!... The only trouble is I get so far then can't think of anything else to add. There was one guy whom I had a meeting with and a BDSM experience. He continues to send messages like 'I want to empty my balls in you.' I just don't know what to say, because I find it too crude...

Well that message he wrote sounds a bit... dumb. Yes, it is crude. Me, I'd say how I had to empty them – can you suggest how? And where?

How and where! Is this fantasy time?

Well it doesn't have to be; I know you're uncomfortable with that kind of thing. I was just seeing if I could do better than that utter muppet you just mentioned.

Oh... so you want me to tell you what I'd like you to do to me... Or are you going to tell me what you want to do to me... or me to tell you what I want to do to you... or do you want to tell me what you want me to do to you?

A bit early in the day to be at the cooking sherry, isn't it?

Actually I'm drinking tomato Cup-a-Soup with Basil having a cuddle on my lap and giving him a bit of apple juice.

Basil makes a perfect accompaniment to anything tomato-y, at least that's what the TV chefs tell you. Lucky fellow!

I've sat and stared at your picture to mentally connect with you and I've decided that your name is Alex or Paul. Then failing that it has to be Eustace... Or Wilfred... Or Winston... Or Tristan... Or Neville... Or Hubert... Or how about Godfrey... Am I close?

I've already told you (daft woman) that my name is **. I'm sorry that it isn't Eustace though. Or Wilfred.**

No you didn't... You're kidding me is it really ****? Good grief not another one! We have a few of those in my family and a couple in the street.

You will be pleased to know, then, that I am none of those people!

Yes… A big relief because the bloke over the road is a right weirdo… Come to think of it there are two of them. And come to think of it again… I certainly wouldn't want to rip their clothes off to play with power tools!

…meaning you want to rip MY clothes off and play with power tools?? Sounds like a drilling prospect. More piercings on the way then!

Can't say I'd given it any thought at all! You have piercings?

Some, yes. Do you?

No, only my ears, childbirth was bad enough! However now I'm even more intrigued by you… a respectable lawyer, with piercings! Spill… Where are they?

I have a stud in my ear. Erm… the rest are hidden when I'm wearing my suit!

Mmmm…

You like? And you're not shocked?

Yes I do like. I'm not shocked. After spending about five years on Lycos and a few less in adult Yahoo groups, I think I have seen almost everything!

Ah, the adult groups. I haven't joined one on here yet – would I be correct in assuming they are something like 95% male populated? Sounds like an utter waste of time for me then! How was it for you?

I like the BDSM stuff, but the erotic compared to the sadistic. I have some little movies which turn me on when I watch them, but the actual experience would be painful.

I know what you mean by BDSM etc., not exactly making one hit the high notes as it were – I think it's a power thing, and more like foreplay than anything else. I like it – but it doesn't turn me on as much as, say, well-shot glamour. I think the BDSM is funny more than anything else. So is there a group on here you think I'd like?

Hmmmm... 'Well shot glamour'... Would that come under porn or pictures of false breasted women with tans and tiny waists? Or are you for the more natural look? I've got quite good legs, apart from varicose veins and you've already seen my nipples. My hair, although it's a bit like hay and I look like a poodle in the damp, is a fairly good feature and I have nice green eyes with full lips all the better for sucking, plus I can bake cakes!

Wow, you really know how to dress it up and sell it, don't you. So if I could go for a haystack-effect poodle that looks like it's eating a paddling pool with one nipple and nice legs albeit with varicose veins... my luck is most certainly in! I feel like all my birthdays have come at once!

'Eating a paddling pool????

Those delicious, full lips... Ooh, I could do things to that mouth!

Right I'm going upstairs to whip myself for having wicked, lascivious thoughts about you... Or if I can't find a whip I shall have to think of something else! ;-)

Look, if you must have these wicked, disgusting, debauched, naughty thoughts about me... share 'em!

No I'm too shy and secret fantasies should be kept secret.

Whatever you're comfortable with. I'm completely un-shockable, but I wouldn't want to make you feel uncomfortable. And don't go telling me you're shy! Didn't you send me a picture of your nipple not so long ago?

24/05/07

You know it's roughly a month since we have been exchanging messages and curiously you haven't run screaming yet! It must be love... either that, or like a horror movie, you have to see what happens next!!!

A month! I haven't run screaming - you don't scare me at all. Is this as scary as you get then?

Yes, I suppose it is as scary as I get... going on about my kids, the guinea pigs, the cat and the garden all the time, (I haven't sent you garden pictures yet!) instead of relating how and in what way I want to have sex with you, which is usually what most of the conversations on here consist of.

Well it isn't a bad topic of conversation in my opinion; I am, after all, completely un-shockable. Considering that most ladies want to talk about my kids, my money, or maybe a free holiday in Tuscany, it's rather refreshing to hear from someone who can actually speak their mind!

Tuscany would be nice, but I'd have to bring the kids, which would kind of ruin the idea of a romantic holiday completely and ergo I'd have to sort out clothes, passports etc., so that's out... and what would I do with the guinea pigs? I suppose everything would work out in the end if love came to me.

Oh by the way I washed my hair before lunch, so while I was at it I removed all my pubic hair and bathed in oil... Bet you wished you lived closer now! Oil is a favourite of mine along with peppermint body lotion, which gives a slight burning, tingling sensation. Of course neither taste too good, but vegetable oil or toothpaste could be used instead. Then I could use my paddling pool lips to suck you as well as massaging with both my hands, and how about I take that penis ring you have (assuming that is what you meant when you said you had hidden piercings) between my teeth just as you're about to come to add a bit of pain and heighten the sensation?

Oh look, is that the time? I must get the tea started before I get too carried away!

What about olive oil? I have got a Prince Albert ring. I've also got rings through my scrotum (they come out when it's

waxed), and bolts through the head of my penis, one from side to side and one from top to bottom. And both nipples. Just so you know! In return for your generosity, why don't I cool you down? How about a little cunnilingus... with an ice-cube in my mouth?

Oh my god... You must jingle like my cat when you walk around! Doesn't the metal detector go off at the airport when you walk through? Olive oil will work too, better use extra virgin as I haven't had sex for so long! Mmmmm... the ice cube should hold me off for a while, the trouble is they melt too quickly. Better put my glass dildo in the fridge... Ahhh... maybe I could use it on you too ;-)

I jingle in a kilt or sarong, when I've gone commando. I haven't set off the detectors yet. I did once with a belt buckle, but not with my piercings.

What happens when your kids find a glass dildo in the fridge? And as for me... how do you know you don't like it if you don't try it?

I really can't imagine you in a kilt. What do you mean 'How do I know I won't like it until I try it?' Try what... ice? Being pierced?

I mean ME! How would I know I don't like taking a cold glass dildo unless I try it? Really, get with the programme! I'm sure we can think of things for you to try too. Can't we?

It's been a long day and you have me really flustered now!

So now you want a picture of me in Bermuda's, a thong, and possibly my 'jewellery' and in a kilt! Did I mention it has to be a long kilt? At least to my knees, or else you see more than my knees! It's been warm lately...

Hmmmm... Will I be able to blow the pictures up to full size and stick them on the ceiling? It might help me to visualise you a bit better.

What could you use for glue?

Blutack... Silly!

That would leave a stain, wouldn't it? Providing that it sticks to emulsion in the first place.

Oh all right clever clogs!... I give up, you can come over instead. See? Who's silly now?

Come over what? (Filthy beast)

Oh... Now you've made me blush! I should have seen that one coming. Well if I have your ring between my teeth it will be over my face, but now you've enlightened me on your vast array of accessories I shall be hard pressed as to which I should choose. Maybe I could try each one then pick a favourite...

All over your face... mmmmm, I'll give you pinker eyes than your guinea pigs. We'll make a list and work through it, shall we?

I'll have my eyes shut and I won't be swallowing either! It will probably be good if I start at the top and work my way down...

It isn't ladylike to gargle. If you start at my bottom and work your way down, you'll end up at my feet, won't you? That's where I like you...

Then you have a foot fetish or you just want me as a slave to do whatever you like... We've been here before, dreams and desires! Actually the thought of being a sex slave excites me. What would you like next Master? Hang on, I'll go get a banana and practise... How many inches should I cut off the banana?

Cheeky monkey! Close your eyes and picture two Coke cans, one on top of the other, with a cricket ball on top. I'm not as big as that, mind, I just wanted to make you wince.
Let's just say that it dangles halfway to my knees. I'm not being coy, I'm possibly the only man to have never measured his penis.

I was going to say 'Hee haw, hee haw', but it depends how long your legs are! Oh come off it, you must have measured it... OK, I'll put the whole banana in then!

My legs are perfectly normal thank you. I run 12 miles or so three or four times a week. Try the cucumber, rather than the banana (although it HAS been cold lately)

12 Miles!!! I can't even run for 3 minutes!!! I'd certainly like to be wrapped in your legs though, but crush me and I'll bite! Ha, ha!

I love good food, so I run and burn all the calories off. I'm forced to use the treadmill these days, when Madam is asleep, which is absolutely, mind-numbingly boring. Ah well. I'm no PT instructor, but try running on the spot (knees up, on tip-toe) for 90 seconds, a few times a day. You can shut yourself in the loo for that one. You'll see and feel a huge difference inside a week, I promise!

Oh yes I like to feel a HUGE difference inside! Changing the subject, the word document that I'm pasting our conversation on now has 26 pages and consists of 12,832 words! Goodness you talk a lot!

YOU do! Utter filth it is, too. Tsk. The woman who has sent me 12+ messages in one day says I talk a lot. Hmmmm.

But you started talking filthy! Now you have me really wanting you with your extra attachments and as I am eating a banana that's not helping either!

Hey, that means you have a new name – 'Rich six-pack jingle jangle thong boy!' I could make up a rap... Hey I just noticed your ass picture... Can I pat him? Would he like me to ride him? I used to have a horse. I have to go now. My daughter wants the computer and I have to get the piggies and washing in from the garden, plus all the other jobs like finish tea etc., which is going to be really difficult now you've made me so hot and wet!

You can do what you like to my ass. I'll trust you. And I'd return the favour, naturally. ;O)

25/05/07

Gosh I just got in from work and you're still on line. I've been thinking about you... Tell me, have you ever been on a date with someone off here? Who looks after madam if you do, or if you need to be somewhere? What are your children's names? What will you be doing over half-term and the bank holiday weekend? Do I ask too many questions?

I've never met anyone from here. I'm not ready yet, to be honest. I haven't met anyone away from Lycos either, as I don't think it's fair on the kids to introduce a new lady whilst they are still grieving for their mother.

No, I felt the same when my ex left. I didn't want a succession of boyfriends or any more children by a different father. I was never meant to end up like this. I had the perfect wedding and was the perfect wife and mother, but it wasn't enough. He was three years younger, but he was always more immature. We didn't communicate properly, which is what caused things to start to deteriorate. The trouble is the years have gone by and I'm still on my own when I thought I would have found someone by now... Maybe I've put up too many barriers?

...In fact the first guy I went out with after my ex left was in September 2002, seven years later! It was the same time that I had my first mobile phone and he sent me a text that I kept. He was also the first guy to give me an orgasm! My ex never did any foreplay except kissing (I did it myself). That was another reason we grew apart!

Wow, this is such a sorry tale. I'm glad that you feel comfortable confiding in me though.

I'm afraid I don't know you or your situation well enough to be of much help to you; I think you'll have to search for the answers yourself. But I do believe that every journey begins with deciding where you want to be. You say "That's what I want" and then endeavour to get there. So, to start things off... are you looking for Mr Right? Or Mr Right Now?

Mr Right... I think I have always been looking for Mr Right, it's just so difficult when children are involved. I have come close a couple of times, at least I thought I was close until I met them in the flesh. The last one was nothing like his photo and his 'smoke occasionally' was way off from the truth, his teeth were so black he looked like he had been sucking coal! Otherwise he had all the credentials I am looking for... single parent with more than one child, taller than me, intelligent, able to hold a conversation and even though it pains me to say it, enough money to support two families. He had a pet shop business too, so I could have helped with that.

I'm still laughing at the 'sucking coal' comment!

But when I meet him... (Look, you have me thinking again) he has to really turn me on too...you know, just by looking into my eyes... *sigh*... In other words I want a whole one this time!

Not too much to ask for, is it?

Well I don't think so. Oh and I want a dishwasher, chickens and room in the garden for trees and bushes to make a secret wood area.

That sounds like my place in Tuscany! Will 120 olive trees, plus a citrus orchard, all the other trees, and an infinity pool do you? Oh, and a dishwasher…

Hmmmmm let me think about it and I'll get back to you. Ok now you are just rubbing it in!

My hands are clearly on the keyboard, I'm telling you!

The Body Shop does a nice olive oil scrub. I could make my own with all your olives (what do you do with them all?) then treat you to an invigorating bathing experience. Afterwards I could squeeze half an orange over your body, licking the juice from all the crevices as it runs down.

You mean, apart from eating them? I have a load pressed; a bottle of Extra Virgin Olive Oil with your own label on it is a pretty cool gift, in my opinion… I grow oranges there too, by the way. And the property is not overlooked at all.

Even better…
God it gets stranger and stranger on here… Look what just came in my inbox! (attached scam letter).

That lady is hedging her bets, because she contacted me too! Part of me wants to delete, part of me wants to investigate. Still the lawyer... .

I reported her for 'abuse' in the box at the end of her profile! It's all some sort of con. Investigate me instead! ;-)

Don't worry, there'll be plenty of probing and body cavity searches going on...

Oooooooh I can't wait... Will you be wearing rubber gloves and will I have to strip down to my knickers? I hope the light is out if I'm naked in front of you too (I forgot to say before) I can't have the light on in front of 'Rich, six pack, jingle jangle, thong boy! Oops, did I just 'sell it again' as you put it? You'll have to punish me for being naughty, the thought is making me squirm!

Well, you can next entertain me by playing a little game, where we see how long you can keep your ankles behind your head whilst I investigate with my tongue... and if you really have been naughty, I've an oily finger to slip somewhere else, to show you the error of your ways.

Probably not very long, and I can't quite get my ankles behind my head (Yes I did just lie down on the floor and try), so maybe you could tie my legs above my head onto the headboard of the bed instead... I was going to add something else but it would kill the moment.

Well, with both your ankles tied behind your head (and your hands tied)... where did you leave that banana? And that cucumber... is that glass dildo still in the freezer? I think I'd better gag you as well, come to think of it...

That's not fair! You have me at a disadvantage. Gt tsh fnkg ggh oof yoo bstd!!!

Now then; that isn't very nice behaviour, is it? There's somewhere else I can slip this frozen glass dildo, if you follow me, should such coarse behaviour continue!

26/05/07

Ahhhh... That's cold!!! Wait until you're asleep, then I'll get you back!

I'm supposed to have a lie in on a Saturday, but once again I woke early dreaming about you... one minute you were there inside me in the spoons position... mmmm... and the next you were gone!

I wonder if I can buy a rubber dildo with accessories. I'm also wondering when you'll next come on line, You didn't tell me what you were doing over half-term, so you could be anywhere and not back for a week... What will I do?

Aside from everything else... you can ignore this if you want to, like the other questions, but on your profile Madam is 15 months, your wife died two years ago, then you mentioned Madam as two, so did your wife die giving birth?

He did answer this, but somehow I lost it. He said his wife was killed in a car accident when his daughter was nine days old. He took over her care, with hardly any help from his family. I think I remember him saying someone suggested that he put her in care, so he sued them and a local TV company who wanted to make a film about his experience and wouldn't take no for an answer.

I can't even begin to imagine how bad that was for you and the boys, but you seem to be coping. Obviously it's not something you would want to talk about to me, so I won't mention it again unless you do first.

People dying isn't one of my favourite topics. In the last seven years I've lost nine close family and friends and attended seven funerals. My dad worries me, he's done a will, paid for his funeral and is beginning to clear his house out. He's had a few scares with his heart, which failed a couple of years ago, but without him I'll be lost, as we meet and chat each week.

I'm off out tonight to my son's team trophy presentation evening. I shall be dancing to disco music and embarrassing all my children, so it should be a good night.

Have a lovely time!

27/05/07

Well... it's the next morning, I'm sat here in my dressing gown (naked underneath), hair all over the place, smudgy eye make-up and slightly worse for wear after drinking a bit too much. One of the lads' parents invited some of us back for a drink to their house, where I got completely sozzled and had to leave the car and walk back with my son. It's a pity you weren't here... I was completely helpless and you could have done anything you wanted to me!

29/05/07

You mean you need to be drunk for me to enjoy Access All Areas? Glad you had a good time!

Well maybe for the first couple of encounters. Ok here's another picture for you, (I'm still waiting for yours. I took this after jogging in the rain to go and get my car back from my friend's house. This is what I mean by Poodle hair. Oh and I have no mascara on either, so probably better that you can't see!

I did that 90 second jog on the spot thing. It's a bit like having an orgasm... You start off cold, but end up hot and out of breath. You need a bra on though.

I do not need a bra! Who's been telling you that? I do need a good jockstrap though. Lined shorts aren't enough.

Why am I not surprised? With all that metal weighing you down I can see that a jockstrap is an essential piece of equipment... No wonder it hangs halfway down your thigh and when you have an erection doesn't it all fly off?

30/05/07

It might come off in your hand too, if you play your cards right...

What, the jewellery or your cock?

Think of it like a bottle of the finest champagne. Put your hand around it. Give it a good hard shake. Sooner or later the contents are going to come exploding out.

You see how naive I am... I didn't think of 'come off' as what happens when 'you know what' happens.

Actually going back to this message, I downloaded one of those little film things from the group with a girl giving a guy a hand job until he came. He was tied up, but she wasn't very inventive – I would have done a lot more to him while he was helpless and at my mercy!

I went to a Glory Hole party, years and years ago. All the men lined up to this curtain and put their willies through the holes provided, to be sucked to a climax. No one on either side of the curtain knew the identity of who was on the other side. Later, out came the ladies... and one gay man! You should have seen the faces of the other guys!

Oh my god! I would never have done anything like that... I was always sweet and innocent! Did you know any of the 'Ladies'? And did you perform? Were you drunk? Did you know the other guys? Did you do it in front of them?

It was ages ago; I was at university, I would have been in my early twenties. Yes, we all knew each other. There were other parties too... 'Spin the bottle', 'Strip Twister', that sort of thing. I've shocked you now, haven't I? :O)

No, we all do things in our youth. I didn't go to college or university. I left school on Friday and started work on the following Monday. The only A level I did was English Lit/Lang when the youngest was a baby. I did go to quite a few parties where I've slept over, but I was always too reserved to have sex with anyone, I fended them off! I didn't lose my virginity until I was 19.

You started that message with "We all did things in our youth" and spent the rest of it saying "except me!" I did some studying whilst I was there; believe it or not, I managed to shoehorn it in somehow. That's when I started modelling, too.

Well I did do a few things... Like got really drunk once at a party I had while my parents were away and was sick... tried drugs at another party once... and was sick... Had sex on a beach with someone else's boyfriend... and wasn't sick, but I didn't enjoy it, it was a stony beach! So that's why you're called Geordie Armani then, you didn't actually say before. Was that your main career then after university?

A stony beach? Ouch! I had sex on a beach in Suffolk once. We got undressed and she more or less said "give me a sackful of money or I'll say you raped me!" I threw all her clothes in the sea and legged it, the bitch. Modelling was my career whilst at Uni. Everyone else left with mountains of debt. I left with money in the bank and I'd bought my first house. Uni is just two 13 week terms, so it didn't get in the way.

I'm called Geordie Armani because I thought it was funny! It was that or Perry Combover.

30/05/07

At the time of writing this we both have 15 votes, but I have 9.6, you only have 9.4... See I'm sexier than you! ;-)

Yes, that's always been something that's seemed more than just a little silly to me. You go to someone's profile, you read it, and you look at the pictures... so why only give that person a 5? It's a bit mean, and if they don't appeal, surely you're more likely to just click off and find someone whom you do consider to be 'sexy'. And people are either sexy or they aren't! What's this points thing all about anyway?

Oh you're just pissed because I got more!

Not in the least! You have more pictures than I do. You deserve more votes. I'm going to put more pictures on there, to accompany my cock and my ass. There will soon be pictures of my chest, my lunchbox, my bread basket, and even my boat race!

Oh very clever, but I'm still waiting for the photos you promised me, can't you send them first?

What colour are your eyes?

Blue. And slightly pink, after this morning's swim. A little too much chlorine…

Oh that's right, rub in the fact that you have a pool again! When I don't even have a shower at the moment. I'm still waiting for the bloke to come and design and re-fit my bathroom. Anyway my eyes are always a bit red from lack of sleep with the cat jumping on my head when he comes in! I sleep in a metal high sleeper with a double bed/sofa underneath to give us more room for stuff in the house.

Just to wind you up… My bedroom is bigger than some people's lounges. There's the big water bed in there, the TV on the wall, and the doors to the balcony which overlooks the grounds and the pool. There are doors to the en-suite bathroom and sauna, the walk-in wardrobe, and my own secret stairs down to the rear hallway. It's a bright, airy bedroom with a vaulted ceiling and Velux windows. But wow, you make yours sound so good! Want to swap?

Hmmmmmm… Yes, why don't you come over here first and I'll demonstrate how well I can tie you up and SPANK YOU!!!

That's fighting talk! When you untie me, you'd better run then. There's a good ass-to-mouth fucking coming your way. Lord, I don't believe I just typed that! What are you doing to me, woman? I used to be a respectable lawyer…

… And I just spat out my mouthful of dinner! I think it's called'I'msohornyIhaven'thadsexforsolongandyouaregorgeo us' syndrome! And as my bedroom is the size of your walk-in wardrobe, there isn't anywhere to run... unless I climb on top of the bed and throw water at you or something.

31/05/07

Well madam and I have just been for a swim, and we're now about to have breakfast before her sleep. I have to go to Tuscany soon as the building work I commissioned is nearly finished! Wanna carry my case?

...Only if I can whack you with it!!! When is soon?

I don't know when, I'm waiting to hear.

I've just thought of a punishment for you. I'm going to wait while you're asleep then decorate you with various objects, take pictures and put them on the Internet! Ha! Or when I have you tied up I could tease you and masturbate in front of you and you won't be able to touch me or get any relief! Or would you enjoy that too much?

I like the thought of you masturbating in front of me... I'd like you to masturbate squatting over my face, making yourself squirt all over me!

04/06/07

Some bitch has just come on my page and asked, straight out, "When did your wife die and how?" One hell of an ice-breaker, eh?

That was subtle! I had a guy who after only a couple of messages got really annoyed because I wouldn't arrange to meet him. He's changed his profile three or four times, but always calls himself 'Lee' and writes his profile in capital letters. He lives in Southampton too, so close to me. I've blocked him twice and now I just ignore him.

05/06/07

I've been going to profiles from your guest book and into those people's guest books. It's a real eye opener to see how many people I already know or have messaged and how similar all their comments are. I'm guilty too, because I always write the same thing, unless someone really strikes me. I also did a search for anyone on line then wrote in their books to hopefully get a few votes. I have had quite a few interesting comments and messages as a result including 'You can tie yourself up naked for me any day... you're bloody gorgeous!' I feel much better now!

Did I tell you I've been sunbathing in the garden topless too? I had to give up though as the ants found me!

The schoolboy in me would reply with something along the lines of "Don't get ants in yer pants" but I shall be strong, I shall resist. But you see what happens when you only speak to teenagers all day, don't you?

06/06/07

Actually I have adult company today. I'm driving with my

dad to collect my great aunt who is going to stay with him for a few days, hence I am wearing a skirt, have make-up on and will be speaking posh.

As a corporate solicitor, specialising in European Corporate & Employment law, with links in Brussels, I can ask for and get £5000 per hour. Yet at this moment, I smell of Marmite sandwiches and Sudocreme!

Oh I love Sudocreme... hate Marmite, well I do lick it off my fingers when I've made marmite on toast for eldest, so I can eat a bit, but if it's a choice between that and Strawberry jam the jam wins. Did that just sound like I eat Sudocreme?
I just ran in the garden to scream!!!... I knew I should have studied law!!!... £5,000 an hour!!!... I didn't know anyone could earn that much money in an hour. I get £6 for cleaning, and my mortgage went up again today. Still I'm happy most of the time, as this is really all I ever wanted, to be a wife and mother. Didn't get the wife bit right though...

07/06/07

You don't imagine all that money goes straight in my pocket, do you? I have – well, had, anyway – an office full of typists, receptionists, research clerks, article clerks, as well as other subordinate solicitors. And a caterer, just to keep office harmony going... I was amazed that anyone would pay £5000 per hour, but some firms charge £20,000 an hour or more, and corporations will pay that when they're up to their necks in shit!

Oh I see... So you're like the boss, and I should call you SIR now? Good morning sir, Here's your tea. Would you like me to pull back the curtains? Shall I pump up your pillows and straighten your bed covers? Oh sir! Really sir! Perhaps I should take care of that morning erection you have... Just wait a moment while I take off my clothes sir and I'll slip in beside you...

Ooops, my minds wandering again... I've STRIPPED all the beds today, but sod's law, the clouds are COMING over and I bet it rains before I get all the bedding washed, although there is a good STIFF breeze blowing. Next is the bathroom to clean, so I'll be COMING on the computer between jobs all day today.

GET one thing right; I am the boss of my own firm. Perhaps I could be YOUR boss one day? You'd spend a lot of time in the KITchen, but quite a lot in the bedroom too, or OFF to the gardens FOR your own enjoyment; I remember you telling ME you enjoy gardening? I have two gardeners who tend to the grounds AND gardens, all around the SPREAD in fact, and they do a good job on 'EM too.

If you are sending me out in the garden for my enjoyment and there are two gardeners there I could be Lady Chatterley! Anyway if you want to spank me you would have to catch me first. Oh hang on, didn't you tell me you jog twelve miles and all I can manage is about three minutes... Ok if you try and spank me I'll... I'll... bite your ankles!

It'll be worth it. I'm picturing your big, bare, white, spotty arse pointing skywards as we speak! No dinner for me then...

Definitely no dinner, unless you eat me first! And my arse is not spotty... well, not until I'm pre-menstrual again!

This is my latest picture that I took today with make-up and nail varnish on. It's not that clear, but it should be enough for you to imagine my nails running down your back!

I went for another walk in the woods tonight and all I could think of was you holding me down and spanking me! Oh, and while I was walking through the woods I heard a scratching noise in a crisp packet. I picked it up and there was a little shrew inside, it was so cute! Off to bed now and it's 10.45pm, so night night.

And quite beautiful you are too! You don't scrub up too badly. You look like you're about to rip that top off... come here, I can probably help you with that... Funny thing; holding you down and spanking you was all I could think of as well! We must be psychic.

Where did a shrew get the money to buy crisps?

Well thank you sir! I was trying to do a sexy pose, but eldest was taking the photo and we ended up in fits of laughter, mainly because she's crap at taking photos. There is a weekly programme that eldest watches called 'How to look good naked.' It features a woman who doesn't like a certain part of her body or thinks she is too fat to look good. She is then given a make-over by a stylist and photographed naked, so I was trying to assume the positions in the photo shoot. It doesn't quite work in our tiny kitchen though. Anyway, Mr Rich Six Pack Jingle Jangle Thong Boy, you would know more about posing than me! You can help me off with my top any time you like honey!

Oh and very funny about the shrew!

I'm aware of the show, and I wouldn't be happy for that twat to have his pervy paws all over MY Missus, I can tell you… Outdoor light works best, but nothing too sunny or you'll get unflattering shadows.

Oooh I can see you getting fired up again. He's a bit over the top for me too. I would like someone who would be a bit commanding, so he could maybe break down my frosty exterior, my practicality… 'Put the dishes down, come upstairs and bend over my knee' would work for me!

"Put down those dishes?" There's a dishwasher for that. Now, get upstairs, Mrs White-bottom, and prepare for correction and chastisement, followed by a quick game of Hide The Sausage.

I'm not Mrs White-Bottom, I'm MISS White-Bottom. I changed back to my maiden name a few years ago. And if you have your wicked way I shall be Miss Red-Bottom!

08/06/07

I see I'm still number 100 in your guestbook, it must have

worked then. I told Youngest this morning that I'm chatting to this guy who's a lawyer and earns £5,000 an hour and how I couldn't believe someone could earn that much money in a normal sort of job. He said "Lawyers are crap, all they do is walk round in suits with briefcases defending people who have murdered people. Footballers earn millions every week, you should find a footballer." I think he inherits my sense of humour! Hey I did have one thought though... for £5,000 an hour I might consider swallowing!

For £5000 an hour, I expect you to gargle! Tell your son that my fees aren't based on a 40-hour week! I also employ people, and that money has to come from somewhere. He should consider it as a career, the law affects every part of our lives, other people's lives, and there's huge money to be made. Do you think my place in Tuscany was paid for with Clubcard points?

Oooooh... urgh... yuk... erh... spit!... ... You can keep your money!!! If you make any more comments like that, I'll bite you again!

You'll bite me? You just love having me in your mouth, don't you?

Oh you get worse and worse!!! I'm blushing again!!! Anyway I couldn't bite THAT, I might break my teeth!!!

Gimme your email address again, and if I'm pissed enough, I might send you a photo of my cock minus the feathers.

You're not going to pluck that poor cock are you? What are you drinking to get pissed? I had a Guinness on my garden bench when I got back from my walk on an empty stomach and promptly fell over. I've recovered now and am just watching 'Big Brother' before bed. I looked at your new pics too!

09/06/07

I had company last night; an old band-mate with a bass guitar in one hand and a bottle of Jim Beam in the other. We had a jam in the den until the small hours.

Maybe tonight…

Oh don't tell me you were in a band too? Is there anything you DON'T do? I've not tried Jim Beam before. What's the difference between Bourbon and whisky? I must admit I am a whisky girl, I like it straight (don't we all!)

11/06/07

As far as I know, the main difference between Bourbon and (say) Scotch is the addition of an extra 'E'. Jim Beam, Jack Daniel's, Black Flag are all 'whiskey'. The first sip hits a little harder, and it's a little rougher around the edges than Canadian Club or maybe Dimple.

I have been in bands, and I still love to play. For want of a suitable babysitter, I'd get back into it in a heartbeat. Well, a heartbeat and a few weeks' solid practice to get my speed and accuracy back up.

What instrument do you play? What type of music? When can you serenade me? Ooooh, does that mean you can sing in Italian as well?

11/06/07

Hey, I loaded Google Earth on my computer. My house isn't on there though, it's just a blur. Your house is. I found three with pools in Norwich, but there was only one with a guy sunbathing with a thong on, so that must be yours.

I haven't looked on Google Earth, but I've seen my house on Live Maps (is that the same thing?) and according to that, I've still got the covers over the pool. There's a set of roadworks in Norwich which have been there since before Christmas. According to Live Maps, they haven't started yet. Oh, I play electric guitar really well, other styles of guitar pretty well, and piano really badly! But I'm practising...

 I was thinking. I'd like to spend an evening with you and listen to you play, with a bottle of whisky, then slip in to bed with you after to make love for the rest of the night... It's my bedtime now ;-)

Jazz and blues... did you ever see the movie Ray? A biography of Ray Charles, and music that'll have you in tears. I like particular songs rather than following any particular band (a little too old for that now). Although it has to be said, I don't like any bands I'm not actually in.

No I didn't watch it. It was on sky movies recently, but I'm not keen on biographies. I like lots of action and adventure movies. Some romance is ok, but I have to be in the mood.

I'm a 'song' fan, not a 'band' fan. Lastly, yes it is conceited, but if you were as perfect in every way as I undoubtedly am, then I suppose you might fall into the same trap. IF you were...

Oh I really want to screw you now!!!

I just opened the back door and my petunias smell gorgeous, you must pop round and smell, I can't send it over the internet.

It must be a full moon, I tell ya... I've had so many "wot u wearin' lol" style messages, I swear I'll go mad... and I instantly regret telling you that, as I know you'll put that in a message somewhere!

12/06/07

Just received this in an email:
Did you know there are five penis sizes?

1. Small
2. Medium
3. Large
4. Holy Shit!
5. Does that come in white?
Which one fits you?

6!

Then you are definitely not putting it anywhere you want!!!

It's not as much fun as it sounds. I mean, YOU try running for miles with a baby's arm tumbling out of your shorts. Quite painful. And trust me, young lady; it goes where I want. Either willingly... or with you 'controlled'!

You're making me horny again... the effect the word 'controlled' has on me... Well, I definitely need to go out now before I ... ermmm... pop!

I have 'ways' of making you pop... So the idea of being my toy doesn't frighten you? Well, not yet anyway.

Do you think it would be right and proper for a Doctor of Law, a respected man of considerable letters, to take ownership and control of such a wayward female?

Somewhat different to "I want to empty my balls over you", isn't it...

13/06/07

I'm not wayward! You encouraged me in the first place!

You need me to turn that big white pimply bottom of yours crimson. Then we'll see who can toss their head back, glare, and snap their fingers to get the other to come runnin'.

Oh yeah!!! You would have to catch me first. I've been

jogging little bits when I go walking in the evening and I've lost 8 pounds now, I can even jog for up to 10 minutes at once! So go on try and spank, I dare you!

I think I'd run behind you, just to watch your bum jiggle as you run! I can see it now, like a hypnotic lava lamp.

Humph!! I am NOT that fat! At least I don't rattle as I jog, unlike some people!

What's your favourite food?

Anything Mediterranean, but especially seafood. All served with plenty of olives, rough bread, and chilled beer or white wine with the sun beating down on you. Are we in agreement?

I haven't tried much seafood apart from cockles, mussels and prawns. I like olives, bread and cheese, salad, pasta etc. I do eat almost anything, but what you describe sounds perfect. I will need to work up an appetite to enjoy it properly.

13/06/07

Good morning. It's a lovely day again today. My daughter has gone off to enrol at college for her second year. I'm going to have a good clear out and dust throughout the house over today and tomorrow.

If the sun stays I shall go out for an hours sunbathing, if I get the time.

I've started my fourth word document containing our conversations... ...Wow.....We talk a lot... .Well you do!

I made up another one just for you:
1. Small
2. Medium
3. Large
4. Holy Shit!
5. Does that come in white?
6. OMG you must be joking, those metal spikes have got to hurt!

Thanks for that. I now have a mental image of you in a French maid outfit, teetering around in fishnets and high heels with a feather duster in your hand. Just look at the way you're bending over! You'll hurt your back like that, at your age…
Do I now have to chase you around the furniture? With a leer across my face, and you yelling "No! Master! Stoppit!" There you go; stick that in your ****ing Word document.

Tut, tut Master, such language, if you're not careful I'll put this duster where it hurts!

Sometimes if it's really, really hot, because our bathroom is basically a cupboard, I clean it with just my panties on. ;-)

Shame you haven't got MSN messenger and a web cam… I'm naked while I'm writing this!

Why are you naked? Have you run out of clean clothes? Those breasts must be heavy, let me help you with them.

No stupid, I'm sunbathing. At least I was when I wrote it. Ok you can help me with my breasts, but only if you're good… very good.

You call me stupid again Ms Pimple-Bum, and you'll find yourself running naked on my treadmill. (How would I do that? Dangle a bar of chocolate in front of you.) Then you're in for a beating of a lifetime! Not from me of course; from your breasts. What with those and the 'lava lamp' behind you, I won't know which to watch first, front or back.

What kind of chocolate?

I can't run naked on your treadmill. My breasts are not that big, but it still hurts to run without a bra, I'd have to hold them and I wouldn't get the beating you predicted. Maybe I could do something else instead, as long as I still get the chocolate.

Italian dark chocolate; the very best chocolate in the world… If not the treadmill, then maybe star jumps? You could be my own little Newton's Cradle. And if your breasts get sore, I can always rub them better with something.

I thought Belgian chocolate was the best? I prefer milk chocolate, although dark chocolate is better for you.

Can't I just give you a hand job with some of your olive oil? I'm really good with my hands!

If Belgian chocolate was any good, they would be famous for their culinary expertise too. The crisp, dark chocolate is wonderful in cakes, with ice cream, in a latte, or on its own. Maybe it's the fact it's in Italy that makes it so special.

Of course I want to know what happens when you jump! Don't you want to know what happens when I do?

Olive oil would be lovely, but make sure you don't use

too much; any excess must be licked off immediately. Think I'll save some for your sore breasts as well!

You certainly put a smile on my face this morning! There are things I'd love to do to those breasts... Do you realise those are the first I've seen in a year and a half?

What things would you do to them? They are very sensitive... just a couple of rubs and I'd be putty in your hands!

Well, a nice gentle rub for starters... but I wouldn't be able to leave those nipples alone! Mmmm, I can feel one in my mouth right now!

Mmmmmm... ow, not too hard... ahhhhhhh...mmm... I could do this all day.

Hey, as if I'd do anything too hard to those lovely nipples! I'm a gentleman...
Are you poking out your tongue in that pic, or are you in the middle of eating an Odour-Eater? That isn't what I meant by "show me something pink".

The only really pink picture I have is my nipple picture, but you've already seen it. I've added it anyway.

THANK YOU!
I feel a lot happier now. You have a beautiful bosom there. And a deliciously, pert nipple to boot.

Well it's amazing what you can do with a good camera angle, a bit of cropping and a few filters...

Maybe you'll show me the complete set rather than just one? Who knows?

Hmmmm... did you just ask me to send you a picture of me naked? Unfortunately I deleted the original photo in case the kids found it, we share the computer. I might think about doing another one, perhaps if you sent a photo of yourself first, I still don't have one of your whole body.

15/06/07

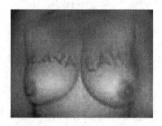

A present for you to cheer you up, as you've been good!

I woke up this morning, sun streaming in through the window, birds tweeting outside and I thought: Oh my god!!! Did I really send **** a picture of my breasts with 'Lava Lamps' written on?

I'm working this morning, so I get a small reprieve from my embarrassment, unless I catch you between school drop off and work.

Birds singing? They weren't tits by any chance? What's to be embarrassed about? They're gorgeous! I think I'll drive over NOW...

No they weren't tits! Hmmmmm... Now I could call your bluff, give you my address and you could be here by the time I've finished work... Nah... I haven't got any mascara on!

You have! It just isn't around your eyes, that's all...

Damn I have to go, so you can send me lots of messages ready for when I get home... Tell me more about you... or something...

Tell me what kind of modelling you did, or if you like tea or coffee, or what you were like at school... or what movies you like, your favourite sweets...Do you walk around looking in windows to see if your hair is ok? Do you like shopping for clothes or food?

You'll have to wrangle with your utter lack of specificity on your own. I shall, however, reply to your questions. I did clothes modelling; Burton, Hepworth's, C&A, Dolce e Gabbana, Next, Top Man to name but a few. Some lovely location work, and a struggle to keep my mind on university sometimes. I like tea and coffee. Strong tea, no sugar and a little milk; or proper coffee, (not instant) either black or espresso. A frappacino in the heat!

I was a swot at school, but I was always being pestered by the girls, even the much older ones, which got me into fights sometimes. I like to see classic movies, just to see what all the fuss was about! I LOVED the Lord of the Rings and still watch them. I like epic stories. But I'd rather read.

I don't really care for sweets. I like fresh fruit and olives though.

Yes I do do that in windows, but not anywhere near as much since I've been on my own. I have to say, I can see why so many single mums let themselves go (I haven't though, and I've no plans to!)

I like shopping for food... but not for kids. They'd eat oven chips and fish fingers swamped in ketchup every day breakfast dinner and tea if they could. I like clothes shopping, but where's the fun on your own?
How's that?

Wow!!! I love Next, but rarely buy myself clothes. At the rate middle son is growing I never have enough money left for me. I don't like rubbish, so I don't buy anything. Tea and coffee the same as you!

15/06/07

Who's that bloke in your guest book? I went to see, but he's 'User not Found'. He seems to know you.

He's a friend of mine, we go way back. He's the one who told me about this place in the beginning. I'm not surprised you can't see him; apparently he's plagued with even more stalkers than I am!

Ooooh... Sounds interesting! Is he as good looking and sexy as you?

On the advice of my lawyer, I shall not answer that question.He does alright for himself, put it that way... '

Well his user name probably gives that away a bit!

Have you looked in your guest book lately...It's getting in a bit of a mess!

You liked my joke then!

Yeah.... You brought a smile to my face; getting to be a habit of yours isn't it?

I do my best Master... I'm a good girl really! ;-)

Well good girls deserve a treat, Would you like something nice and creamy for dessert?

Yes please Sir... clotted cream is my favourite, on banana with sugar... Oh sir, you didn't mean that did you? Oh dear, is Master going to spank me now?

Well you were half right when you said 'banana'. And it's been so long, I wouldn't be surprised if my cream was a bit clotted... Ah, what the heck. I'll just spank you anyway! Bend over...

Oh thank you Master... I know I'm naughty... ow, ow. More Master, I've been SO bad...

You're not hiding a book inside your PE knickers, are you? I thought as much! Ah... good old Yellow Pages.

Humph... I don't wear PE knickers! Oh no, don't take them off... please Master, I don't want a red bottom... Oh... *Struggle, struggle*... Not over your knee... Let go of my arms! Ow, no! ow…this isn't fair… Let me go Ow! I'll be good!

You'll wear PE knickers if I tell you to! Uniform must be worn, that's what it's there for. Whilst you're over my knee, squirming, I think I'll explore for a bit. Do some probing (isn't that what lawyers do?) I've a friend who might help me. He's all excited! He has a real 'buzz' about him. It must be the new batteries…

Thank you for giving me so much attention Master, but if you use your friend on me I might make you wet!

Well I said I'd make you squirt! Although if it turns out to be an unpleasant experience then you will feel my rage. I'll tie you to these little hooks I have in the en-suite ceiling! And see how you like being tickled… and I might even make YOU wet if the mood takes me!

Now you're making me blush again! I'm very ticklish, I might pull the ceiling down in my efforts to get away! You wouldn't really string me up and make me wet… would you? And make me wet with what?

The ceiling is reinforced. It could bear your entire weight if it pleased me. There's a thought… when you're hogtied and gagged, would you like to be suspended at a workable height? Or the cold marble floor? You'll be 'under my control' for certain, one way or the other!

Oh god... I'm practically having orgasms just thinking about it!

There is a site called Hogtied. You have to be a member to get on properly, but they let visitors see photos of sessions. A lot of my group email backgrounds include photos from there and sometimes I get videos sent through. I have plenty of pictures mirroring your description of what you want to do to me! Can I be suspended... Please? All my kids have gone out now, it's a pity you live so far away, and my daughter could baby sit whilst you played with me!

18/06/07

I'm aware of Hogtied, as well as www.alt.com, both of which appeal to me. Have you seen the 'water torture' pictures? And you'd like to be suspended in my wet room... You're so naughty, aren't you? I like it!

I told you I went without sex for seven years until I got a computer and discovered L@L dating... now If I'm lucky it's once a year!!! Well if it wasn't for the three kids I have running around then I'm practically a virgin!

I've been without sex (that is, sex involving other participants!) for eighteen months now. It's been difficult to get 'in the mood' since my wife's passing, and I don't have much of a social life now, as the profile says.

OK as I'm bored, and all the kids are out, as no one is allowed in with my youngest ill, then I'll write down a fantasy, although I'm not that good at putting things on paper.

I'm asleep, but wake to find my wrists tied to the metal headboard and my legs spread apart and tied either side of the bed, with a cushion under my hips. 'He' is rubbing oil over my 'bean' (as you call it), which is what woke me. Sometimes I pretend that I've been drugged with something and I'm there for a group of men to watch. They play with themselves while 'He' brings me to orgasm using a few toys as well.

Another fantasy...

There's this guy I like who I chat to on a dating site. I meet him for a drink with the intention of chatting then returning home, but its winter and a blizzard starts, so I can't drive back and end up going to his house. We're both wet from the snow and he takes me up to have a hot bath. In his bathroom there are hooks in the ceiling with handcuffs hanging on the end of chains. He grabs me, holding my arms behind my back, forcing my head back by pulling my hair and then he kisses me passionately. I gasp as he starts to move his hands over my breasts and begins to remove my clothes; before I know it he has the cuffs in the ceiling firmly attached to my wrists and I'm helpless... heh, heh, heh...

Well me writing this isn't having much of an effect on ME, but when I read yours, it's wonderful. Best of all is when I look back through the messages to your breath-taking, wonderful breasts! I'm a very visual person, and they work a treat on me.

No clothes pegs then. Just G clamps, sash clamps, and your head in a vice... although at the minute, I'll just have you naked, face down, with your wrists bound to your ankles

with your vast white spotty bottom in the air. Out comes the baby oil, and I'll play with both your holes at my leisure.

Oh thank god you haven't sent me your email address then or you might end up persuading me to send a video of me masturbating. No you definitely wouldn't get that until after our date in February and then I'd probably do a new one...I've lost some weight now!

I've no idea what those clamps are... Now I'm scared! And my bottom is not spotty. (Although I haven't checked lately). If the bloody sun would come back out it wouldn't be white either!

I don't think you'd need much persuasion to send me anything! You know I find your sexy, compliant body a turn-on, and I think you want to show me things... Do a Google picture search on G clamp and sash clamp, and set your eyes to 'water' mode. Your bottom might be white; I think it would benefit from a big red handprint or two across it. And never mind a video, I'll set my camera up with a screen so you can watch what I'm doing to your body from behind that big spotty bottom! How about a gag too, so you can't tell me 'no'?

19/06/07

You know you definitely have a dominant evil streak!!! Where on earth are you going to put those clamps? I did the picture search and there is no way you could clamp those to my nipples and still have me standing, they're too big!

And if you have all that equipment for your camera then there is no excuse for not sending me a photo of you. I only want one with your clothes on so I can see ALL your body at once. Anyway you are NOT filming me. I don't have that good a body to appear on film, it's bad enough stripping off with the lights on!

Who said anything about filming you? You'll get your picture! Be patient.

As soon as I've hung up the washing I shall go and sunbathe so there won't be any pasty white bottom!

20/06/07

I've started reading a bit more now. I used to read a lot and have hundreds of books. I like the modern romances for a bit of light reading before bed. Anyway where were we? I'm suspended from your ceiling, naked, wanton and waiting...

I love a good read! I'm reading 'Jude the Obscure' by Thomas Hardy right now, and I recently read 'Crime and Punishment' by Fydor Dostoyevski. I read a few Dan Brown books recently, finishing 'Angels and Demons' in a little under two hours. There's nothing like being an adept to the Law to sharpen your reading skills... I try to encourage my daughter with books. She has a few, and at 18 months has a library card of her own! But the boys? I say 'Do some reading', and what book do they get? The Argos catalogue.

Okay, so you're hanging there; I have shown mercy on you by a support taking your weight (under your pelvis) and by tying your hair to another hook so your neck doesn't ache.

Now I can take my time. I think a latex glove and some lube are in order. It's time you became my glove puppet! And I don't want to hear a word of protest, or it's a spray of cold water for you! Remember, no one's gonna hear you scream…

Oh… *Lets out a low moan as he inserts a finger* Ah… *Tenses up as he inserts three fingers*… Ah… No… No… No more… You can't… Not your whole fist…It won't fit… Ow, stop!

I still haven't done the bathroom. I went to town to get a new cat flap and some hay and grass for the piggies. I also went to Iceland and got some 'Nobbly Bobblies'… hmm… They remind me of something, but I can't think what.

Oh, and instead of suspending me on ropes or something why don't you get a 'love swing'? they look really good and we can take in turns. ;-)

You think I don't already have a love swing? The love-swing is for when you've been good! If you've been naughty, expect to be punished. Go on, be naughty!

One minute talking about books, the next minute talking about you doing things with a glove! So if I took you in the shower, wet you with warm water, lathered up some soap, washed you slowly all over in every nook and cranny, followed by body scrub to remove all your impurities. Then afterwards if I dried you with a nice soft towel, laid you on towels on the floor then oiled you all over using my body to slide up and down covering you completely…

Can I please, please, please go in the love swing?

Yes, I believe you can! That's rather excellent behaviour, isn't it? I'd prefer you to 'dry' me off with your tongue though; all the towels are, erm, in the wash I think...

Mmmmm... Now why didn't I think of that, licking off the water? Would I be able to contain myself though in order to finish off all your body? I might get stuck half-way down!

What about after a swim? By the pool, with the sun beating down on us...

Oh yes, I forgot you had a pool! And you would need drying off after, although if it's really hot the sun would do the job for me, perhaps a little wine or dry martini and ice would help...

After regular trips to Tuscany, it won't require much imagination on your part to guess how my wine cellar is stocked! I'll get the corkscrew, shall I? Join me under the parasol, it's a scorcher today. While we're here by the pool... I've accidentally spilt my wine all over your breasts! Oh no, and again! What a mess. What a waste, too... I'll just lick it up. Hold still...

Now it's run all the way down my front and between my legs...

Well I'll lick it up anyway. It's just as well you're naked, wine stains can ruin a bikini!

Oh look, some of it's gone down you, I had better lick that off for you too… I tell you what, I'll lie one way, you lie the other, then we can both lick at the same time and get it done in half the time!

Thank goodness we're both naked then! Those wine stains can be terrible on, erm, black trunks. I suppose… Aw, would you believe the whole bottle's gone and up-ended itself all over your body now. Mister Clumsy! Well, here I go with my tongue again, lie still…

Oh you just wanted to drink it all yourself! I'm going to get another bottle!

Really? I might just follow you indoors. Only to show you where the bottles are kept.

You men, you have sex on the brain. Hmmmmm… have you any different shaped bottles? Perhaps I could try a few out while I'm tasting them…

My daughter's planned this play evening for her birthday and needs 30 people to pay and go by Tuesday, well so far she has 8, not including herself and her brothers, whom I'll pay for of course.

I'm eating a Feast lolly at the moment, it's got knobbly bits on too. I think I like knobbly bits in my mouth.

I like knobbly bits in my mouth too… your nipples, your clitoris (though not simultaneously)… lick… suck… bite! But not hard, yet…

Mmmmm... just how I like it! One of my favourite positions... You between my legs sucking, with your arms wound under my knees and holding my arms, so I can't stop you when you bite me... I'm getting hard just thinking about you there!

That's funny, I'm hard too...

I tell you what, I'll come over with my kids to your house; we can leave them all by the pool and go up the woods together. ;-) Do they have woods in Norfolk?

22/06/07

I'm bored. If you don't hurry up and come on line I'm going to carry on ranting at you. Where's my picture you promised? Can I chain your nipple rings up on those hooks in the bathroom and play with you?

I've been visiting lots of profiles and putting tens on, but I still haven't got on the hot list. *Sulk*. Now I can't think of anything else to write... I'm still bored.

What's your natural hair colour? It's streaked in that photo. What colour is it now? Have you had that body hair waxed off yet? Ouch!

Still bored... What did you have for tea?
OK that's it, I'm going to have a banana.

This is message seven. You have been hit by the bored witch... God it's only 8.20pm, What can I do for the rest of the evening?

22/06/07

La, la, la, la, la, la, la, la, la... I was just singing before I go to bed, although I might watch another film, because my son hasn't come back from his friends yet and I don't want to walk down the road in my dressing gown.

23/06/07

Good morning... although as you're still not here a lot of good this message will be! Not sure what I feel like doing today. What will you do?

24/06/07

You know how stupid men are... Well my son and his friend have just come in and they have put about ten small temporary tattoos on their faces. They're in the bathroom now trying to get them off, you should hear the laughter and the screams, it's hilarious!

Did you go to Tuscany to check your building work? You never say what you do at weekends, it's one of those taboo questions like... what are you kids' names? It took me over a month just to get you to tell me your name, remember?

Anyway I'll shut up and be patient.

25/06/07

Now I'm beginning to worry that something has happened

to you...Next time you plan to go off somewhere at least let me know that you won't be online, then you won't get so many bloody messages to read when you get back!

27/06/07

Ok. This is like going on a date. You're sat opposite each other chatting away and getting on really well, finding out that you both have lots in common then... in mid conversation your date leaves to go to the toilet... AND DOESN'T COME OUT FOR FIVE DAYS!

SIX DAYS counting today!

Here's a joke for you. I rear-ended a car a few days ago. The driver of the other car was a dwarf. He angrily swung open his door and scrambled out of his car to confront me. Man, he was pissed! He looked up at me and loudly said, "I am NOT happy!"

"Well" I said, "then which one are you?"

WELL... I'M NOT HAPPY EITHER! Now you're going to come on line and tell me something terrible happened... bollocks!

02/07/07

Typical... just as I start to fall in love with you, you run screaming... I knew that would happen! I've been waiting ten days now for you to come back on line. I wish I knew why you haven't come back. I can only speculate. Either something happened, you're working, you've gone away or you're depressed, because of your wife and still need more time, and you haven't had much time yet have you? I've been jogging and walking every evening now, if only to have time to myself to think… Mostly about you. I've been going round in circles. Say nothing, wait and hope to pick up where we left off. Give you an ultimatum, say I can't do this again, shut my profile and leave you with my number, even though I know you won't call and I've probably cut off my nose to spite my face, it's not fair on you anyway and what about the other 160 women after you? Shit, I'm nearly 46, you're seven years younger and who wants to support a women with three kids, even if she does like kinky sex?

03/07/07

You've turned me into a crazy woman. I just bought a jar of Dolmio Taste of Tuscany, because it made me think of you… fat lot of good it will do me! I suppose I could use it to masturbate with, it might make a bit of a mess though, don't you think?

My bathroom should have been started this week, but because of the floods the stuff couldn't be delivered, so I have to wait until next Monday. Guess I'll continue to run in the rain when I need a shower, unless you invite me over to use yours… Oh but you're not on line to ask anyway and I'm talking to myself again.

06/07/07

Hey, I've altered my profile a bit (well I'm really bored with missing you now) and changed the photos, so if you ever come back you can have a look. I nearly took a picture of my arse too as it is spot free, but what's the point if you're not going to see it? I bet you're getting a tan somewhere... I shall just go and sulk under my duvet now!

07/07/07

I'm now getting hounded by older men on here between 50 and 65... yes, 65! How can that be good for my fantasies? How can I visualise taking off a 65-year-old's clothes, telling him he can't touch me, as I tease him with my tongue, gently run my fingers and nails down his body until he is erect and wanting me to touch his hard cock, but I don't, I make him wait while I undress myself slowly sucking my fingers, playing with my clitoris before taking his cock in my mouth making it wet ready to go inside me. I thrust him on the bed mounting him, rhythmically riding him up and down, and making him hot urging him to come for me... hang on, would a 65 yr-old even have an erection or should I get out the Viagra?

02/08/07

I see you're back. I still think about you every day, goodness knows why! I still want to suck your cock and bake cakes for you, though not at the same time. I know the you-me, Norfolk-Southampton thing is futile, but couldn't we still chat sometimes?

03/08/07

I don't see why not. I had a bit of a family emergency, hence my absence. The odd thing is I didn't miss this website at all! I can bake my own cakes. As for the other, I'm not double jointed.

Oh good... I think! Didn't you even miss me a little? Not even a tinsy, winsy bit? You disappeared for two weeks, came back, read my messages, didn't reply to any of them, blocked me and shut down... I've been doing my nut! And YOU didn't miss ME! What was the emergency?

05/08/07

Coming straight to the point. I'm looking after my friend's house, the one I clean, from Monday to Monday. She said I can 'use' it if I want, as it's empty. If you wanted a night away, with me, even if it's just coffee and a chat, then let me know by Thursday, if you come on line that is. You have all my numbers in messages somewhere and I know the logistics involved with a journey like this and a family, so I don't expect a yes, but I thought I'd ask anyway, because I'd really like to see you and it would be on neutral territory and maybe you could do with a night away. Think about it.

09/08/07

I don't know, I give up with you... you read messages, but don't reply to them, then disappear again!

Are you going to talk to me again?

I wish you would come back online. I'm bored and depressed. It's a lovely evening too. Just right for sitting in the garden drinking red wine while the sun goes down and discussing the day's events...

I wrote the messages below in an attempt to get him back; each message was in the subject line, so he could read them without having to open them.

WHAT'S WRONG?	28/08/07 08:17
WHY WON'T YOU	28/08/07 08:17
OPEN MY MESSAGES?	28/08/07 08:16
STUPID!!!	28/08/07 08:16
COME BACK AND I'LL	28/08/07 08:16
SHOW YOU MY	28/08/07 08:15
TANLINES :-)	28/08/07 08:15

31/08/07

Sigh... It's no good, I've shuffled the men in the picture shuffler over and over again and the only guys that come close to looking as handsome and sexy as you are in their early twenties, but not one of them can spell! What am I going to do?

I'm reading 'The Story of O'. It was mentioned in my group, Dominant-and-Submissive-Incredimail, so I bought it. You may have heard of it; it's about a girl who becomes a slave to her lover and the 'cult' he belongs to. It's quite erotic in places and stirs hidden fantasies within me, although I wouldn't want to be whipped quite as brutally as she was. If you haven't read it, then I recommend it, especially with your penchant for 'Hogtied'.

Catch you later?

(Maybe next year, huh!)

04/09/07

Can't a man spend a little time in his new pool in Tuscany without mad panicky types filling his mailbox? Scary.

If you gave me a proper email address I wouldn't fill your mailbox, I could put everything in one letter and send you some erotic photos too.

11/09/07

On another subject. I was reading about the Madeleine McCann case and the fact that DNA evidence suggests that she was killed in the apartment, then moved in the boot of the McCanns' car. If they killed her by accident, then why would they want to cover it up? Even if it was done by one of them losing control and not by her falling or injuring herself, surely it would have been better to immediately call an ambulance and confess, then to cover it all up like this?

13/09/07

Being involved in the case, I cannot comment.

Oh... I see. I was just trying to make normal conversation to see if you would reply, as you don't reply too much lately. Guess you won't reply to this either, if you can't comment and find me annoying too.

I'm not THAT scary... am I?

No, I'm used to you now. More 'annoying' than 'scary'.

I'm sorry for being annoying.

19/09/07

I should imagine that you are indeed sorry; there are only three messages this time, as opposed to the tirade one has come to expect. I cannot discuss the case you mentioned at all. Yes, it is difficult to cope with everything. And I hate this time of year anyway; it gets colder, darker, and gets near Christmas and the anniversary. I think another picture of your ample charms would cheer me up!

I hate Christmas now, without my mother it's just not the same. Each year I try to make some sort of new tradition, but it never works. I wish I could just pack up and go somewhere else, without all the palaver of presents and being nice to everyone.

I did try and take a picture of my tan lines, but my top half was not distinct enough. You might have to wait until next year.

Could you translate this please, it's in my guest book: 'un beso para una chica preciosa tienes un 10 de mi parte'.

Into which language?

English of course (bloody smart-arsed lawyer!)

Bloody too-thick-to-be-specific, blonde-bimbo piece of fuckmeat!

That's not very nice and it definitely doesn't say that. I put it into an online translator and this is what I got: 'Un tipsy protects a chica preciosa tienes a 10 says leaves me'. Which is a load of crap!

21/09/07

Well if you had brains – a stretch of the imagination, I'm sure – then you might recognise one or two of the words' sound, y'know, Spanish and not Italian. So a translation would be "A kiss for a precious girl, you have a 10 vote from me". Too smarmy by 'arf if you ask me.

No wonder! I should have asked my son to do it, he does Spanish at school. And anyway you still owe me a photo!

Erm – NO! I shall furnish you with pictures when it pleases

me to do so. You however, should drop 'em and smile when you're told! There is no debt here; I'll send you a picture when I'm happy to do so. So make me happy. That's the way it works. Silly girl for not knowing that.

Stroppy aren't you! Here's the requested photo, although it's pretty difficult to hold the camera, smile and drop 'em all at the same time and if you sent me an email address I'd be able to send you the others without making them so blurry to fit on this Lycos web site!
Happy now?

Ah, that's the tonic I need. Thank you! It would appear to have done the trick and I'm immediately finding myself a good deal less stroppy. My compliments.
How about a picture of your face and your bare shoulders?

OK, as I'm in a good mood and you need cheering up I've attempted a more provocative pose. This was even harder than the previous photo. Is Sir feeling better now?

Much better, thank-you. That's the kind of start to the day I enjoy. You have wonderfully inviting nipples! I'm sure we would be the breast of friends.

Ah well... ... At least I have done one good deed today. It's a shame I have to go to work now or I could have teased you a bit more. ;-)

Likewise. We are off to Bath for a wedding this weekend. Madam is a bridesmaid! Have a lovely weekend.

Oh that will be fun. What colour is her dress?

Madam is in an ivory bridesmaid dress. And she looks so beautiful. Her Mum would cry tears of joy and pride, just like Dad.

Did you mention to me once that you tried to find my house on Google Maps? How did you get on?

I was only joking and it would be like looking for a needle in a haystack without your postcode, besides I wouldn't want to stalk you, I'd rather wait until you invited me... see if you can find mine!

26/09/07

********** Street in ******* so you can find mine! I'm on the corner of ******** Street and ****** Avenue. The one with the pool! And I do trust you not to just turn up - you'd never get past security, even if you did!

He gave me his full address here. If only I could turn back the clock, if only I had got my dad to babysit, jumped in the car and gone to his house. I might have met him and things might have been so different.

Oh, do you have guards then? So if I fluttered my eyelashes and stripped, that would get me past?

No, just huge gates with an entry code system and video surveillance. Nothing exciting. And don't strip today, you'll freeze your tits off! And I wouldn't want that...

Well it's definitely getting a bit nipply in the mornings; I shall have to put my bed socks on soon to keep my toes warm in bed.

A bit nipply... just what I was thinking when I looked in your photo album! Have you no shame, woman?

That's art. I wouldn't put the other photos in there. I'm not even sure how I got persuaded to take the other photos and send them to you!

All I'll say is, if you put pictures like that in your album, EXPECT to get pervy messages! And not just from me! ;O) It may be art to you... but it's as sexy as hell to the rest of us.

So if you were sending emails at 4pm how did you get to Bath in time for a champagne reception if you have a five-hour drive?

On my WAP mobile! The same way I always log on here. And no I wasn't driving.

I was supposed to go on a date tonight with the guy I've been talking to for at least two years on here. We both got stuck in traffic, so we had to abandon! I said it must be fate that we are not supposed to meet.
Tell me how the wedding went when you get back on here, please, oh and who was getting married, and don't forget to describe what the bride was wearing will you?

Damn, you have a sexy body. An honour to be shown it. And you have a beautiful family! Your youngest though, he looks like trouble to me...

The wedding went quite well, although I couldn't stop thinking how much my wife would have enjoyed it all. It would have been easier had not every Tom, Dick and Harriett f*cking gone on about it all the time! What about the boys? Eldest had some really good GCSE results, so why don't we talk about those instead? Celebrate the living – it's meant to be a wedding after all, not a wake!

The bride, my late wife's sister, wore a white dress. Kind of 'minimalist' as it had no lace or frilly bits, but it was cut and designed to devastating effect. Someone said it was a bespoke dress made by Jean Paul Gaultier, but I don't know if it was, nor even if he does wedding dresses. His suits are shit, at any rate.

Thanks, although if I was a bit taller it would be better and there are a few bits I don't like about my body, which I've told you about before. If I keep up with the running at least I won't put on any weight in my looming middle/old age. I'm 46 soon, nearly 50, but friends say I look more 36, so not too bad.

I found your house... not exactly in the middle of nowhere, so when I come round and you spank me you'll have to play loud music.

Go and see my photo album, I have a cute duck picture.

Oh, if you insist. But I don't find ducks 'cute', not after what they do to my pool! Put the kettle on, I'll be there in a minute.

Ahhh… You get ducks in your pool, I love little ducks. That was one of my list of things I wanted: a house in the countryside with chickens, ducks, guinea pigs and a dishwasher!

It isn't so cute when the ducklings die. Expensive and inconvenient too, as the pool then has to be cleaned. I mean, would you want to swim in water that's had dead birds floating in it? Nor would I!

Why are they dead? What did you do? You don't shoot them do you?

Goodness me, NO! They swim in a pool of chlorinated water and can't get out.

Poor little things. Perhaps you could make a little ramp for them, or give them a floating house to live in.

OR, just maybe, they might like to stay the hell out of my pool! It's all a bit academic really, as the covers are going back up pretty soon and the transformation back to 'indoor pool' will be made.

Well, leave a lilo in or something, just in case. So now you'll have a huge erection in your garden again!

I'll have some big strong men and a crane to help me with it too!

Careful, don't tease me too much, remember I know where you live!

27/09/07

Thank god it's lunchtime. I was supposed to be dusting and vacuuming, but I decided to apply for three passports. We will all have one then, although I just need one for my middle son who is going on a football trip to Malta with his team next May half-term. What are you having for lunch?

I'm really lucky when it comes to applying for passports, as many of my contemporaries are considered to be suitable signers. So am I, and we all help each other out. It's quite strange when someone's there for you to countersign their passport application whilst they countersign yours. Lunch today is a grilled chicken salad. What are you having?

My friend is a teacher, so I'm ok. I had left-over vegetarian stew from about 4 days ago, with dumplings... hmmm, no wonder you're skinny. I'll need a work out now.

You think I'm skinny? You should've seen the chicken!

Oh my God! You ate a whole one! You naughty boy, go to my room, I mean the gym, immediately!

No I didn't! Like you, all I've had to enjoy have been the breasts! And where would I get the greater workout – your room or the gym?

It depends on how long and hard you spank me before you put your long and hard jewellery holder inside me, then how long you can keep it up and how hard you can bang away until I come! If you can't play with me for at least a couple of hours then it's the gym for you!

How hard do you like to be spanked? Just playfully? Or a shit-that-hurt-I-can't-sit-down-for-a-week kind of beating? Perhaps I might like to play with your body for a while. You'll be blindfolded of course, as my pleasures would be private and none of your business! Just between me and your body – my property!

My boys are about to walk through the door, they have a half day so next Septembers intake can visit the school... there goes my computer for the rest of the day. On with the dusting!

I've got another PC now – a small one that fits under the TV. It's about the size of a video recorder. It has a TV & Freeview tuner built in, and you can record (video+) onto DVD or the hard disk. It'll play any movie files, look at pictures through the card reader, play the sound through the surround sound speakers, AND you can surf the net with the wireless mouse and keyboard.

Ooooh new toys, I love new toys. It does everything then, like you, Mr. Perfect (That's quicker than Rich Sexy Six-Pack Jingle-Jangle Thong Boy). If it plays movie files I could send you some bondage films, including 'The Story of O' on Pando, although on second thoughts, they are probably illegal... Oh look I'm thinking about sex now... Time for a cup of tea and chocolate!

You send it to me, and I'll send you a copy of Beating Amy. That's guaranteed to scare you away! Time for a smoothie. I won't have any more coffee now or I won't sleep tonight.

You won't scare me away, remember nothing scares me, except if you get angry with me. I'll give you my email address, again, if you want to send it. Yes, no caffeine after 5pm, or else I don't sleep either, even with an orgasm :-)

It's 10pm... I'm drinking whisky with one hand and thinking about you spanking me while I struggle to get away... Mmmmmm... I wish I was a duck then I could fly over... but you wouldn't want to f**k a duck, so that's no good is it? Now what can I do with the ice left in my glass? Any suggestions?

28/09/07

Hey I just went through your guest book and you've replied to the wish entry I left you.......I had to look negates up in the dictionary......Good word, I'll remember that one, but then you lawyers have loads of interesting words that normal people know nothing about.
Sooooooo.........If telling me your other two wishes negates them........then.......your only wish is to have me! Yay!

We lawyers spend many years learning (and in some cases, creating) long words. How else would one justify such huge salaries?

Yeeeees........Along with the huge egos!

No question of it!

And especially if they look as sexy and handsome as you! Normal people don't stand a chance against you!

That has been said before, in many a courtroom. Who am I to argue?

Oh no!!!.....Scrap that last reply.......I've probably just made it worse!!!

You don't think that your constant messaging, naughty pictures on demand, and indefatigable adoration could have possibly done that already?

I'm going in the shower now, as I just got in from work and will be taking myself and the boys to get our passport photos done after school. I need to look my best. I might even try on my black stockings!

I'm sure you'll look truly beautiful. Don't try on the stockings in the shower.

So I went upstairs, took off my robe, dried my hair, put on my black lacy suspenders, carefully rolled one stocking up my leg... THEN MY DAUGHTER TURNS UP WITH THREE BOYS FROM COLLEGE AND A GIRL! I had to quickly rip off the stocking and suspenders and run into the bathroom where my clothes were and get dressed! It's all your fault if I've snagged them!

02/10/07

My apologies! I'll pay for any damage. Or I'll just replace things. Let's see... from your pictures, you look like a size 12, maybe a 36C. I'm probably way off though!

No you're spot on! How did you do that? I was a 14 until I started the running and less snacking, although with college (I decided to do my ECDL) and two nights a week at football training, my running has lapsed a bit.

(Sent picture in stockings and suspenders)
Ok this is as far as I go, you've turned me into a naughty, slutty, whore who definitely needs spanking!

My goodness me... and THANK YOU! There, that's a smile on my face for the rest of the day. And I know that you trust me enough – these pictures stay with me. They won't turn up elsewhere on the Internet! Wow...

Yes, but you can't see much, it's a bit dark and my head got chopped off. I'm glad you have a smile on your face.

Well you look absolutely fantastic. As sexy as hell. And the first naked woman I've seen in nearly two years! The first one I actually know, anyway: I still get strangers sending me pictures of their bits. I don't want to see them! Just yours, that's all!

I'm not completely naked. If you want me completely naked,

then you'll need a room with the lights off! I'm not that brave to send you a completely naked photo and I don't think I'm THAT sexy, in fact I'm not like this in 'real life' as my youngest would say, I'm just playing with you, because I like you… quite a lot.

Going back to that message, it would have to be a 'shit-that-hurt-I-can't-sit-down-for-a-week' kind of a beating.

I've never been blindfolded either. The thought of you gently and playfully playing with my body using whatever you wanted, doing whatever you wanted, keeping me waiting, my senses heightened, bringing me to the point of orgasm, then back down again… Well, I can't stop thinking about it!

Neither can I! Tell you what – you've only got my word for it that it's ME doing things to your body.

Oh now who's being naughty!

That's just it – you won't know for certain! Maybe I'll introduce you afterwards…

Bad boy!

Getting badder by the minute! Boy, what I could do with that body…

When I say I'm playing with you, it doesn't mean that I wouldn't do any of the things we've discussed at all in 'real life' and I'm just playing with you knowing you can't do anything about anything being so far away, because I have this fixation on you, or was it 'indefatigable adoration'... I mean I would do things if you asked me to, if we ever met, or if you made me ;-) but not straight away, but then you wouldn't want to either, straight away, or at all, I don't know, maybe you're just playing with me? Well you are, playing with me, or you wouldn't reply to mail and the ones you don't reply to are the emails when you don't want to play with me. So I wonder if one day you won't want to play anymore, as in meet me, but that would seem odd after all this playing don't you think... am I making any sense? At all?

Some. You're basically insecure. When I don't reply, it doesn't mean anything other than I'm unable to keep up! You try reading and replying to 12 messages on a mobile! Some ladies are repeatedly ignored! Be thankful.

Oh I see, I forgot most of the time you're on your PDA. It's like texting, I can't stand it. I find it annoying having to press those little keys. It's OK for one or two messages, then I've had enough, which is why if you did take my mobile number and text, you certainly wouldn't get as much back as you do on here, so you would be quite safe from me pestering you.
I'm not insecure!... *sulk*

No, not much you aren't.

Humph! I shan't talk to you anymore then! I'm going to cook tea then go in the bath and make myself beautiful and soft and I'm not taking any pictures, so you'll just have to imagine how soft and wet I'll be and what you'll be missing.

Wrong again – you'll take whatever pictures it pleases me for you to take! That's how it works, young lady. See you at bath time. I'll be in the suds, just after I've lit the candles and poured the champagne. How would madam like a neck rub while she relaxes?

Tyrant! You can't make me take pictures! Anyway it would just be a picture of bubble bath and steam, so there! Yes I would like a neck rub... I need one after all the stress. Are we in your bathroom or mine? There's no room for candles in mine.

Yes I can, and yes you will. We'd better be in my bathroom where the tub is in the middle of the room. There's a sofa in there too if you're tired! And heating under the tiles. Then into the en-suite shower wet room with hooks in the ceiling.

OH NO NOT THE HOOKS AGAIN!!! PLEASE NOT THE HOOKS... I'LL BE GOOD AND TAKE THE PICTURE, I WILL HONESTLY... I'LL BE REALLY, REALLY GOOD ;-)

Too late! It's the hooks for you – both hands, while your bottom is coated with baby oil, then paddled until it's crimson. Then I think I might like to take that bottom and slip my lubricated penis into it.

Oh you... you... beast. That's not fair, at least let me have one hand free so I can rub myself while you put THAT up my bottom! Damn, you just made me wet again!

That's OK – I'll indulge in a little 'double bassing' whilst I'm wrecking your ass. Fair?

Double bassing? What's that supposed to mean? Is that some sort of college slang from your glory hole days? And I'm not sure I like the sound of the word 'wrecking' either!

03/10/07

No, this one is straight from Roger's Profanisaurus, published by Viz, which the boys gave me for Christmas once. We all read it and all laughed until we cried. Imagine I'm inside you from behind. My right fingers are on your clitoris, my left are on your left nipple. My posture would therefore be as if I was playing the double bass. Make any sense? No? Then go and look at your Bill Haley and the Comets record sleeve and remind yourself what a double bass is!

Thank you, that makes it very clear! It's a good job I haven't changed yet to go out, I'm cleaning the bathroom, because you've done it again (made me wet) and so early in the morning! My nipples are VERY sensitive and the slightest touch sends me wild, you have to hold the nipple between your thumb and second finger whilst rubbing them with your first finger, but I do like them pulled hard when I'm about to come… can you manage that in your current position?

Yes, I can manage it. I don't know what it is about you, but you seem like a lady who cums like a freight train coming off the rails! Are you loud? Maybe you squirt….

Oh gross!!! If it's done right I can be loud, but I don't 'squirt', I'm a lady!

We'll see if you do or don't. Who knows, perhaps you just haven't squirted YET. We'll find out. Maybe if I tie your elbows to your knees, then just see what I can do with my tongue?

Oh god! No comment!

Ok, I'm sending you the last piece of the puzzle, which is me, which somehow you've persuaded me to send... I don't know how it happened. Maybe it's your commanding voice. Maybe it's the whisky. Maybe it's what I imagine you could do if I was there hanging from your ceiling... mmmm... I did put a few filters on with Adobe to disguise it a bit and give it more of an artistic edge. What do you think?

04/10/07

Well it's the next day now - I hope you don't feel so embarrassed about that picture. Not that it's anything to be embarrassed about, you have an amazing body! It's just that last night you were on the whiskey, and today you're (hopefully) sober. But I think you KNOW that these pictures stay with me and only me, don't you?
What a sexy body... Grrrrrrr!

Oh I wasn't drunk, really. I know the photos stay with you.

I shouldn't say this - and I cannot discuss this at all in any way - but I know that you're interested. Here it is: expect BIG news in the McCann case within days.

05/10/07

Go and visit my profile, I have new photos, well not new to you just old ones with added text, as I decided to get rid of the witch pictures, they were too out of date... like yours!

I see you've been in my guest book again, I hope you wiped your feet first, it may be sunny outside, but there's still a lot of mud around. I've left a comment with your comment, so you have to go back to read it.

All this running around you make me do - tsk! Okay, I'll be along in a minute. It had better be tidy.

Well Madam has been to a birthday party this afternoon, straight after Nursery, so I've been kind of busy, including a nice little 10-mile run. I could do with a backrub now though, getting a bit stiff.

I'll rub yours if you rub mine ;0)

You're a pain! All I can think of now is massaging and I'm supposed to be getting on with the dishes. We need a nice quiet room with the curtains pulled, a few candles, preferably scented, dotted around, maybe some background music. Put some cushions on the floor to lie on, so I can work my way all round you without falling off a bed... Now take off your clothes and lie on your tummy, I don't want my eye poked out just yet! OK, I'm opening the olive oil, your home grown of course and adding a little lemon oil unless you have another preference? I shall start at your shoulders with hard, long strokes going back and forth, working my way down your back to that nice little tight arse, I might even insert a finger or two... well, it's so irresistible... Your legs are next, but I need you to turn over now so I can roll my hands round your ankles, working my way back up... Gosh I'm getting hot with all this work and the heat of the candles, I think I'd better take my clothes off...

06/10/07

Honestly... why do you have to live in Norwich? It's Saturday morning and I'm still really wet thinking about massaging you. You realise once I've turned you over and got you really oily, it's going to get a bit slippery as I work my way up... now how can I stop myself from sliding off you? Hmm... what's this poking up? Maybe if I just eased myself on top, I could anchor myself down and carry on with massaging your shoulders... mmmmm, that seems to be working, I just need to go up and down a few times to get myself comfortable. There that's better, now if I lean forward to reach your shoulders I can bite your bottom lip too and play with your tongue... See I can do three things at once! Aren't I clever?

I was going to tell you something, but I can't remember what it was, something to do with the words in a song... Oh well, it will come to me later I expect.

08/10/07

It isn't going to be Mr Blobby, is it? The boys bought me that when they were much younger – I still have no idea why!

Now why would that song come to mind... are you putting on weight? I went to the theme park with the kids where they had Mr Blobby. It was absolute rubbish. I did remember two things though. One was that I passed the first module of my ECDL course. The second thing was that I went to town on Saturday and got some half price lingerie in La Senza, so I have a really sexy basque with suspenders to wear for you...

I keep thinking about doing the ECDL, but I don't know if I can be bothered with it. I have a friend who was one of the first to do the Computer Literacy & Information Technology course, and proudly displays a certificate with CLIT written on it. That's why they hurriedly changed it to Computer Literacy AND Information Technology, CLAIT.
I look forward to seeing the lingerie.

If you want to see the lingerie then ask me out and I'll wear it. ;-) Oh I know what you'll say... "That's not how it works young lady, if I say wear it and send me the picture you'll do exactly that, blah, blah, "... I may as well just go upstairs and spank myself now.

Did you see the menswear in M&S? Go back and check out the La Collezione range with all the Italian fabrics – feel the fabric and imagine it on ME...

Yes I did see it, I was looking for a shirt for my son for the wedding. You're making me horny again... do I have to imagine it on you? I want to feel it on you, I want to breathe you in... then I want to take it off...

Well, buy one of the shirts, douse it in Clinique Happy for Men, and leave it on your bedroom floor!

Oh ha ha! Next you'll want me to lie down on it and masturbate!

Well be careful you don't ruin it. And wash your hands when you've finished.

08/10/07

Good morning. I suppose it is a good morning. It's sunny now, but it wasn't when I got up at 5.20am. I was actually lying awake thinking of having wild, passionate sex with you when I heard some noises. I thought my daughter had got up early to shower, but I hadn't heard her bang any doors, suddenly it occurred to me that my son had been up the loft yesterday and the cat must have been shut up there all night. I put up the ladder and lo and behold there he was and very pleased to get out for his breakfast. Fully awake now, I made a cup of tea and read for a while, considering the fact that I was highly unlikely to get back to sleep. I then went off for a run to return in good time for a shower, before delivering my daughter to work at 8.30am. I'm now having coffee before cleaning out the piggies, then after lunch at

2pm is my son's match, so not too much to do today, although I have to take my daughter to a party in town later. Do parents ever get a completely free weekend? What do you do at weekends?

Not as much as you do, in comparison! I just like to spend time with my children. They won't be here forever, and I just want to cherish every moment that I can with them. I owe it to their mother, after all.

That's exactly how I feel and probably why I haven't made any progress with anything at all in my life. I gave up work etc. to have the kids, and then my ex left us. When my mother died in 2001 my ex cut off contact, the kids had therefore lost their nan and their dad. My dad nearly died too, which just left me. I couldn't just pack them off into childcare and go to work, apart from the fact I had no real career to go in to and couldn't go back to my old job, because my ex worked there.

Here's your picture. I don't like it, I'm too pale and I never look good in daylight!

I think you're right - you'd look better taking it off ;O) Joking aside, I think you do yourself a disservice. You look absolutely gorgeous! Sexy as hell. And if you're a little pale - try swimming in a certain pool in Tuscany and drying off in the sun on the terrace. Can you smell the barbeque? I'll wake you up when it's ready!

It's quite difficult to get off. There's a catch at the back, perhaps you could help? You see with your charm and

imagination you have me completely and utterly hooked...
It sounds perfect, lying in the sun getting an all over tan,
with someone else doing the cooking... Heaven! Send me a
plane ticket and I'll come over!

It isn't caught at the back – there are a couple of things at
the front that are impeding it. Let me help you with those...
I'm in Norwich at the moment, but we'll be over there for the
olive harvest at half term week. They are removed from the
trees then soaked in the sea from sacks off the end of the
pier. There's going to be a big citrus harvest too. We eat well
in autumn out there!

That will be nice for you. What do you have with the olives
and citrus? I can't see me just eating those... Can I see on
Google Earth?

According to Google Earth, my place isn't built yet! It's also
too rural for the 3D view. Those aren't buttons! More like
chapel hat-pegs.

I have a friend who is an excellent butcher and pie maker,
who also deals in game when it's in season. He does all
those gorgeous smoked meats as well as all the usual
butchery, including veal. There's a deli in town that does
everything from cheeses to creams and an array of different
coffees. Fish and seafood can be bought straight off the
boats, at the harbour. If you like, we can pick armfuls of wild
herbs as we walk back to the house. In the kitchen garden
are all the grapes, tomatoes, onions, garlic, leeks etc. that
you'll ever need. And what do the boys want to take with
them? Ketchup!

Well my daughter will eat all your grapes, my middle son will join your boys with chips and ketchup, although presently he's only eating sausage rolls, and my youngest and I will eat the rest.

That leaves me with lobster, octopus, and langoustines, all done on the charcoal grill in the outdoor kitchen. Yes, I'm happy with that! I think I'll have some peppers to go with that... We'll take all the kids to the sea afterwards. Have you ever been jet-skiing?

Not sure I fancy octopus, but I'll try a bit before I make up my mind. It's a bit of a contrast to my lunch; left over mash with melted cheese, done in the microwave!

No I haven't jet skied, I don't like water much, at least I'm quite happy to swim around, but I prefer my head above water. I'm bound to come off one of those things!

Our passports arrived, by courier today and yes, we all look like convicts in the photos! Then my book came, recommended by you, 'Under the Tuscan Sun', and I've passed my second module on my ECDL course. Oh and another thing... you woke me up at 5.30am again! ;-)

How did I wake you up that early? Did you feel my lips on your neck, my hand on your breast working its way down to your clitoris?

Octopus is a chewy texture like seafood, but a fishy flavour that suits lemon juice and white wine vinegar. You'll come scuba diving with me, won't you? Beautiful scenery isn't just on land!

Scuba diving? Will I get my hair wet? Aren't there sharks about? I'll give it a go as long as you don't leave me! Hey, do I get to wear one of those tight rubber suits? More importantly, do you wear one? ;0)

Yes I do – even in the Indian Ocean, it's only warm near the surface. I wear one with sleeves and short legs. Even my mother said "mmm, nice legs!" shame on you, Mother…

Yes you'll get your hair wet. And it'll be worth it! I've heard of a fantastic dive off the coast of India and I'd love to see it myself.

Mmmmmmm… Now THAT will be interesting, giving you a hard on in a rubber suit… I wonder if my nipples will stick out as much through the rubber?

Quite possibly, although it's quite thick neoprene. It's like a quarter-inch of foam inside the rubber. I remember being on a dive once, and there were around 12 of us in our party. A certain Dutch lady (50ish) seemed nice enough – but she had the strangest, biggest nipple piercings, which were immediately obvious, even through the thick foam rubber. They were the size of Christmas tree decorations. Bizarre.

10/10/07

Send me something nice to read later, a bit of your life story perhaps. How did you meet your wife? Why do you have such a big gap between the kids? Or something about your travels? Failing that we could go back to the HOOKS!!!

I started the Tuscany book last night. It sounds idyllic. I used to dream of moving into an old house in another country and Italy sounds perfect. I once went to Sardinia, which was lovely, but haven't been to any other part of Italy. France I don't really like and Spain is so common, I know I'm a snob, but from watching documentaries about families moving to another country, they all seem to go to Spain and they all seem really rough and common, turning Spain into Blackpool.

I suppose I could be considered 'snobby' but I think it's largely because I wish to protect my kids and myself. I do know a snob among snobs though. He is Lord Whatever of Somewhere (titles don't mean much to me – I can break anyone in or out of the courtroom) and despite me having Money, he looks down his nose at me: "He had to buy his own furniture"! He lives in an inherited stately home that's been kitted out for generations. Wanker.

Oh do go on, I love listening to you… and you see that's the biggest attraction that you have, for me anyway, you're a dominant male and I'm drooling at the idea of you breaking me, getting inside me and weeding things out!

I have to say, that notion appeals to me too. ;O) I'll write something good for you; that's a promise!

I did mean in my mind when I said getting inside me, not sex.

It's difficult to tell with you.

Sorry I wasn't very clear, I could have meant either, still it is hard when you can't see me...

Fnaar . . . . . "it's hard when I can't see you" . . . . . . fnaar! My goodness me - I'm turning into my boys!

I had another stat through my group today. It said: I suck so hard you'll be pulling the sheets out of your arse! I wouldn't mind trying that one.

Hilarious!

15/10/07

I do believe congratulations are in order! I bet you can't guess why? Go on guess... no... try harder! It's six months since you started emailing me, so you deserve a pat on the back for having so much stamina and being so stubborn! Stamina, because you haven't blocked me yet or run screaming. Stubborn, because you still haven't sent me a proper email address, a mobile number so I can text you, a different photo to the one on your profile, a photo of you naked or told me your children's names!

Congratulations on your persistence!

Gee thanks honey!

Well, I'm just sticking to what I told you at the outset - I'm here purely to establish and maintain human contact with

people older than teenagers! I don't know about 'stubborn', I'm just doing what I feel is best for me and my family. It's lovely to know that there's a (slightly) bonkers lady out there who I'm getting to know, bit by bit. You are persistent. And patient. And I like that.

19/10/07

I'm sending you a letter in parts, so follow the numbers for the correct order.

I can think of a thousand replies to that and as I am pre-menstrual, irrational and depressed I may as well go for it!

I too state on my profile that I'm only here to email chat and am not looking for a relationship, but that all goes out the window, if I find someone I like. I found you, which couldn't be any worse really, with your situation; your recent bereavement, (Even though two years have passed it doesn't make it any easier) location; bloody Norwich and lack of any free time for dating. Oh, not forgetting that you're seven years younger, which should actually be OK, because I look much younger than I am and men age so much quicker than women, so we're equal really, but you can't possibly say you're sticking to what you told me at the outset, when you have related so much to me, so many details, so many things that have kept me glued to Lycos looking for you every day. I know men don't think like women, but you've turned something on and I can't turn it off.

I still need to know if it's worth the effort and if I should carry on. I need to see you. You say you're not ready for that or that it's not fair on the kids. Now I go round in circles again. Do I carry on? The answer is yes, because I am stubborn and I am persistent. Equally though, I certainly don't want to be where I'm not wanted i.e. waiting in your inbox.

This leads on to the other annoying aspect of my personality, the way I jump ahead to try and work out all possible outcomes of all situations without having any solid feedback from any of the persons involved first and consequently getting myself into a state. So the next question I ask myself is, why do I like you so much that I continue to hang on your every word, when I should cut and run by now and get off this useless dating site with creepy old men and rough, uncouth youths hounding me? Is it love? No, I haven't met you yet. Is it the money you earn, which would be enough to support both our families? Yes and no. Yes, because we would need money to live with six kids and three on the way (Get lost! That was a joke!) I have my house, my ex pays maintenance, although he would try and get out of it as soon as he knew I was with someone and I'd save you nursery bills, even gardening bills... I'd keep the cleaner though! (Now do you see the annoying habit I have of jumping ahead?)

Is it how sexy and handsome you look? Oh come on, how can I tell from one f**king teeny, weeny photo. Oh well, maybe a bit.

Is it the fact that you can cook? Yes.

That you can play the guitar? Yes.

That you can drink a whole bottle of Jim Beam in an evening? Yes.

Is it the way you say "You will do as you're told" to me? Oh most definitely yes.

Is it having three children? Yes. I know I've discussed that before three is different from two, plus I wanted six kids, but have now resigned myself to the fact that I'm never having any more, which is one of the things I'll never forgive my ex for. I think I've covered a lot of other stuff before too, including having piercings, a six-pack, wearing thongs, running, hooks, spanking, Dominance, you like reading, wine, tranquillity. Oh not to mention your superior intelligence too, of course. The two most important things though are that you make me laugh AND turn me on and that's all I really want.

I don't know what I'm trying to say. I do tend to go off a bit when I write and I would never tell you any of this to your face. It just doesn't come out as words, which is why I like the idea of you 'breaking' me, making me tell you what I'm thinking, or else ;-)

Anyway it's taken me over an hour to write this, now I have to break it down to send it! Oh god now you are going to be annoyed with me!

30/10/07

A 'proper' email address? Do you mean like geordie_armani@jubii.co.uk or perhaps @hotmail.com or maybe something similar?

Oh I hadn't really thought about it, (he he)but the Hotmail one sounds OK.

I'm in the process of carving my pumpkins. One is two hands pulling apart its bottom, the other I'm still waiting for inspiration, but it's bigger and I have some gourds I can stick on. What will you be wearing tomorrow to scare off the kids? Hey, if you go naked to the door that should work quite well! ;-)

31/10/07

Did you get my emails? Go and read my mouse story in my journal, if you have time.

It was at this point that we began to email with our personal addresses, but here are some of the entries that we put in each other's guest books on the dating site for all to see.

Guest Books

17:22 | 31 May
Hmmmmm... your cock has spurs on! Just flying through!

How good of you to point that level of detail out to my dear Guestbook readers. xxx

16:33 | 6 June
Ooooooh!!! Looks like I am number 100, so all you girls can stop bickering now, because I win the trophy!!! There is a trophy right? May be a bar of chocolate? I'll settle for a packet of Maltesers then...

Come on, you heard Mother... We've all had a good night. Now, can you see your drinks off please? Some of us have got homes to go to!

9:25 | 14 June
Where's the sodding joke then? You persuade me to trudge all the way over here, on the promise of an incredibly funny joke, and look at it. I've coughed up funnier stuff than that. Frankly madam, I'm disappointed.

9:23 | 15 June
Did you see that, Lava-lamp Lady? The gentleman two messages below me DOES know how to tell jokes. Watch and learn.

14:03 | 15 June
Here's a better joke for you, Jingle Bells... Part One
This is a story about a fly, a fish, a bear, a hunter, a mouse and a cat. There is a moral to this story, but not exactly the one most of us are expecting. In the dead of summer a fly was resting on a leaf beside a lake. The hot, dry fly said to no one in particular, "Gosh, if I go down three inches I will feel the mist from the water and I will be refreshed." There was a fish in the water thinking, "Gosh, if that fly goes down three inches, I can eat him." There was a bear on the shore thinking, "Gosh...if that fly goes down three inches that fish will jump for the fly...and I will grab the fish!"

It also happened that a hunter was farther up the bank of the lake preparing to eat a cheese sandwich. "Gosh," he thought, "if that fly goes down three inches and that fish leaps for it, that bear will come out and grab for the fish. I'll shoot the bear and have a proper lunch."

Now, you probably think this is enough activity on one bank of a lake, but I can tell you there's more...

A wee mouse by the hunter's foot was thinking, "Gosh, if

that fly goes down three inches and that fish jumps for that fly and that bear grabs for that fish... the dumb hunter will shoot the bear and drop his cheese sandwich."

A cat lurking in the bushes took in this scene and thought, (as was fashionable to do on the banks of this particular lake around lunch time), "Gosh, if that fly goes down three inches and that fish jumps for that fly and that bear grabs for that fish and that hunter shoots that bear and that mouse makes off with the cheese sandwich, then I can have mouse for lunch."

The poor fly is finally so hot and so dry that he heads down for the cooling mist of the water. The fish swallows the fly, the bear grabs the fish, the hunter shoots the bear, the mouse grabs the cheese sandwich, the cat jumps for the mouse, the mouse ducks... the cat falls into the water and drowns. The moral of the story is: whenever a fly goes down three inches, some pussy is in serious danger.

3 July
Is that it? How dare you waste everybody's time! That joke took seconds from my life to read... and I want 'em back!

13:58 | 3 July
Came by on my broomstick to drop another ten, shame you're not here or I could have dropped it on your head, knocked you unconscious and had my wicked way with you!!!

10:24 | 29 August
Now what are your other two wishes?

It is my understanding that if I answer that question, then it negates any likelihood of those wishes ever coming true.

9:17 | 5 October
"Come and look at my profile!" she says. "I've got some new pictures!" And what do I see? Blatant exhibitionism and an infantile sense of humour! Fantastic! ;O)

I know, I'm fantastic :-) and at least I have proper photos in my album not cut-outs from magazines!

11:51 | 10 October
I thought it was about time I came by and soiled your guestbook again, so here's another joke...

On a farm lived a chicken and a horse who were friends. One day the horse fell into a bog and shouted for the chicken to get help. The farmer was out with the tractor, so the chicken took his BMW, tied a rope to the bumper, threw the end to the sinking horse and pulled him out. The farmer was none the wiser when he returned. A few weeks later the chicken fell into a mud pit. He shouted to the horse for help, who thinking for a minute then straddled the mud pit and told the chicken to grab hold of his 'thing' and he pulled him out.The moral of the story: If you're hung like a horse you don't need a BMW to pick up chicks.

30/10/07

If you get this, then you gave me your email address... Did you get heat stroke in Tuscany?

No heatstroke – just fed up with the moaning… ;O)

Well I have no idea what to write now I have your 'proper' email address, but then I haven't finished running round the garden shouting "He gave me his email address, he gave me his email address, he gave me his email address!"

The thing is, I can actually imagine you doing that.

31/10/07

How was Tuscany? Did you get the olives in? I've just got to that part in the book I'm reading recommended by you, of course.

01/11/07

Where are you?

You finally give me your email address then you disappear… Again! I've had two orgasms already just thinking about you and now you've made me write another email to you, which is going to be too many for you to reply to… again, which will make you annoyed again, and there are loads of things I've thought of that I want to ask you now, about all sorts of stuff… One is, is that your real name? If so, are you Jewish? Or religious at all? Did your eldest go to college? My daughter is picking a university, but I'm completely confused. How's the potty training going? Did you go scuba diving? Did you see any sharks?

You see it's too much now, I'm going back to dust!

02/11/07

Bless my soul… Yes, I am partly Jewish (American Jewish). My family tree takes in elements of Kennedy and Onassis along the way, and my late wife was part of the Guinness family. My only ties to religion would be to do with Freemasonry – I'm involved with Bilderberg but that's not a religion, nor a belief system. But we meet once in a while.

Tuscany was glorious! Just as beautiful in the autumn as the UK with all the red and gold leaves, but still twenty degrees! We gorged ourselves on produce (apples, apricots, pears, citrus, all the others) and I'm expecting a box of 48 bottles of my own olive oil any day now! There will be several boxes, but they don't all arrive together. We went shooting whilst madam stayed with my friends for the afternoon – they've been far more help to me than their own grandparents. Tragic, in my opinion. We had our last Italian barbecue of 2007, which included a spit roast hog. You've never had crackling like it.

We did go scuba diving, but we just saw crabs and a few small fish, I've no idea what they were. Plenty of coral though. And far too many jellyfish than I'm comfortable with!

God you are posh then!!! But I love Guinness. I used to belong to a scooter gang. We all wore those black satin puffy jackets on top of green army overalls (we were scooterists, not Mods) and mine had a Guinness beer mat on.

You go shooting! What do you shoot? My youngest son will be your friend for life! He is fixated on guns, fighting games and anything to do with the army and war.

I'm not keen on jellyfish either! We lived in Singapore for 14 months when I was 8 years old. We once went on a boat trip to an island for the day, but as there was only a couple of dinghies to get to shore a lot of people decided to swim and got stung by baby jellyfish on the way. I'm off to work now. We have a wedding on Sunday in Braintree. I'm driving there at 10am and back at 12pm, so we won't get to bed until 4am I expect, on Monday morning.

I looked up Bilderberg on the Internet. Is that where a load of posh guys go to chat like a load of old women about how they'd like to run the world over tea and cakes?

Sigh You're definitely way out of my league! It also means I have to add to your ever-growing nickname you've just become: Posh, Rich, Sexy, Six-Pack, Jingle-Jangle, Thong Boy! Oh well looks like I shall just have to be your cybersex slave!

05/11/07

Morning... well it's actually 2.50 am on Monday morning. I just got back from the wedding.

It was a black and white theme, which wouldn't be my choice, but worked quite well and there was a games room, with sweets and a PlayStation that kept the youngest amused for most of the evening, but I'm still fed up going on my own, everyone else seems to be in couples at these things and once again I have to drive, so I can't drink and I have to cope with arguing children, as my eldest son gets a bit hyper on long journeys, plus I only have a small car and he's much too tall for it now.

Sounds like quite a wedding. 'Black and white theme'? Are they minstrels? Goths?

You're 100% right about Bilderberg, it's where business leaders can meet heads of state and financiers, lawyers without any media pressure. In fact no one is allowed near – partners, the public, hotel staff (we have our own caterers!) and certainly no reporters or journalists who aren't members.

It sounds like you need a bigger car! Or a trailer. You should get a decent deal on a 4x4, everyone I know can't wait to get rid of theirs! I never had one, I don't go off road in the UK so I didn't see the point. Why not travel in style?

Now do you see the advantages of giving me your 'proper' email address, you can see me in 'Large'. No more eye strain trying to look at those tiny Lycos pictures! Mind you now you can see my grey hair and age spots… not good! You can send me a picture now, preferably one where you look a bit older, unlike your Lycos picture where you look about 22! (another six months of pestering until that happens, I expect).

Well I had a nap, but couldn't really sleep, so I had a long bath and read some more about Tuscany. I'm going to do the soup now and Tesco's will have to wait until tomorrow, I'm knackered… … Not too knackered to think about sex though… mmm.

I saw a site recently which held my interest (but not long enough to subscribe!) It had 'Ultimate Surrender' in the title. Anyway, two ladies wrestle, and the winner gets to do whatever she wants to the loser, be it tie up and torture her, fuck her with a strap on or spank her. Whatever she feels would degrade her defeated opponent sufficiently. Different – and that's what I like. Any flavour other than vanilla.

I have a stat for that!

I don't know what "I have a stat for that" means, but oh look! ******'s heard of it. Those are rough-looking women aren't they? Tell you what though – you tell 'em that. I'm not going to...

I used to have a profile on alt.com ages ago before I married. I had a nice sex slave who I'd just use and degrade whenever I felt like it and then I suddenly had two! The first was slightly younger than me, the second was only about 19 with a girlish, somewhat underdeveloped body. You should have seen their faces when I brought them together! I'd already tied the older one and put a gag in and a hood over her head. Then the second one arrived, and I did the same to her. Then I put them next to each other, touching... then pulled the hoods off. 'Panic' is a good look for a sex slave.

Anyway, I soon had them doing whatever I wanted. Sometimes I liked to see them kissing deep and passionate, sometimes I liked to see them lick and fuck each other. Sometimes I'd fuck one or both, sometimes I'd administer discipline to one or both. But I especially liked days out with my sluts – doing whatever I told them to. If I wanted them to snog in a posh restaurant, then they had to. Topless on the beach, they had to do it. Take off their underwear and pass it to me (or each other's underwear!) they would do it

happily. I had some male friends over one night, and they waited on us in their lingerie and high heels, before putting on a show for us afterwards. Falling asleep between two gorgeous sex slaves every night – you couldn't beat it!

Before you were married? How old were you then when you got married if your eldest is 16? OMG... You do have a 'dark side' or should I say 'hidden side'. I knew you liked the Alt.com and Hogtied web sites, but hey it's all coming out now! Were you rich then? Only it sounds like a typical bored rich boy pastime, having sex slaves. I thought Masters were usually a lot older, but I suppose they have to start somewhere. Was your wife into BDSM too?

I think I've just led a really sheltered life and then when I do discover 'other' sexual activities I'm stuck in my prime with three kids and no one to play with! Typical!

You've surprised me again. I'm nervous now!

I just got out of the shower... my hair needed washing, so did my two dildos. I'm supposed to be going to Tesco to get the food, but I'm compelled to stay here.

So... you're just out of the shower, still wet, with some lovely clean dildos and a webcam.

No, the dildos are back in the drawer. And I'm dry... on the outside... And yes I have a web cam!

I've only been in Tesco once – as far as I know, its main purpose is to keep the riffraff out of Waitrose.

SNOB! Well I don't have a Waitrose close by and it's expensive. I used to go to Sainsbury's, but my ex is a manager somewhere and I have a fear of bumping into him, so Tesco it is, which is where I'm going now... With my 'wet' pants on!

On third thoughts... Can you have third thoughts? If you send me a picture of you, I could make a video of me 'getting wet' looking at you... mmmmmmm... oh no, see you're turning me into a slut again!!!

When I married my ex, I hadn't had many men and had only had one orgasm with one of my boyfriends. With my ex sex wasn't ever really good either. I can't for the life of me remember why I married him, I suppose it was because I wanted to be married and have children. Once we had the children we practically stopped having sex. He worked late a lot and I was always tired from the kids waking up, so I was in bed when he got home. He never once gave me an orgasm when we were together. I had to do it myself. His idea of foreplay was to kiss me until my face was sore. I used to get it over with as soon as possible. He was never in right, so sex was painful. I used to hope that he would come quickly and go to sleep, but because I hadn't come I couldn't sleep with no release, so I would avoid sex at all costs. This was part of the reason that we broke up. It wasn't until after we divorced that I became more aware of his failings from reading Cosmopolitan and it wasn't until 2002 when I got my first computer that I discovered L@L, Incredimail and then the BDSM Yahoo group. You could say I'm a bit of a late starter!

The Dom/sub thing lures me. I want to be overpowered and controlled and played with. I want the attention that my ex never gave me. I want someone else to give me orgasms... to make me orgasm... to pinch my nipples, spank me and warm me up with mental manipulation. Not too much pain, just enough to enhance, not needles or drawing blood, I've never swallowed and I wouldn't suck you off if 'it' had been in the back door! There's a lot I'd like to try and stuff I've tried, but felt I didn't really go as far as I could have done- a good Dom is hard to find! At least Norwich is closer than Spain...

I'm going to bed now, It's 11.30pm already and I'm still not that tired, I must have gone past it... now what can I do to get myself to sleep?

12/11/07

Guess what? I woke up at 5.15am (when I could have slept in) dreaming about being tied up, gagged and blindfolded! Only you were there and although the idea of other men involved does have a certain dangerous appeal, in reality having a couple of drunk, lecherous blokes seeing who can think of the most degrading thing to do to me, doesn't appeal at all and definitely wouldn't give me pleasure!

My spanking book came, but I haven't looked at it yet, I've been too busy. Having tossed in bed for a while I got up, showered and washed my hair, put a load of washing on, stripped all the beds, hung the washing out, took my daughter to work and made the boys get up and go with her, so we could go to town early.

."A certain dangerous appeal" would be right. However, gentlemen of breeding would be unlikely to bring you to any harm. Degrade you, perhaps, but then again you need it. You need to be shown the correct path, and this would be a memorable way for you to learn. No, please, don't thank me.

Gentlemen of breeding are the worst kind! They are the ones with money to burn who think they can do as they please, because they can afford it and the ones that are bored enough to try anything! I do not need to be degraded! I do not need to be shown the correct path!

Yes, I would say that you have "gentlemen of breeding" down to a tee. My reply would be... "SO?"

'So'... That was a short answer for you... are you feeling well? I still don't think I could do any of that stuff though, if it came down to it. I'd have to be in a very stable relationship to even consider it, being insecure, nervous etc. I'd much rather be spanked, just by you and hooked up for a bit of double bassing.

13/11/07

Good morning sir, how are you today? I'm tired, as usual and about to go to work. I had college last night and haven't had time to wash my hair, so I've put it in plaits and... LOOK... the ends of my plaits nearly touch the end of my nipples! I wonder if you have anything long that you can nearly touch to the end of something else? ;0)Just sending you some more pictures. I'm bored and you're not on line. I'm horny and you're not here to take care of me... I think I must be ovulating again... Can you tell?I think I need you to control me!

15/11/07

Well, actual physical harm is not really me I'm afraid. I know a member of Her Majesty's Government who calls himself a Dom because he likes to tie ladies up and then beat them black and blue. That is not being a Dom; that is being a Wanker. Being a Dom is about controlling, owning that other person; heart, mind, body, spirit, and soul. But you should still be able to have a cuddle and a laugh about it afterwards, shouldn't you?

Well that's a relief, because you were beginning to worry me with the olive trees and the yacht thing. No, these pictures only fire my imagination; I wouldn't want to be tortured in any way. You have my mind, some of my heart, some of my spirit and a tiny bit of my soul... Oh and a photo of my body!You also didn't answer the question: 'How come you didn't pay for your furniture?'

Simple. My family come from "old money". Although I've made a fair stack of my own!

Ohhhhhh... hand me downs.

19/11/07

Something wonderful has happened! I've worked out how I get to see the pictures you send from your mobile! I did it all myself; no further need for a teenager to show me how to work my own PC. Madam has been dreadful these last few nights – unable to sleep with some sort of irritation. She scratches away at her nappy, saying her 'poofy' hurts (I wonder which of her darling brothers taught her to say that) but there's no sign of any irritation on her skin. She has a bath with baby oil in, Sudocreme and a fresh nappy, but she still writhes away, unable to sleep, and then cries in frustration. A worrying time. She's fine during the day of course!

Clever boy! Have a gold star. You sound pretty bright considering you're having sleepless nights. I've just got home from the 'Riff Raff' store, so I must unpack, hang up the washing then I can have coffee and a doughnut... Why don't you pop round? Incidentally I now have a coffee bean grinder, so I can make whichever coffee I want with fresh beans instead of three different packets of coffee in the fridge.

22/11/07

I have a coffee bean grinder, and an espresso machine I brought back from Italy. Eldest asked me once "What do coffee beans taste like?" so I told him to eat one. He buzzed around the house for a good 20 minutes like a child possessed, and then suddenly went silent. We found he had

crashed out on the sofa, fast asleep. It turned out that Madam had threadworms, probably caught from some disgusting working-class peasant child. One spoonful of expensive banana-flavoured medicine, and she's alright again. It was fun explaining to the boys that they had to have some too!

Well of course you would have a grinder and an espresso machine and I bet you have one of those really expensive ones too, not the little stove-top pot that I have!

Talking about spanking, I'm getting through the 'Consensual Spanking' book slowly. I didn't know it was so involved. According to the book spanking sessions can go on for over an hour, building up from hand spanking to implements, while taking breaks and continuously changing positions. Also slowly removing clothes to increase the embarrassment for the spankee… No wonder I'm still left wanting after the five minutes or so that I had from the other two Doms that I experienced! Have you read the book? There are also tricks mentioned to stop the full force of the spank going into the bottom and sending the force through the spankers hand instead… At least it's written to show the spanker how to avoid this, but it's quite useful for me too.

It's nearly a full moon. I managed a short run today in the last of the daylight and the moon was already out in the sky. I love to go out on a clear night with the moon and the stars; all I need is you to come with me. I can imagine walking with you, maybe we met on a date and you decide that we should go for a walk, the pub being overcrowded and noisy. There would be a full moon overhead with a chill in the evening air. We would walk down a footpath through a field, perhaps alongside some woods. A light mist would be settling across the fields with ponies finishing off the last of their grazing. I'll be prattling on just as I do online, annoying you with my incessant talk disturbing the peace, oblivious of your real intentions... Then 'Shh!"

What was that? In the woods...'

'In the woods where?"

I heard something... Follow me.'

You take my hand and lead me into the woods, our feet cracking fallen branches, pushing through the undergrowth into a small clearing, the bark from a silver birch reflecting the moonlight. You take me up to the tree and stop.

'I can't see anything,' I say looking at the tree, my back to you.'

No, that's because you're not meant to."Huh?'

Quick as a flash you snap a blindfold over my eyes, I cry out in surprise, my hands go up to remove it but you grab my wrists, bringing them round behind my back and fastening a pair of handcuffs onto one wrist, then coming round in front of me, you force my arms above my head to link them over a branch in the tree with the cuffs.'

Oh that's not fair... You can't do this... We've only just met... I'm not ready, it's too cold!"

Enough talk! You're ready if I say you're ready and after months of teasing me on the Internet I think it's time I assert my authority and make you a bit more obedient.' As you speak you place a gag around my mouth.'

And now I shall do exactly as I please to you and for as long as I like, and don't worry, you'll soon warm up.'

Well it's your fault, because I'm drinking Jim Beam, which I only bought because it was on special offer and you told me about it and I need something to help me sleep because I'm not going to have you am I and that would help me sleep a lot better if I did! So there... With brass knobs on the end. That's appropriate because you have got a knob with brass on, well not brass, but you know what I mean... And I'm not going to see that either, or you come to think of it... Not even in a photo of it or you, because YOU WON'T SEND ME ONE!

Goodnight!

26/11/07

Do you go to parties? Not now I expect, but I'm sure there must be lots of posh, pompous, lawyer parties that you've been to when your wife was with you, being rich and posh and in those circles of people that have parties all the time! Well if you have to go to any and you need an escort I'm free... Well not actually free, you'd probably have to buy me something suitable to wear, as I only have 'clothes like everybody else' and pick me up, I'm not driving to Norwich and partying all night and I'd need to sleep in your guest room, if you have one, which I'm sure you do, failing that I'll sleep in the car in the garage... What car do you have? Will there be room to lie down? I haven't asked what car you have yet...

Blimey. She's been at the meths again. Yes I go to parties, and yes they are usually full of pompous fucking lawyer

types with no necks and walk-in wallets and 'partners' that their wives know nothing about. I'm sure I can find room in the guest wing. I'm changing the cars around a bit; I'll keep the Aston Martin but I don't know what else I'll get yet.

Is meths the same as mouthwash?

I don't know if you could use meths as a mouthwash. Dropouts in Victorian London used to drink it as a cheaper alternative to alcohol – remember to take the paintbrushes out first though.

I know they drink meths, I'm not stupid… I meant is drinking the mouthwash the same as drinking the meths! Dur!

You'd know. Can you afford mouthwash?

I'M GOING TO COME OVER THERE AND HIT YOU NOW!

You ought to work on that anger – violence is not a trait one admires, nor encourages, in the lower strata of society.

Pompous a******! As I'm a lady I really cannot reply to this in the manner it deserves, besides I shouldn't be writing while I'm driving to your house!I'm nearly at your house so you had better be ready for me!

28/11/07

Yesterday the cat chewed up my daughter's homework, which she left on the floor in the bedroom. My son thought it was hilarious that she could go into college and tell the teacher that the cat ate her homework. Anyway he just came home for his breakfast, he tends to disappear for hours sometimes days at a time, went upstairs and did it again; she had still left it on the floor! I stopped him and gave him some plain paper, then did a little video.Here is the video of the cat eating the paper.

By some miracle, that worked! A dire taste in music (why Rockabilly? What does that have to do with a lunatic cat eating homework?) But I am seriously impressed. I could never make a video, I haven't the first idea how.

Rockabilly because I was looking for some fast music and that's all I had loaded already. I used to be a Stray Cats fan.The movie thing is easier than I thought. You just go to Windows Movie Maker (Start, Programs, Accessories) then drag and drop in the big space what you want to add, music, video etc. At the bottom is a time line where you then move your items to in the order you want them. You can add titles and fade music in and out and cut the video down just by dragging it! Clever!The finished product appears on the right so you just keep replaying it until you have it how you want it.

Have I got Windows Movie Maker? I just checked – and I have! Mmmmm…

It's interesting what you can do with a PC; I have a friend who is in the process of making big money with his, from his laptop. He told me what to do. Time consuming – but free, and lucrative. First, he said to find out from Google what their top searches are. Let's say that most people search on Google for 'baby's names'. So you borrow library books on baby's names. The most I've ever seen is 80,000 names. Let's say that you've found (and made up) 101,000 in total. You then write your book, "101,000 baby names". You then make a website to sell the book. It's written in such a way that it creates the desire and SELLS the book. It should also be one of the first websites to come up when people search on Google for 'baby's names'. That bit might be tricky – but do-able.

So someone reads the website, and buys the book. They pay online – PayPal or some such – in their virtual shopping basket, and they get the book in pdf format via electronic download. Your 'shop' is open 24/7, around the world. The money should (if it's done properly) roll in all on its own. Leaving you free to write a second book, either (say) one book for boy's names and one for girl's names, and/or a book on Google's second most popular search, be it 'tracing your family tree' or whatever. Then one on making your own PC, or getting your poetry published, or how to learn a language online, how to do your own plumbing, whatever.

I think it's a brilliantly simple idea! You could do it from anywhere on the planet (being a virtual shop) and earn money in your sleep. He's written six books so far, and is well on his way to making his first million. He says you don't need to be an expert in any field, but you need to research it and write about it properly. The hardest bit was the website/shopping basket/pay online thing, but once it was done, the second book was easier and the third easier still. He bought the software, but I'll bet you could get it from Kazaa or DivX Crawler, or maybe just make do with demo versions until the money rolls in. Like I say – it's great what you can do with a PC! I'll give this 'video' nonsense some thought.

See, I'm useful for something. I can see how that would work. I have in fact bought a PDF book on guinea pigs from a well-known guinea pig vet. Guinea pigs have 'special needs' and are completely different from rabbits or hamsters. The book, however, I'm sure I could write better myself also by having a PDF book there is no need for a publisher or any paper… Gosh, I could even write a whole book on Internet conversations on dating sites!

30/11/07

Why don't you? My associate is currently making another bundle with his eBook about 'how to make £££££ in the internet porn industry' or some such. It's ridiculous – how many people who buy and read that eBook are going to make a go of it, let alone succeed? But that doesn't stop him waking up in the morning and finding another 1,000 copies have sold while he's been asleep. His readers, in this regard at least, are dreamers and he's comfortable with that. I understand he and his family will be taking Christmas in the Seychelles this year, which is his deadline to get his next eBook and its sales website finished. Good work. It doesn't have to be a brilliant book about Guinea Pigs – but the website you make to sell it with has to be spot-on.

30/11/07

I've found something you can do at a 'party' – you can help me entertain a select group of guests.See what you think of the picture – and relax, you can always find out later who was doing what to you afterwards, from the video! Could I be more generous than that?

Hmmm...........I think YOU are asking for trouble!I will not be attending those kind of parties and if you're not careful you'll be the one wearing the spreader bar!At least you have established one fact by this.........You can send photos if you want to.

01/12/07

I made you a little something... (Sent Dec 1ˢᵗ vid)Oops, that last one probably didn't work, as I didn't save it properly to send to you, but this should.

No. There's still nothing there.

03/12/07

I've just eaten a whole packet of white chocolate covered strawberries! What have you just eaten? If you haven't just eaten anything, what would you like to eat?... apart from me of course.

06/12/07

Where are you? You closed your L@L profile. Has something happened again?

I closed mine too, because I can't be bothered with it at the moment and it all seems pointless anyway.

I don't know if you'll come back on line until after Madams birthday and Christmas, so I've sent you a little movie of me looking how I look most of the time with the coat on that I wear to football and my new wellies. It will either scare you or make you laugh, but it's certainly not sexy!

07/12/07

I wish you wouldn't just disappear without a word. It's been a whole week and likely to be longer, as you don't email at weekends. I'm patient, but I'm not that patient. You could at least send me a little message to say that you won't be online for a while.

Or is it that I've said the wrong thing in a message? The only thing I can think of is asking how your wife died. Did I overstep the mark?

How many times am I going to sit here and write messages to you like this?

12/12/07

It's December the 12th, which means there are 12 days until Christmas and this is my 12th message to you since you disappeared 12 days ago… maybe 12 is my lucky number and you'll send me something back this time.

17/12/07

This is probably about my sixth attempt to write to you this morning, each letter I've deleted. I wanted to wish Madam a happy birthday tomorrow, but if you're not even going on your Hotmail then there doesn't seem to be any point. I was going to make an e-card, but without her name it's a bit stupid. You don't share much do you? I've told you almost everything about me and the kids over the eight months we've been emailing, yet still you stick to the same line of 'protecting your family' (from what? from me?) and that you're only here to chat and once again you've disappeared without a word!

This should be a happy time of the year, but it never seems to be for me I just end up depressed and stressed. Yes I have the kids and they do surprise me with gifts etc., but I'm still lacking someone special for me and I was hoping that by now it could have been you, with at least a bit more from you i.e. a photo. I know that it's too soon for you to date and things must still be raw, but it doesn't get much better, you just have to decide to carry on in a different way at Christmas and move on.

It's obvious you don't think of me in the same way that I think of you or you wouldn't have left me like this. I would drive over to see you for a couple of hours, for coffee, to see if there was a spark, to make or break this non-relationship, but you won't ask me and then I think it wouldn't be a good idea anyway, with our age difference, social situations etc. I couldn't possibly be what you were looking for, when you decide you're looking, if you ever decide to look at all!

I won't send any more emails, I have to let you go now and go back to being a sane organised mother and not this infatuated woman in love with a man who doesn't exist, who can't possibly be as perfect as you sound and exactly what I was looking for... Apart from being a pompous arsehole sometimes!

23/12/07

Well I wasn't going to email or speak to you again, but maybe that was a bit harsh knowing what you must be going through, and besides six days of not speaking is probably my limit.

So why am I here? Why am I back? I don't know and I have thought about it a lot and I've tried to think about it in a sensible way instead of the fantasy way and I've tried to not think of you at all and block you out and get on with being normal on my own for the rest of my life, but it's not working. I go in a shop and there is a book on Tuscan cooking, I go to bed to read and I'm reading 'Bella Tuscany', which is next to 'Consensual Spanking' and 'The Story of O'. I turn on the telly, flicking through the channels and there are programmes about lawyers, escaping to the sun, even adverts about 'complete wet rooms!' I can't get away from thinking about you and sadly I'm pretty sure that you haven't given me a second thought since you 'disappeared', so I'll just have to hope that eventually you'll fade away like everything else...

Failing that, and this negates everything I've said in the last few emails... Oh all right twenty or so emails... What I really want is to submit to you.

07/01/08

Hello ****, how are you? Are you still alive? Are you reading any of this crap I'm sending? Yes/No (Delete as appropriate)

08/01/08

Hello *****

Well still no answers from you, so I give up and admit defeat, not just with you, but with all men. I have to face the fact that after 12 years of singledom I'm never going to get the relationship I want, which is in a nutshell, (if you can put something like this in a nutshell) to find a man who is intelligent, good looking, successful, single, under 50, with children, (preferably younger than mine, as my 'baby' is nearly 13 now and I'm not going to have any more) and a preference for 'kinky' sex.

I've thought long and hard (Have I told you that already?) and unless I can have it all then I'm not going to bother trying again. I say again, because all the dates and the two small relationships I did have off Lycos compromised each time on one or more of the preferences on my wish list. Even with you to start with, because at the beginning I had no idea you were Dominant, sexually that is, also you were too good looking (Good looking men are always too cocky and full of themselves) and too young.

I was looking for someone a year older than me, as they would be more compatible according my horoscope, but apart from the obvious attributes you have it was the little things that attracted me to you, even thinking of you smelling of Sudocreme and Marmite, which brought back memories for me, as my daughter had Marmite on toast all the time too. Then there was the mental picture of you playing with dolls in a pram and getting up in the middle of the night, something my ex never did or telling your boys off for staying on the computer too long, I have the same problem with my youngest. Oh and having a house full of teenagers in the summer round the pool, I always have other people's kids in all the time. The really agonising thing though is picturing you in a suit and a crisp white shirt, with the scent of your aftershave wafting over to me and being completely under your control as you remove my clothes and tweak my nipples, though you'd have to work on the 'control' thing, I can be quite Dominant and bossy too.

10/01/08

Please come back, I miss you.

15/01/08

I wish I could speak with you properly instead of going into fantasy land all the time, because that is where I am and where I think I'll always be. I will have to go back on Lycos before I go insane talking to myself, but I shall be incognito and not share any of myself this time.

17/01/08

Jesus! Why can't I just forget you? What have you done to me? How long have I waited already for you to reply to all these emails I've sent you? I told you I was persistent!

I was going to propose that we met up and had sex just to see what it was like. Apart from not having partners we both have complete, busy lives, where at present a relationship with regular dating would be difficult, so this would probably be a one-off and it would be your call if you wanted to repeat it again, but I hope that we would still talk afterwards, even if you didn't want to repeat it.

Failing that you could ask me out on Valentine's day and we could have a normal date, like normal people. You would like me, promise, I'm not really this insane, not much anyway...

22/01/08

It's been nearly two months since you last came on line, and I still miss you. Maybe I'm already your slave...

24/01/08

...or maybe you took my soul? Because even though you've been gone so long, I still can't forget you or function normally. It's almost as if I'm on hold... I even tried to get a proper job, to move on, to fill up the time I spend pining for you and I couldn't even do that.

17/02/08

I just cut my finger on the ice in the birds' water dish trying to melt it! I hope I don't catch some nasty bird disease, which would be ironic after all I do for them.

We have two robins in the garden today, which means they are a pair and will hopefully mate. I lost one last year, the cat killed it. He was called Stanley. I think Robins only live for a year anyway, but we, or rather I, always call them Stanley and Jemima.

My great aunt died on 29th Jan after just making her 104th birthday. It's the funeral tomorrow. I shall miss her and wish I'd written down some of the stories she told me, especially about family members, as there is no one left who is old and remembers all that stuff on my mothers' side.

I still miss you and think about you, but I have signed up to another free dating site called 'plentyoffish.com' so I can at least talk to other adults.

29/02/08

Well here I am again, and yes, I know it will not do me any good whatsoever, as either you've blocked me, or you are never going to reply again, or you've done exactly what I do when things get too much, which is shut off from pointless distractions.

Defining 'pointless distractions' in my case, would be talking to men on dating sites who will eventually want to go out with me, and if I did would obviously want to go out with me again, being that I am gorgeous and sexy, but with whom after that one date I'll have no more interest in and would find it difficult to then get rid of them. I suppose I am your 'pointless distraction' too and being on the other side I should take my own medicine and give up on you....Even though you haven't even been out with me yet, which is part of the problem, because until I meet you, I won't give up, I'm just too stubborn, especially when I found what I was looking for in you and yes I am trying to find someone else to get over you, but no one else is as good as you in my list of what I want in a man.

Moving on... I've told you all this a hundred times before and the whole point of this letter was to propose to you, being February 29th in a leap year, and they told me on the news that I was allowed to do so today without fear of social rejection or retribution! Ergo, will you marry me and re-balance both our lives and the lives of our children?

Ah well... of course the answer is no, you'd be insane to write back and say yes, I know I certainly wouldn't say yes if some mad man kept emailing me months after I stopped emailing back, but it's worth a try and I am, trying am I not?

******

This is the point where I gave up and stopped emailing him. I cried a lot, went for long walks, which turned into running, and I've continued to go running once or twice a week since. I joined more dating sites, had a few dates, but always my thoughts came back to him, so at Christmas 2009, two years later, I decided to give him one more go and sent him an email wishing him a happy Christmas. He replied.

23/12/09

Merry Christmas ****,Hope all is well and the coming year is good,Love ****** x.

30/12/09

And a very Happy New Year to you too! I remember you from Lycos – though I never kept any of your rude pictures. It didn't seem right, with two teenage boys in the house (though that's all changed now...) I hope all is well with you and your family.** xxx**

31/12/09

Well you didn't send me any pictures, so I had none to keep, remember!

So where are the boys now? And is 'Madam' still a little madam? I still have all mine at home except my daughter (19) is at university studying Sociology, Culture and Media, so she's only around for the holidays. I'm still exactly as you left me apart from growing much older and fatter. I did run quite a lot, so was fit and healthy, but I haven't been able to for four months, because I injured my foot, so now I feel like a hippo! So you must have a few grey hairs and wrinkles now I bet!

03/01/10

I have one son who is in the Army now – he's completed the Public Services course that your son is currently doing, and

is currently at Sandhurst, training as an officer. The other one is completing his GCSEs, in between game consoles and a girlfriend I'm supposed to know nothing about. My daughter is a stroppy little madam who looks more like her Mum every day.

Were we really talking for eight months? My goodness... there are no grey hairs yet, nor wrinkles – though everyone I know seems to be looking for them. Even my daughter tells me I have 'cuts' on my forehead...

Hope you had a great New Year – we stayed in the UK, as middle kid has GCSEs soon. We now have a home in Gozo, and I'm looking forward to spending some time out there once the exams are finished!

Gozo! That sounds like the name of a puppet on the Muppets. You left Tuscany then? Malta is where my grandfather is buried. He died in his forties. He had a heart attack whilst out walking the dog.

So, Gozo... What's in Gozo?

04/01/10

What's in Gozo? It's the jewel in the crown of the Mediterranean – it's where the Maltese themselves go on holiday. The most expensive real estate around the Med, with the exception of Monaco (where we also have a place, earning me a degree of tax-free status). I recommend that you examine Gozo on Google Earth – you have the natural beauty of the Azure Window and the Inland Sea and the ruins of the oldest free-standing buildings on the planet.

If you've ever read Homer's Odyssey, you might remember that Odysseus was shipwrecked and rescued by the mermaid Calypso, who held him captive for seven years as a sex-slave on her island. Her cave is on the north coast of Gozo, and my daughter was mortified when we visited her cave and Calypso was nowhere to be seen. I explained that even mermaids have to go grocery shopping from time to time, and we bought her an inflatable mermaid for the pool instead – which she has christened Calypso. That sounds fair enough to me.

There are plenty of forts and castles around the coastline, what with being just a short distance from the North African coast (and the constant threat of Muslim attacks). These forts are still used by the Maltese Army, and are 800 – 1000 years old. It's also the reason why Malta remains fundamentally important to Masons. I was welcomed with open arms, naturally, though family reputation had a large part to do with that (there's a statue of one of my ancestors outside the Citadel). The British Royal Family also enjoys a similar connection.

Being a deeply religious country – you could be arrested for being topless on the beach – each village has a saint, and they celebrate the saints, week by week and village by village, all through the summer, in style. Street parties, brass bands, churches illuminated with coloured lights, and the loudest home-made fireworks I've ever witnessed. That, ******, is what is in Gozo.

05/01/10

No thongs on the beach for you then! I bet they welcomed you with open arms! I expect the whole island turned out to see you arrive, especially the women. They probably thought Odysseus had returned! By the way, sorry I wasn't there in my cave when your daughter called, you were right, I was doing the grocery shopping in Tesco's. I'll check my diary and see when I have seven years free. When were you thinking of coming round next?

06/01/10

We have SNOW! Enough to make balls with and everything!

07/01/10

It was actually unbelievably hot in August. I was in Iraq meeting their Government officials a while ago and it was never as hot as that, even in the open desert where some of the soldiers drink ten litres of water a day or risk serious dehydration. It was a case of dashing home, jumping into the pool, and staying in it up to your shoulders. I returned home resembling a Swan Vesta match. You ought to read the Odyssey – it's got all the components of a great novel – sex, mystery, action, double-dealings, a hero's triumphant return, and plenty of action at the end. And it's between 7,000 and 11,000 years old.

Yes it's been snowing here – but I don't care. We're off to Morocco for a little winter sun in a few days anyway!

A Swan Vesta match? Did you dye your hair black too? And you've just ruined the fantasy... all I can picture now is a short, burnt, peeling, skinny, wrinkly Adonis!

You're always jetting off somewhere, when I'm quite happy at home and would get really stressed having to organise everyone's packing for one trip a year let alone the amount you do, although I suppose you have enough money and staff to make it easy. I did two camping trips last summer and that was just with my youngest. The photos are on Facebook, not that it would interest a foreign land, visiting person like you.

Well I would write more, but I'm about to see if I can thaw my car out to take my daughter to her friends to collect some stuff, so I'll mail this now just in case I don't get home again before you go off for your sunshine fix...

08/01/10

Swan Vesta matches have a red head, you state-school educated imbecile. You stay cool in the pool in the heat of the day, but it doesn't stop your face getting a bit sunburnt, even when wearing a hat. I'm not on Facebook so I'm unable to join your camping experience.

I'm not averse to camping myself – I packed a tent and rode down through France on a motorcycle not that long ago. You ought to try it – the solitude, the countryside... Usually, when I travel though, I go alone. A small suitcase of essentials, and an American Express Black card. That's all I need, though the list expands a little when I take my daughter. As long as she can take Lamby or Mr Snuggle-fit, she's happy.

There was a section I had to miss out here, as it was too complicated and long to put in the book. We had an argument over him calling me 'state-school educated' and me calling him a snob.

11/01/10

I love it when you're angry; tossing back your blond hair, flashing your blue eyes at me and calling me young lady!....Should I go and stand in the corner now and wait for my punishment?

You may find that my tastes have developed somewhat since we last had a 'little chat'...could you handle it? There'll be more than my hand across your bottom...

12/01/10

The snow's melting... But I suppose you're sunning yourself in Morocco now. I'm in all day cleaning today interspersed with adding bits from my old computer to my new computer, just to make the day a bit more interesting. I sorted some animations/images out last night. I saw this one and thought of you...

Is this how your tastes have developed? Or should I go and hide in a cupboard?

17/01/10

I've finished sorting my animations for Incredimail, which are the little tag things, and have now moved on to the stats.

I think I have about a thousand to sort, maybe three thousand, I can't remember, although I'm deleting a lot of them as I group them, I'm hardly likely to write that amount of emails to use them, so I shall just keep the best ones. Still I thought I would send you this one, which is grouped under BDSM Spank. I particularly like this one, because he is holding her wrist to prevent her from stopping him from spanking her. It demonstrates how I feel about the whole BDSM thing. It's not the idea of receiving pain that I like, but the control and the strength of the man or Master, if you prefer...She's helpless and cannot win...What do you like?

20/01/10

Good morning Sir

Are you back from Morocco yet?...I've been waiting patiently for your return and I so miss being chastised by your sharp tongue, in fact it's probably worse than a good spanking, being chastised by your tongue, not that I've experienced a good spanking yet, which brings me on to the fact that while you've been away, or busy, or just ignoring me, I've managed to sort all three thousand or so letters for my Incredimail and I have a grand total of 58 letters to do with spanking!

I also have several more extreme BDSM stats and I especially like the sketches and the slave type letters, although somewhere along the line I lost some of my favourites, which were more torture than BDSM, although it's just as well, because I wouldn't want you to get any ideas if I showed them to you, you being so young and impressionable that is...

Well...maybe I should talk about something else? I always seem to get stuck on the subject of sex with you. How's your garden after the snow? I have a broken pot and it looks like the Camellia buds are damaged by the snow. Hey how was your pool? Did it freeze over? Or do the chemicals you put in stop that?

There that was a normal conversation. Oh and I almost forgot. This stat (the picture in the bottom, right corner) reminded me of another conversation we had a long time ago about stringing me up in your wet room and 'double bassing' back onto sex again!

Catch you soon.

25/01/10

Photo of a Vesta match and model like *****

Ok... So out of the next two photos, which one is the most accurate? If it's the second one then you definitely need to lose the socks!

28/01/10

I would suggest that I have rather more meat on me than the first picture - and a better haircut and socks than the second.

27/01/10

Sent a Valentines document, (A present for you and don't worry it's not slushy crap) This was a picture of three different types of Jim Beam, with an invitation:

Happy Valentine's Day

Thought you might like a drink on Valentine's day, as it is most likely a day for reflection, rather than action, for you. However if you fancied the action too, then I'm free that weekend. If not, then it looks like I'll be watching Saints V Pompey instead....Normal Valentine's Day for me then.

28/01/10

I'd hate to see your idea of Slushy Crap then, young lady. Valentine's Day - an interesting invitation, I'll check my diary. It's been years since I've 'celebrated' Valentine's Day.

01/02/10

Gosh it's a frosty one this morning. I had to wear bed socks last night.

I can't decide if I like the snow best or the frost when I take photographs, I wish I had a camera that could take proper pictures of the moon. I picked my daughter up Friday night for a weekend stay; it was mesmerizing as I drove up. It's outside now, but not quite so full of course. I'm taking my daughter back this morning, so might stop for a walk on the way back if I have time, I have to do the food shopping and collect my son from college at 4.30pm.

Are you in this country? Can you see the moon?

07/02/10

Where are you?

I don't know, it's like trying to get blood out of a stone,

getting an email reply from you. I've waited eleven days for you and I haven't written for five days, which is a record for me to be quiet. Have you any idea how hard that is for a woman?

Anyway... While I've been sitting here, waiting, I decided to compose my idea of a slushy Valentine, as requested, sort of, by you...And oh I somehow got carried away and wrote two. Now don't go getting any ideas when you read them. I don't want you getting a bigger head than you already have...

11/02/10

Why? I mean, I appreciate the fine form of the lady in the picture (though I believe she ought to call an Interior Designer). Sorry to have been out of touch recently – it looks as if I'm going to be somewhat busy until the end of the Chilcot enquiry (and perhaps for a long while after that). It's a nuisance. I don't care to be this busy, I believe I've earned the right to take it easy for a while!

Good morning sir. For your information it appears that I am at more of a loose end than I first anticipated when sending you the original Valentine invitation... Did I send more than one Valentine?

The lady I clean for on Friday morning has cancelled me due to her and her husband re-decorating after they get a new hall floor fitted. Also the following week is half-term (for us state school educated, incendiary bomb making imbeciles), so I don't have to worry about getting the boys to school on the Monday morning. Therefore it would be good if I could take a much needed break away from the boys trying to kill each other and revitalise myself before the half term starts. If it would suit you and make it easier, I could drive to Norwich, stay in a B&B and be available to meet for a few hours and a couple of drinks on the Saturday or Sunday. According to Google Earth it's only 3 hours 41 minutes from my house to Norwich, but it will probably take me a lot longer, more like six hours, after I get lost a few times and take time during the journey to rest my foot, which is still giving me trouble.

Let me know what you think, as I shall make other plans if you're not available, or going off to Gozo (or are you there already? Can you get an Internet connection there?) But it could be fun, seeing as I'm probably clinically insane, and it will definitely be an experience you'll never forget, especially with the addition of alcohol. I haven't had much fun this year yet, apart from mailing you (with or without a response), although on the plus side nobody has died yet or had any accidents.

I'm off to work now.

11/02/10

You do push it, don't you? I'm not actually in Norwich at the moment, as inviting as your web sounds, but if you're going to Norwich anyway please drop in and make sure the domestic staff are behaving themselves, would you?

11/02/10

Alternatively, instead of the normal meet for a drink thing, or as well as, you could lock me up in your basement for the weekend and instruct me on how to be a good slave. Then you could demonstrate in person how your tastes have developed, seeing as you still haven't answered the question!

There would be a few provisos of course. You can't clamp or peg my nipples, they are too sensitive and I will need to be able to sit down at the end of the weekend so I can drive home, else you might be stuck with me!!!

Just think of the satisfaction that you will get from keeping me quiet for three days... your email box will be quite empty.

Please Master...

Thinks to herself, if this doesn't work nothing will and it will be another two years before he speaks to me again, by that time I'll probably be a granny and no use whatsoever, but at least I can take out my dentures and suck his cock like in the Jim Carrey film 'Yes Man'.

11/02/10

What about sharing you with a few friends? Is that off limits too? Just think – you, tied and blindfolded. You won't know who is doing what – all you'll know is how many penises are inside you at any one time. Oh, and not all of my friends are male. Have you ever sucked another woman's tongue? You'd do that for me – it isn't like you'd have a choice.

Suck another woman's tongue? Yuk!!! I'd vomit! It would be like forcing me to eat blancmange! I see you're still stuck on the gangbang fantasy! Come on, you don't actually do that stuff, do you? It's what porn stars do and old, fat people who try to recapture their youth by having swinging parties... Haven't you seen the pictures on the Internet and talked to the freaks on alt.com? I chatted to one married 'gentleman' who wanted to take me to a hotel room, get me legless, tie me up and play with my breasts until I had an orgasm... Sorry, but it just wouldn't work on me. I'd be cold, I'd need to pee every five minutes from all the drink and I'd need much more stimulation than just having my breasts played with to have an orgasm.

Ok I admit the fantasy turns me on too (gang bang), but the reality is a different matter. I'm not slutty enough to take part in those kinds of activities. If you took me to a party where sexual activities were on the agenda, then I'd be scared to death and straight out the bathroom window!

I suppose if we had a proper relationship, well a relationship in some kind of form where at the very least I belonged to you... This is complicated to explain and difficult to put on paper... I actually hardly know you, having not met you, YET, but on the other hand I seem to be totally infatuated with you, which, considering it's been two years since we last spoke (apart from recently of course) and I have tried really hard to find someone else and even managed... ooh... three dates with two men, this infatuation hasn't gone... at all!

I am a one-woman man and I am still looking for that man and if it was you, then I wouldn't want you to have any other woman, or me to have any other man even on a casual basis, even at a party that was for that purpose... I have done things on impulse myself, but none of these activities ever left me with any sense of satisfaction.

Now here you are talking about having me used sexually for your friends, which would make me a classic slave/submissive in this context. I'd be yours, which is what I wanted, but, because you'd want me for your friends too, then I wouldn't be yours. Rich people don't seem to have the same boundaries as us mere mortals. If I was married to you then it might be different, I'd definitely be yours and the men you offered me to would also know that I was yours, so I'd be safe, because they would use me, but knowing that it was an honour to be allowed to use me and not that I was just some slut that you were amusing yourself with for a time. But still I'd rather not, so in answer to the question, yes sharing me with a few friends is off limits. After all you are hardly likely to want to marry me and as I just explained it would still feel wrong, besides what would I do with my cats and guinea pigs when you wanted to jet off to Gozo? Do domestic staff look after pets too?

I suppose what we are left with is... Will you go out with me when you're not busy, just to see what happens, knowing that I'm quite boring, frigid, not prepared to have sex with your friends and probably not what you wanted at all, along with all the other things, you know, like having grey hair, varicose veins etc? Or are we just going to continue swapping fantasies until one of us, probably you, gets bored again? This is, however, what attracts me to you, the fantasies and the danger that you might actually mean what you say, that you might actually be what I'm looking for and be the one man who knows exactly what I need, without me knowing it's what I need myself – in other words my true master.

Another reason I'm attracted to you is the fact that you were left to cope on your own after your wife died and had to get up in the middle of the night to see to a crying baby, which mirrored my life when my ex left. Oh and not forgetting the pompous lawyer way that you talk, and when you call me 'young lady', and that you have such good taste, even though I don't like to admit it, because it would make me look like a gold digger (seeing as I have nothing and you seem to have everything), if I agreed with you, wouldn't it? Anyway it's more fun disagreeing with you and winding you up and you can't be right about everything.

Well that's about it. I think I've covered just about everything, but no doubt I'll think of something else right after I press send. I have included a stat for you, which I think just about covers your fantasy and if you do decide to put me out of my misery and you suddenly get a slot free, here is my mobile number ************, but don't expect me to be coherent if you ring!

12/02/10

Sent Torture/BDSM Artwork

15/02/10

Sent Comixx BDSM cartoons

15/02/10

Being a Monday, I awoke feeling, you know, 'badly drawn'. It looks like I'm not the only one. Doesn't Fifi look like a male 100m sprinter with breast implants?

15/02/10

Well, yes. I don't think the drawings are accurate, although Katie Price would come close. It was the concept of a secret bondage society in a remote jungle location, just the sort of place rich people could afford to maintain.

16/02/10

The jungle would be unbearable – too many biting insects, too humid (dehydration issues) and impractical. I know of several places in London though – including Whitehall, Pimlico, and Covent Garden. 'Know of' does not imply 'been to', before you jump to your utterly predictable conclusions. I've also heard of such activities on the deck of a sailing yacht in the Pacific. That would be pretty secret, though I'm not sure what would happen if one were accosted by Somali pirates, what with people already being tied up and held prisoner.

22/02/10

I'm having one of those days. Couldn't you just come over, take me to a room, spank me, use me, and then chain me up in a cupboard or something? Well you're no good as usual. I suppose you're holed up in a court somewhere...Anyway I've eaten chocolate now, then I'm moving on to a bottle of wine to drink myself into oblivion, maybe things will be better tomorrow.

23/02/10

If I'm a good girl will Master treat me to a clit pump?

25/02/10

So... when are we going to get together so you can discipline me?

26/02/10

Do you check this email address every day? In other words I know you're too busy to answer, but are you at least reading what I send or am I wasting my time? It's the 'Men are from Mars, Women are from Venus' thing. Women like to talk about stuff; men like to go away in peace to sort things out themselves.

Of course for all I know you could have remarried by now, or are at least going steady with someone, but you did answer me in the first place, so I was hoping you might be available this time and I did nearly wangle a date out of you for Valentine's day, so I'm pretty sure you are 'available' even though I'm not getting much back at the moment, which leaves me prattling on MAKING A COMPLETE FOOL OF MYSELF!

I found your picture. The only picture I have, because for some reason you won't send me another, along with all the other things I've asked for, like what your children's names are and things like that, so I'm not even going to ask for another one, but this is the one I have;

This is me two days ago taken on my mobile, so not brilliant clarity, aged about... oohhhhh... Let's say 38, because I definitely don't look my age, green eyes, grey hair... Well you can't see that either in this picture. Dimples? Just about see those...I have them in my bottom too if I clench it, see what you're missing!

Now I'm going to go away and get on with my work, I have a long day ahead and I've forgotten what point I was trying to get across, other than are you going to talk to me again? Or should I just wipe you out of existence, grow old, never have sex again, never experience a clit pump or a violet wand, or double bassing, buy a few chickens and spend a lonely, frugal life selling eggs to pay the bills, living in a cottage, in the middle of nowhere... Oh stop a minute, how am I going to live off selling eggs if I'm in the middle of nowhere?

02/03/10

The last time I saw something akin to this "clit pump" was in Nigeria – as a part of a female circumcision ritual. I bet you don't want one now, do you?

I DID hear about two female members of the traveller community (as a lawyer I'm prevented from thus employing the colloquial mannerism 'thieving, tax-dodging gypsy

scum'). Anyway, they were pulling up carrots – stealing carrots, more like it – and one of them pulls out a massive one.

"Hey, look at this" she says, "it reminds me of my husband."

"What do you mean" comes the reply. "Do you mean the length or the thickness?"

"Neither" says the first one, "I mean the f**king dirt on it."

I had a nice drop of wine last night – the last remaining bottle of 1955 Bollinger in Groucho's stock. It cost a few pennies – hell, yes it did – but it certainly beats chocolate. If I were to give you 1955 chocolate, you wouldn't want to eat it.

I've vaguely heard of Bollinger. I have no idea what 'Groucho's stock' is… you're talking posh crap again and anyway you couldn't find 1955 chocolate if you tried, no matter how much it would cost!!!

03/03/10

A Jewish boy was walking with his girlfriend on the grounds of his father's house. His father was a successful doctor, and was carrying out a circumcision in the on-site surgery.

As they were walking, they heard a scream and a foreskin flew out of the window and landed at the girl's feet."

What's this?" she asked.

"Taste it," he replied, "If you like it, I'll give you a whole one."

This is in poor taste considering the implications of circumcision for both male and female. I'd be interested to know the full story from the last email, as to why you were in Nigeria and in what way you were witnessing a circumcision, or if you were at all?

My daughter went to Africa for a month's volunteering last year. She was at a bush camp near Kruger for African town children to go to for a week at a time to learn about the countryside and animals. They also did simple English and Maths, which my daughter taught as part of the placement. One of the weeks they only had a few children from the local orphanage to stay, because the usual children had started school holidays and the organiser said that it was the time of year when they all went off to be circumcised and that many of them didn't return!

I didn't know girls were circumcised until I was in my thirties. I read Waris Dirie's book and the whole thing just makes me go cold to think that a mother could put her child through the same thing she went through, knowing how awful it was! Did you know they do it to two-year-old girls? It's cheaper to do then, when it was initially done to enable them to become women and be able to marry, so really the whole point of doing it is lost. I'm glad that there are people trying to stop it, women who have been through this themselves, it's not something I could do.

I had a man come over this morning to give me a huge erection... OK, he put a digital aerial up on my back wall, as since buying a Free view TV for the kids room my reception has been less than satisfactory, ie no sodding reception at all, which is part of the saga I didn't bother to tell you about, it's something I'd save for when we meet, you know to chatter and fill up embarrassing silences, although I can't see you being that silent, but everything is hunky dory now... Hey, if I attach a cable to you I might get a good reception with all those metal bits...

15/03/10

Dear Sir *****,

It has come to one's attention, indicated by his Lordship's apparent disregard for one's prodigious correspondence, containing one's indefatigable adoration and worship of your Lordship's person, that your Lordship is currently engaged in more pressing activities than satisfying his Lordship's proclivities of a more delicate, but highly enjoyable nature. Ergo if his Lordship could perhaps spare a moment of his time, then one would make oneself available to his Lordship whenever it was convenient, hoping that one's quiddity would be pleasing to his Lordship and one's nymphomania could be satisfied.

Or, in simpler terms...

Hello gorgeous, fancy a shag?

P.S. I don't actually use the word 'Shag' at all. I don't think any word suitably describes the act of sexual intercourse, it's more an emotion, a power, an insatiable urge that over takes two people compelling them to make love...So I suppose I'd use 'make love', but then the problem is that sex and love don't always go together, at least not where most men are concerned...

21/03/10

Hello, are you still there?

31/03/10

Happy Easter Sir.

I just ate a Galaxy ripple with my coffee and it was only 9am... am I bad?

So what do you do at Easter? I don't celebrate it at all. I don't think I'll even get round to doing a roast dinner... I have bought eggs for all of us though, so Easter to me means chocolate, I hope you have some for me too! It's snowing in Scotland...If we didn't have kids to look after you could have picked me up, taken me to Scotland for the weekend and we could have played in the snow...That would be a good present, although I still want the chocolate...

Am I keeping you entertained?

31/03/10

If I hadn't made myself entirely clear in the last message, I am available this Saturday, but not the week after, if you fancied an alternative activity to lawyering (is that a word?) and parenting, like clubbing or something...It's years since I went to a club, but I've told you that before too...

03/04/10

I have four Easter eggs and a chocolate cake, so lots of

chocolate inside me... But I'd still rather have you inside me Master.

12/04/10

Is it your birthday yet?

15/04/10

Not yet.

12/04/10

If you had the money, what would you like to do?

15/04/10

I've got the money. And I already do whatever I like. I suppose, in my wildest fantasies, I'd like to disappear, in Cartagena, Columbia - just vanish. That's the way to experience REAL freedom. I know how to make this possible, and I can even source 'fake' IDs (they would actually be genuine, but with made-up names). Add that to a few Bolivian and Nigerian bank accounts (which don't require names, just numbers) and you have the facility to come and go as you please, anywhere on the planet. The trouble is, I can pretty well do that already. And I'd miss the power and influence I wield over the Judiciary, Parliament, and the Monarchy. And too many people would notice I've gone. What about you?

15/04/10

That's just like that film with Michael Douglas 'Romancing the Stone.' It was set in Columbia, but snap, I'd love to be able to go off somewhere remote… a little house, chickens and unspoilt countryside for my back garden. The kids could have this house to live in, or at least my eldest son, my daughter would be renting somewhere and my youngest would come with me. I don't have any money though. Oh and I want to see a volcano!

I like to keep as fit, healthy, and as lean as possible. It's most enjoyable to see practically all my contemporaries bloated, stressed, and lining themselves up for a heart attack. That's what a desk-bound existence does for you. I trust that answers your question – money cannot buy, after all, a fitter, healthier body. You can change the one you have (a Government Minister of my acquaintance has just had silicone breast implants (yes, really!) to give him the pecs he's always dreamt of) but you can't change into a completely new one. And body dysmorphia isn't cool in my estimation.

Do you want to go to bed with me?

Once you lose your inhibitions, yes. I don't find your conditions a turn-on – 'you can't do this, you can't do that'. My pleasures do not depend upon your permission. Isn't that what trust is all about?

I didn't think I had any inhibitions… the conditions are

mainly to have you break them... Reverse psychology perhaps? The trust will take time, it depends on how we get on I suppose.

Oh, I think you have plenty of inhibitions. I'll have to 'take you in hand', as it were, until you surrender completely. And I do mean completely.

Yeah... You keep saying that too! What car do you drive now? Jeremy Clarkson on 'Top Gear' played a car racing computer game. He had to choose his track, car etc... he chose an Aston Martin DB9 and said 'That's not really a racing car it's just pornography.' It is a sexy car though...

Clarkson talks out of his arse. That's why most of the clubs in London won't accept his membership. I know a lot of people who drive a DB9, so there's no way I'm going to have one. I keep a Porsche Cayenne with blacked out windows so I can drive myself - and others - around London in anonymity, whilst I still keep my father's Jaguar E type for weekends. It was made in the year I was born and I'm its second owner ever. And it's still in amazing condition, not surprising given the money I spend on re-plating the chrome and general restoration work. Other than that I change my vehicles regularly (bikes as well as cars and boats) and I have different ones at different locations around the globe. If I had a few clear days, I'd take a scooter along the west coast of Greece, watching the sun set as I wind along the mountain roads, unimpeded by a helmet, and with my rucksack between my feet so my back gets tanned. Heaven.

20/04/10

I'm doing a crossword in a magazine. Twenty-two down is: The most powerful, rich, gifted or educated members of a group or community. But it's only five letters, so your name doesn't fit.P.S. Is it your birthday yet?

22/04/10

The answer is probably 'elite'. The best crossword clue I've ever seen was in the Times once – it was as follows: E(13) Can you get it?

22/04/10

I've had a letter from my endowment company telling me my direct debit has been cancelled and they can't get the payments. My ex pays this and it is part of our divorce that he continues. It seems as soon as something gets sorted out, something else goes wrong!

Is it your birthday yet?

I pre-ordered 'Avatar', which came yesterday, so I watched it last night, before I went to bed. It was really good, although slightly far-fetched, but I can see why people are raving about it. I have the X-Box game too, but I couldn't get past the first bit of alien dog killing, so gave up. Still, the computer games are enough for the limited spare time I have, to keep me amused. *Sigh* a real, live man would be nice to play with too…

I think the big deal with Avatar was that it looked so good in 3D. I thought the story was crap, but the 3D was good – like Alice in Wonderland, the 3D was amazing, but the story was mediocre. Nothing like the book.

By the way, Roman Abramovich has his own 3D cinema. Where? In one of the submarines in his new yacht! You would have thought that being in a submarine would be entertaining enough really, wouldn't you? I can't abide that man. A complete and utter tosser, who "can't speak a word of English". Yeah. Right. I've said things in front of him and I've seen his body language – he understands all right.

Name dropping again sir! You're just jealous because he's richer than you and he has a football team.

I read the 'Rich List' in The Times at the weekend and I can't see you anywhere... Well I need to pick my next victim, Heh, heh, heh...Actually no I lied, after the first couple of pages it just got boring, I have better things to do.

I haven't seen any films in 3D yet. I usually wait until they come on DVD, but apparently there are going to be 3D televisions for sale soon and Sky will have 3D films available...I bet it will cost a lot more though. Avatar was like cowboys and Indians really, when you think about it.

Yes it was like cowboys and Indians – and Clash of the Titans was typical princess-saved-from-impossible-odds-by-a-boy-from-the-wrong-side-of-the-tracks. I've heard that there are only seven basic plots – if anyone claims to have invented a third, you know it's going to be rubbish.

Sky are about to unleash 3D television. BUT.

You need Sky + HD, a full subscription, and a 3D television. You'll need to wear 3D glasses (my daughter calls them 'Goo-goo goggles' as in Dr Seuss) and the only thing they intend to broadcast – for now – is the odd football match. The range of TV is pretty rubbish and nobody's releasing the technology so you can buy a 3D Blu-ray player. So that's what all the secrecy was about – I saw Baron Peter Mandelson and Rupert Murdoch in private talks at Bilderberg, so that must have been on the agenda.

That Times Rich List is a load of stuff and nonsense. They only look at UK income, and not assets held nor income derived from outside the UK. The Monaco Rich List is the one to watch (or the Isle of Man, or Turks and Caicos, or the Channel Islands).

I don't want riches, (my concept of having money is very different from your concept of having money) maybe someone who could at least pay off my mortgage, so I could leave a couple of kids in my house and live with my chosen rescuer somewhere else relatively child free, would be nice, but then all I really want is to be in love completely. I want someone who will cherish me, love me, look after me, see to all my needs, someone I can trust. In return I wouldn't mind what I did. If I have to clean other people's toilets for the rest of my life, then so be it, but I have this picture of being somewhere nice and warm, with the sea nearby, pottering in a large garden pulling up weeds, making salad for tea with wine, sunset and candles... Did I say candles?... .Hmmm... I wonder what you would do with those Sir?...Maybe you just found a slug in your salad?... Would you then force me to strip on the patio and tie my hands behind my back with the skipping rope that 'madam' left lying around and then would you grab my hair pulling my head backwards making me struggle to stay on my feet, while you slowly dripped hot wax over my breasts...Then because I've made far too much noise and complained far too loudly that the wax is burning, would you then throw me over your back and follow this with a dousing in the cold swimming pool?... But wait in my struggles maybe I've grabbed something I shouldn't and causing you to become aroused beyond your control you don't manage to get me to the swimming pool, but lay me on the grass and use me very thoroughly until we are both exhausted... Then perhaps a dip in the pool before bed?

Most amusing.

23/04/10

Hippo birdie 2 ewes. Do you get it?

Yes I do. Hippo, Birdie, two Ewes. Laugh? I nearly did! Have you solved that crossword clue yet? E, with thirteen letters?

No. You still haven't told me the exact date of your birthday. I don't want to keep getting it wrong each year.

26/04/10

Hooray, I finally managed to do a three-mile run with my iPod sensor and loaded it on the computer. Still can't imagine running a marathon that would take me two days. If you chose to be my master, would you be pleased?

It depends on the running – would you, for instance, run naked on the spot for my entertainment? Or bounce naked on a trampoline with people watching? What about being my own 'pony girl' or whatever they are called – complete with a plug-in tail?

There are two answers to this question.

The answer you want to hear is: If you were my Master and I became your submissive, then the only answer to this question would be 'I will do whatever pleases Master.'

The answer you won't want to hear is:

Do you have any idea what running on the spot naked looks like? Is that really going to give you pleasure? And me jumping naked on a trampoline will be twice as bad!!! Do you really think your friends/ acquaintances will thank you for that spectacle? And a pony girl? Where did that come from? I think I stopped pretending to be a pony when I was about six! That's about as bad as men who want to dress up in nappies and have their bottoms powdered. No I can't go on with that one I'll throw up in a bucket!!!

Why don't you just go out with me and then make suggestions, at least you would then know what you had to work with.

29/04/10

I wish you were closer... I'd love to go out tonight for a

couple of hours. A drink in a pub, stimulating conversation, a little light flirting, some time to relax and forget our troubles...

I've attached the song I'm listening to at the moment, whilst sorting out my running tracks playlist. Not sure what they are singing, but it sounds nice and bouncy to run to.

30/04/10

The answer (to my crossword question) is the word 'Senselessness'. If you have the word 'sense' and take away ('less') the word 'ness' you're left with an 'E'. John Major used to pretend to do the crossword, and say out loud, musingly, "Hmmm - 'A Postman's dilemma'!". There would always be somebody new, some ridiculous sycophant, who would always try and be helpful; "How many letters?" And he would reply "A sackful!" This would perhaps explain the Labour landslide of 1997.

Oh... Well, there was no way I could have guessed that!!!

When I used to participate in triathlons, a friend showed me a new bike he was building. One of the components was a titanium & magnesium alloy seat pillar (the shiny part that sticks out of the frame and the saddle bolts on to it). He was going to drill a few holes in this £250 seat pillar "to save weight" because he'd seen it done elsewhere. We told him that holes would weaken it, and he'd be better off turning it down on a lathe, making the diameter smaller. So he did, the moron. He wasn't happy the next time I saw him - "It doesn't fit now!" £250 wasted.

I also know that Mohammed Al Fayed spent £110,000 or so on ONE bottle of wine from the 18th century. And then found out that opening it would turn it to vinegar within seconds. The stupid fucking Arab grocer ought to know better.

Most of the time I'm talking to you on MOD or Government computers. They're funny about me loading files onto them – blame the Official Secrets Act amendments, and those stupid MPs who keep leaving them in taxis and everywhere else.

I'm a bit tired – I'll be happier once this election nonsense is over and Mr Cameron and his lovely wife can pick out new carpets and curtains. At least it's taken everybody's eye off the Iraq Enquiry – I think I planned the timing quite well, don't you?

Are you telling me that it was you who decided when the election should be? That's funny, I thought Nick Clegg was going to be the clear winner. Round here we have to vote Lib Dem just to keep Labour out, but usually in a general election I vote Conservative, however I may stay Lib Dem this time, I haven't decided yet. It's Inquiry not Enquiry.

02/05/10

I take it you don't like Mr Fayed either then? In fact you don't seem to like anyone who is rich, famous and successful. That gives me the advantage then, being poor, invisible and stupid.

Have you been to Bilderberg this year? It's a bit early isn't it? Normally it's later... not that I've spent any time at all looking through each and every link trying to find information about Bilderberg, to see if you're in any of the lists!

Actually, while I'm on the subject, I'm beginning to doubt if you do exist in the flesh or if I've just somehow got so psychologically unbalanced that I really am talking to myself and I've made you up as my perfect man? I have no pictures of you and I can't find you on the internet anywhere at all, not on any web pages of places or meetings you've mentioned, or in any lists of clubs you've mentioned (oh, except that brothel...) and your name doesn't bring anything up at all, except the Goldman Sachs bankers and you can't be them, can you? Don't you even have a personal web page for your clients to read all your achievements and for them to contact you? My brother does. I suppose you do but it's obviously not open for every Tom, Dick or ******.

You are just Mr Elusive, the black panther hidden in the forest, moving through the top branches of the trees, and I'm the little mouse tucked in the roots on the floor of the forest, walking in all the shit, waiting to come and get the thorn out of your paw, so you are forever grateful to me and protect me for the rest of my life... Nah!!!... .I preferred the candle story! I'll make up another story while I'm at work for you. I'm at work all day today and tomorrow, my legs will kill by the time I get home tomorrow night, so I need something to keep my mind busy too. Perhaps a 'Hogtied ' story would suit Sir?

04/05/10

It's the Bilderberg collective who choose the next Prime Minister. Not me on my own. Nick Clegg is not a Freemason, to the best of my knowledge. Cameron and Brown are both high up in the orders – Cameron is a relation to our Queen and his whore of a wife is a descendant of Nell Gwynn – and both have attended Bilderberg and pledged their allegiance. Whoever wins will inherit an economic disaster and it will be near suicide for their party and their political careers, but we always knew that. The recession/economic downturn/whatever you want to call it will be extended until the banks return to form, and this will be applied across all European member states. It doesn't actually matter who wins to be honest – as long as he has our approval – because since the ratification of the Lisbon Treaty pretty much all laws now come from Brussels. We kept that quiet, didn't we? Hold on to your hat.

Why would I be numbered amongst the attendees of Bilderberg? The lists represent the elite, the invited. Basically I'm the one who does the inviting. Yes, I am related to the banking family. Do you like my little cloak of invisibility then? It took a lot to construct – including a small legal practice in Norwich which is now defunct – but it is absolutely necessary. Can you imagine the furore that would explode if my status were suddenly in the public domain? Political meltdown, legal chaos, financial ruin. And it would all lead back to me. I think it is better for Europe, for the World in fact, that the current façade of Government, National Identity, and the Financial Markets and national economics remains intact.

By the way - do you like my little 'no fly zone' over Ireland? I'd buy some Aer Lingus shares soon if I were you; a takeover looms in the wings, you could say.

When I wrote my first novel, I made a summary, bullet points, for the whole thing and put them into a Word document. Then I put it to the end and wrote my story above it, referring to the bullets now and then as a guide and deleting them as I wrote a particular section. You then know that (1) your book remains true to the original plan, and (2) the story, characters, plots, everything else, already works because you've read through those bullet points a million times and polished them until they shine. Let me know when it's ready! I'll have a publisher call you.

04/05/10

I don't like Mohammed Old Fathead, because he is disrespectful. He has tried to buy his way into a high degree of Freemasonry, but nobody is impressed by his gaudiness or wealth. He is a pauper by our standards. Furthermore he keeps playing the 'race' card - the Muslim card to be exact - in spite of the fact that Prince Charles is a convert to Islam. I have no time for either of them to be honest. It's a shame that our Queen is as old as she is, as nobody trusts Charles and Prince Bill refuses to acknowledge his place within our hierarchy. It looks like the end of the monarchy may be approaching - it exists purely because of us, and Bill, Harry and Charlie would do well to remember it.

05/05/10

You've written a novel! I needn't bother then, yours is bound to be so much better and anyway it was a story, not a novel, and definitely not one that could be published. It was sort of about you and me, at least how my imagination imagined how it would be if you did call my bluff on some of the previous sexual fantasies we've discussed. You know you sound exactly like that chap I emailed who was a writer and lived in Norwich too. Before he disappeared he was writing a novel and said exactly the same thing about bullet points... maybe he was you? Maybe he was one of your so called 'smoke screens' and when I thought you had gone, really you hadn't and you were still talking to me?

English was my strongest subject at school, apart from the fact that my subject matter was immature; I have always been naive. I don't catch on very quickly and tend to see things differently to everyone else. Perhaps I would do better writing children's stories!

Perhaps you'd be better off writing a screenplay – you're a very visual person, and your idea sounds like it would translate to the screen very well. You would earn £2,000 for your first novel, but anything up to £200,000 for your first screenplay.

12/05/10

I looked up 'Coalition' on 'Thefreedictionary.com' because I was going to say to you, "If the Conservatives can make a coalition with the Lib Dems, and you're Conservative and I'm Lib Dem, then want to make a coalition with me?" But after reading the definition's I'm not so sure!

1. An alliance, especially a temporary one, of people, factions, parties, or nations.

2. A combination into one body; a union.

3. A group of usually two to six male lions that drive off and replace the male lions in a pride in order to mate with the females and protect the resulting offspring.

The first definition was the one I was aware of.

The second definition is the one I'd really want with you.

The third definition I'm not so sure of... Is this where you men got the idea of gang-banging?

Ah, the coalition between the Liberal Democrats and Conservatives. I'm quite pleased with my baby. Do you remember the Governor of the Bank of England saying last week, "Whoever wins the election will be in the financial shit and won't be re-elected for a generation" or something along those lines (sorry but I'm pretty tired). By joining two out of the three parties, I've managed to negate such an eventuality. Pretty good, I thought. Next stop – Bilderberg. Though I might stop off at the pet shop and buy a poodle. And call it 'Clegg'.

The third definition sounds pretty good to me. And I'm sure my property will be ready and waiting. At a time of MY choosing. Not hers.

Oh go away! How did you have anything to do with it? You would have to be a king or something! And don't get a poodle, get a Chihuahua, they are in at the moment.

13/05/10

I'm not a king. You just don't understand how these things work. Our societies (by which I mean Masons, Bilderberg, Skull and Bones, et al) MAKE kings. Freemasonry is one of the reasons why Mugabe remains untouchable, in spite of committing more atrocities than Saddam. It's why we still have a monarchy. You really ought to Google these things more...

I'm still pleased how things have worked out. The British public are about to get stung pretty heavily you might say – and ultimately join the euro – but now the political system has been substantially and successfully obfuscated, nobody will be able to do anything about it. However you vote in future, you'll get a subservient Freemason 'running' the country.

I'm set for an easy week or so now before Bilderberg. After that, it's time for another little crisis to sharpen everybody's minds. I think I should like to enjoy a little tongue-piercing distraction in the meantime.

No, no, no, no, no, no, no, no….My tongue is too small and delicate… (Angry Mouth pulling smiley) And now I'm late… .

If you're late, don't make any long-term plans without a DNA test.

You watch too much Jeremy Kyle!

There is no such word as NO when I tell you to do something.'

Bite Me'

I think I might like to clamp those nipples of yours too. Did you ever wonder why there's a trouser-hanger conveniently placed in every hotel bedroom (with the two pegs on it)?

I don't go to hotels. I don't have any money. I go camping, but yes I have seen them and have a few at home and no, I wouldn't use them for that!

I told you my nipples are very sensitive, but I didn't mean sensitive to pain, even though what you're suggesting would really, really hurt, I meant sensitive to any friction at all, meaning that they are my 'on' button, just a few strokes and the sensations created elsewhere can have me writhing about in a few seconds.

I see in my news email that Cameron has got rid of people against gays in the cabinet, I wonder why? And he's looking at Nick Clegg in a rather odd manner…

I understand that the comment was passed on Have I Got News For You last night, when a clip of Clegg and Cameron waving together from the doorstep of Ten Downing Street, "It's Britain's first Gay couple at Number Ten" or something like that. They aren't that far from the truth.

19/05/10

I've received an invitation from someone in Kuwait to come and watch a pony girl contest. Basically, the women are dressed as ponies – all black leather, plug-in tails, and impossibly high heels – in the desert sun, in between sand dunes in the lonely wilderness somewhere. Then you're

supposed to watch while they perform tricks, race, show jump, and then kick the shit out of each other. You're then supposed to bid for the one you wish to ride, so to speak. You know what, I think I'll pass...

I really don't know who you are. If the things you tell me are true or not. I don't know why I am drawn to you. There are things about you I don't like, but other aspects that I really like about you. You tell me so much about some things and so little about others and the things you do tell me I think you probably shouldn't tell me and the things you won't tell me don't make any sense. Am I to keep what you tell me secret? Like how you supposedly run the country single handed? Or do you make it all up? I don't have a photo of you, so you could be anyone... Do I think too much? Am I so caught in your snare that I am now dependent on you whether I like it or not?

I know I think too much. I always have.

I'll tell you what I like about you. I like the way you try to shock me telling me you'll tie me up on a yacht, tie me up in public, make me submit to your friends etc., when really if you are as important as you say you are, then it would be impossible, because you'd end up like Max Mosley! I like it that all your fantasies match mine.

I like the fact that you keep fit, even though you are a bit short... but then without a recent photo how do I know you are not fat, bald, over fifty etc.?

I like the fact that as a father you have exactly the same problems, with or without your money.

I want you to be in charge. I like it when you say 'There is no such word as NO when I tell you to do something!' I'm still not having my tongue pierced though. I can't work for the National Trust and greet customers with a metal bar in my mouth, I'd get the sack and it can be dangerous and swell up for weeks!

I like it when you answer my emails, even though some of them are written when I'm not 'normal' and I think after I've sent it you probably won't reply again.

I do want to travel the world and meet the wealthy, beautiful and powerful, like normal people. I want money. I want to live somewhere sunny. Yes I could probably scrape enough together by the time I retire, but then I'll be old and I want more than that before I get too old and even though I'm cautious and scared and stupid and don't really know who you are... I still want you, so please:

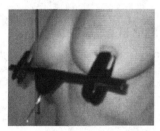 By all means toy with me Sir, but don't leave me hanging around too long. Soon it will be too late to enjoy me fully.

And am I not pleasing Master?

P.S. Actually, in my opinion, I've probably drunk too much whisky to be let loose with a camera... What do you think Sir?

P.P.S. Surprisingly I enjoyed the coat hanger, which I had to keep on for quite a while to get a satisfactory picture, but it would have been so much better to have you tie me up and force me to orgasm before releasing me from its 'bite!'

18/05/10

Oh dear, did I send you naked pictures last night? My nipples are sore...

'I really don't know who you are?' That's the way I like it. And it's the way it HAS to be, because of who I am and whom I represent. Remember I have naked pictures of you – AND, you have to question, who is likely to believe you if you were to approach Max Clifford or someone? I do not run the country single handed. I am simply on the Bilderberg steering committee, amongst other things.

29/05/10

I had this little video [of the Kennedy assassination] sent to me through one of my groups this morning. It certainly makes one wonder about conspiracy theories. Look at Princess Diana's accident. People still believe that she was killed to prevent her marrying Dodi, but if it was because he was a Muslim then how come Charles is a convert? Muslims will rule the world one day anyhow, because they have more children and will outnumber us.

Then I was looking up items about Bilderberg, only to see that the steering committee is made up of two people from each country, or thereabouts and that would make you really powerful and important, seeing as the people who attend really do rule the world. I'm beginning to feel worthless and insignificant; my very existence is a waste of time. I may as well be a flea, but even a flea would get to suck your blood and have some physical contact with you! The Internet has a lot to answer for! I can't get my head around any of it.

How do you? How does one sort it all out and keep it all in perspective? How can you keep it under control? I suppose you have one advantage, being male, you don't get pre-menstrual and hormonal, but you must still get stressed. Who do you go to when you don't know the answer or you feel you can't cope? I go to my dad, when he dies I don't know what I'll do. Otherwise I like to sit in the garden, with a drink of some sort, listen to the birds and just think, relax, maybe read a book. I'd like to do that with you, but will that ever happen?

It's no good thinking any more. I'm pre-menstrual. I've put on four pounds. I'm tired and miserable and I want you, just you. I love you... but I'm still not getting my tongue pierced! Hey, actually I won that one. On 13th May you said:"

I'm set for an easy week or so now before Bilderberg. After that, it's time for another little crisis to sharpen everybody's minds! I think I should like to enjoy a little tongue-piercing distraction in the meantime."

And I haven't had it done so I won!

I'm off to work for the day, so I'll be half dead by tonight, being a Bank Holiday weekend, and I have a lot more shifts next week, so not much playtime either.

Take care at Bilderberg.

01/06/10

It is the 1st of June today Sir. This slave begs to have the privilege of increasing Master's luck this month and comes before him naked to be pinched and punched. Will you not grant this slave's wish, Master? Does Master not find this slave pleasing to pinch?I miss you.

04/06/10

(sent some BDSM pictures)By the way Sir...When will you take me in hand?'

07/06/10

In her ass would have been funnier – and then she can lick the toes clean.Of course – you would make an excellent wine bottle holder like that. The colder the bottle, the better.

That's revolting!!!
    You can't fit a wine bottle in and anyway it wouldn't be cold for long, which would ruin the wine completely!

If you ruin my wine by warming it up – or if you refuse to open up and take it – then you can expect to be punished, publicly.
    That's your point of view. And as my property, I shall disregard it and do whatever pleases me. Let's not pretend that you're entitled to a say, shall we?

Am I? Well it's not fair if I can't fit a wine bottle in 'you know where' and if you want chilled white wine, when I'm so HOT!!! (Stamps foot, runs up the stairs and hides in the bottom of the wardrobe)

Follows her upstairs, and places a chair against the door of the wardrobe.

Slides a hanger under the door, knocks the chair over, then sneaks down to the kitchen for a cup of tea.

Suddenly finds herself restrained with a bag over her head. The next thing she sees – when the bag is removed is a roomful of strangers, all staring lustfully at her naked body.

We were in the house on our own… You can't just suddenly get a load of strangers round!

I didn't say how long that bag was on your head for, did I?

Hears him approach from behind, quickly ducks under the table, out the other side and runs off out the back door to hide in the garden…

You are assuming that you are faster on your feet than me, aren't you? I shall just have to clap you in irons whilst you undertake your daily duties…

I might be faster. How do you know that you would be faster? Have you scrambled under a table before? And I can't be in irons, you had my legs apart trying to ram in a wine bottle at the start of this… remember!

11/06/10

I believe that "irons" exist where the wrists and ankles are attached to bars, as opposed to chains. I think I'd attach you to bars that are slightly too long – it would amuse me to watch you falling over a lot. Mind yourself near the swimming pool, won't you?

I've just found this message from you – this pose ought to form one of your duties, though I would remove your knickers first... (picture of public spanking)

Do you mean one of my duties would be to be spanked in public every day? That's mean, especially if I've been good, it would be a nasty punishment, not daily duties!

Given your propensity to question my command, I think it would be in order to remind you who is the boss – every day, in front of anyone who happens to be around. A daily dose of humiliation will be good for you! You may find it 'character-building'!

No I wouldn't. And anyway wouldn't people interfere if they saw you spanking me and I screamed loud enough? They might take pictures and you could end up on Crime watch... "At 9.30am this man was photographed beating this woman, the police at Norwich are anxious to speak to him or anyone who witnessed this attack."

"Experts believe this is the same man, leading the same woman with a collar and lead through Norwich City Centre. The woman was apparently naked, gagged, and handcuffed at the time."

You missed out blindfolded with a wine bottle stuck out her ass!

That's one way to carry my shopping home – will I get green Clubcard points if you do that?

Well obviously if you bring your own bag!

That would be my recyclable, wipe-clean one then...

09/06/10

Ah, JFK. First, think about the Masons/Protestant Church (C of E and American Fundamentalists/Baptists) – together with Skull & Bones, Bilderberg, Mafia, and all that. And then wonder why nobody wanted that Catholic boy in charge.

There are many theories about Diana. My favourite – Did Dodi do Di, then Di & Dodi died? And the jokes! "I said 'beat them all', not 'eat the wall'!" "I'm so tired; I can't wait for my head to hit the pillar!" And of course the Princess Di satnav voice – "Put your foot down, I think we can shake them off!"
    Wasn't it wonderful, how the entire country united, tied by the grief at Diana's death? That's the value of a Royal Family – to bring a country together. So through this economic downturn I'm prolonging, I think we ought to put a Royal to death, just to pull everyone together, starting with that jug-eared embarrassment. And yes, he is a Muslim.
    It isn't for you to keep things in perspective – you aren't even supposed to know about these things. It's just as well

that we control the press too, so this misinformation, this silence may continue. I get my head around it by thinking about numbers, as opposed to people's lives. I don't know everyone in the EU personally! The fact remains, to enjoy an omelette, you have to bankrupt a few countries. Sorry, I mean 'crack some eggs'.

Your hormones are alive and well I see.

My hormones are alive and well and I'm still waiting to be controlled, mastered, dominated, used, fisted, tied, sucked, squeezed, pinched, whipped, electrocuted, rubbed with chilli powder, tooth-brushed, wine bottled, hung, paddled, kissed, tickled, taken out for a drink, stripped naked and have cum all over me... but not in that order.Bedtime...

09/06/10

(Ken Marcus) *Sent 7 'Wrapped and Waxed' photos*

Good Morning Sir,I had a set of Ken Marcus photos sent through my group, 46 altogether, called 'Wrapped and Waxed.' Here are a few to give you a taster...

I like her collar, but would prefer something a little finer and less heavy round my neck if it's to be worn continuously.

Your horoscope today is: Taurus

Your romantic side is fully energized right now, so sweep your mate off their feet or go looking for someone to fill that gap in your life. It's easier than you think, so take positive steps now!

What time shall I expect you?

09/06/10

I would love to ride along the Greek coast and swim in the sea, they have beautiful, clear blue water and the food is good too. I once went to Lindos on Rhodes for a week or so with three other girls, but I think I've told you that before. It was quite a long time ago. I remember that the song by Arrow called 'Feeling Hot, Hot, Hot,' was popular, but I don't remember the year. I remember the sand on the beach being too hot to walk on, sunbathing topless for the first time and coming home examining my reflection in the mirror with only one white bit on my body. Drinking grapefruit juice out of tins, which the barman shook and tossed in the air, before he poured them out and eating funny cone-like, kebab things, but can't remember what they were called either...

10/06/10

It isn't as hard to move, live, and work abroad as you might think. Might I commend to you the website http://www.escapeartist.com which, despite its heavily Americanised disposition, remains a useful authority on the subject.

With all the kid's stuff, I would just make an appointment with one of them – just one evening would do it, or maybe a day. I'd have all the stuff from the loft down in the lounge, and spend a quality evening sorting through it, reminiscing, enjoying, and chucking out all the old crap that nobody's missed in the last few decades. Have you considered Nicaragua – a Mediterranean climate, a gardener's paradise (if you put up a fence with wooden posts, the posts are likely to sprout leaves) and you can live like Royalty on $300 a month, employing a cook and a cleaner. They speak pretty good English, and the views are incredible. Yes the country has its problems, but they need not concern you (the UK has problems, but you're still happy to live here!) Your mobile will still work, and with Skype, your family are never far away.

10/06/10

Thanks for the suggestion, I'll have a look later, but it will be a long time before I do get to the stage of considering moving somewhere else, especially if it's going to be on my own.

Agreed. You have to get rid of the kids first! I think my daughter will be around for longer than yours though…
I've spotted a lovely seafront taverna that's for sale along the western Greek coast - right there on the beach. Imagine the sunsets. You know, I'm seriously considering buying it just for a laugh - someone else can manage it of course, but that kind of investment is a lot more rewarding than just sterile zeros on a bank statement.
I'm with you on that one - the soft, baking hot sand, the clear and gentle seas, the smell of the amazing food. Remember that thick, sweet smell of all the flowers after dark? I think I'll go and pack…

I could do with a few more sterile zeros right now, but then a taverna does sound good too… I wouldn't mind working there, I'm good at pouring coffee and tea now and putting cups through dishwashers... I even have tea stained fingernails to prove it!

I can do the Greek cooking – and many other Mediterranean cuisines – though I'd rather pay someone to do all that hot sweaty stuff for me. I'll do front of house, dispensing Ouzo amongst my guests, and setting off Chinese Lanterns into the dying sunset across the sea.

I've not done that before... set off Chinese lanterns, the opportunity just hasn't arisen. I can't recall what typical Greek cooking is either, but I love anything with goat's cheese and olives. And yes the only thing that should get you hot and sweaty should be playing with me, not cooking!

You should try the Chinese Lanterns – I think they are going to be the next craze, unfortunately, so they will be for sale on every street corner. Goats' cheese and olives sound good to me – how about some barbecued octopus or tuna that was caught just a few hours ago? Washed down with orange juice from our citrus orchard, and grapes from one of our vines. Sound good?

I've never had octopus either, but it all sounds very good, I could just lie on the shore and let the waves roll over me like that famous movie... would you make love to me too sir?

Of course I would – that's what you are there for. I'll use you as my spunk dustbin.

Yuk! That's not a very nice expression.

Just another of your daily duties! Think how much money will be saved on Kleenex...

No!

It will be your greatest honour to consume each and every last drop that your Master gives you.

That's something I've never done either, along with eating octopus! I've tasted a teeny, weeny bit once when a guy came on my face, but that's all.

You will be doing PLENTY that you've never done before. I'm kind to you, rewarding you with all these new experiences, aren't I?

Yes sir. I want them all, sir (well most of them).I have had other email chats, with other men claiming to be Dominant, but so far the only three experiences of actual meetings were disappointing... It's not so much the physical side, although I got spanked a bit twice, it's the lack of actual dominance, the mental side.

So how am I doing?

Hmmmm... quite well sir, enough to scare me, thrill me, make me smile, turn me on, have me bite my lip just contemplating playing with you, but of course this is still in imagination form...

You shall be invited, from time to time, to voice an opinion. It shall be purely be at my request – and I had better like what I hear.

When I replied 'Am I?' I meant 'Am I your property?'

Obviously.

Well how does that work then?
Do you really mean it?

Since when is it your place to ask ME questions?

Do you always own things you've never seen? Do I get a certificate as proof? Or will you come and take me to get a tattoo done?

Sometimes. I apparently hold title to an estate in Scotland and another in Zimbabwe that I have never been to.
    Why? You will not obey me when I give a simple, explicit, not-hard-to-get-the-wrong-end-of-the-stick instruction, such as "You will get your tongue pierced for me".

I can't get my tongue pierced, haven't you read all the warnings about getting it done, plus it can break your teeth, I already have two broken ones, so it wouldn't be good at all...*Pouts.*
    What if you don't like me when you see me?

Then you will become something more pleasing to your owner and master.
    Do not question my authority. Ever.

Does 'ever' mean 'never' or is it just a tiny bit flexible sometimes? You know, like grey areas.

What have I told you about questioning me, or hesitation? Are you too stupid to understand? Teeth are like servant girls - they can always be replaced. Would you like new teeth (I might have my initials engraved or embossed on them - I haven't decided yet.) While I'm at it - I might choose for you to undergo cosmetic surgery! Hmmmm - what shall I have?

But it would hurt sir. Would you really want to damage your slave girl, beyond recognition, when she is already perfectly formed and so passionate for her Master?

WHAT? You'll be telling me she is WORTHY of her Master next! Firstly, she is mine to do with as I will. Her life is mine - wholly and completely. She will depend upon me for food, shelter, and clothing as and when I see fit - even air to breathe. And I will be the one to decide if she is perfectly formed or not. If I wish for her to have bigger breasts - or more of them - then she will take them without question.

Yes sir. I shall do my very best to be pleasing sir, after all I don't want to end up in the 'chokey!'

You WILL end up there - if it pleases me, regardless of whether you deserve it or not. But the knowledge that you are pleasing your master will ease your suffering - so it's not ALL bad.

It's not like I'm your normal, single submissive, with a toned, brown body and various piercing's/tattoo's.

Good, because I can get that just anywhere.How quickly can you get to Paris tonight?

I don't know. I'd have to wash my hair first... oh, and I have work tomorrow.

11/06/10

Sent video of subbie tied on a remote control cart with an automatic vibrator (For wife that has everything)
     This might take your mind off work.

Wow - I would love to try you out in one of those! Fancy a few laps of Tesco's car park? Or along the promenade at Brighton when the beach is packed? Don't worry - no one will recognise you in a mask. Will your breasts jiggle as much as hers? I bet your screaming sounds just as pathetic...
     Thank you for that - I'm still laughing!

Yes, my breasts would jiggle like that, I don't like them if I'm on all fours, they are just too 'loose' now and somehow disappear to nothing but two little, saggy sacs... Oh and my screaming would probably be pathetic too.

Who would recognise you with a gimp mask on? Apart from your gynaecologist?

I don't have a gynaecologist. I took pot luck at the local NHS hospital when I had my daughter and ended up with a midwife who was crap at sewing and not brilliant at birthing babies either. I ended up split inside needing over 16 stitches, and then later I had to go and get scar tissue cut off, because it was such a mess... oops, TMI?

I've just watched it again – if you scream like that, I'll make it go through that hedge!

Oh no sir, please don't put me through the hedge. (Next he'll want to see if he can drive it into the sea, or a car wash or something... men!)

You know I keep every email you send, with my replies, and put them in order into a word document. It's going to take me an hour to cut and paste all these emails!

He knew I was writing this book. He could have stopped me at any time or warned me to stop, or was he waiting until we were together, when he would have read it, then destroyed it? But I can't believe that someone so important, in control of so much, could leave my book to chance in the event of his death; he wanted me to publish this.

12/06/10

I've just downloaded a complete movie in four parts from my group. It's titled 'The training of O' and is about a submissive called Holly Heart being trained over four days as a slave for a men's club. It starts off with her being interviewed and asked what she does and doesn't like by means of a check list, then armed with her safe word the training begins. The whole thing is really just a movie for hogtied fans. It's not bad, but she makes a god awful noise when she comes and is forever repeating 'Yes Sir' in succession, which is just annoying.

Anyway just before it comes to the end of her training, her trainer accidentally catches her clitoris with the end of a small cane as he's caning her thigh. She swears like mad and they cut her loose. The next scene finds her with the trainer and another man, plus a bag of ice on her pussy discussing whether or not she will be OK to continue and film the final scene at the club, which kind of destroys the whole 'this is for real' feel to the movie. If you had any doubt at all that it was staged, then you realise now that it was.

They do film the final scene where she is chained hand and foot and taken into the gentleman's club for questioning and a bit of sport, something you would probably like, with your fetish for having other people watch, but it's all so, creepy, nasty and yuk... not at all nice really, just false people pretending to be upper class. I wouldn't want it to be like that. As your slave I want to be only yours, for your amusement, to love you and have you love me back, not strung up by some weirdo I don't know for 'training,' then put on display in a room full of creepy twats.

Anyway England drew with USA. I had a busy day at work, kebab for tea, because I was too shattered to cook. I shall sleep well tonight and have a day of rest tomorrow, apart from cooking, cleaning, washing, gardening etc.

13/06/10

Good morning Sir, is this how you would take me around as

a travelling companion? *(Picture of a woman tied to an old trunk)* Nicely packed and ready to go!

Or perhaps, if you are tired of Gozo and decide to visit a different climate then perhaps you will keep me 'hanging ' around until you need me like this.

(Picture of a woman hanging from a tree by her ankles dressed in an open jump suit in the snow)

Or maybe you would just stash me somewhere safe out of the snow?

(Picture of a woman tied on her tummy, hands to feet, on top of a tree trunk in the snow)

And then sir, if you leave me in the hotel, will I be permitted to amuse myself? Or will Sir leave me like this handcuffed and wearing a chastity belt? *(Picture of a woman tied to a bed, gagged, with a chastity belt on)*

13/06/10

There is absolutely no reason at all to stay put where you are. Some of the biggest European movers and shakers I know don't even live here! You've been to some beautiful places though. It's a beautiful world, isn't it? I could spend hours on Google Earth – or just make a few phone calls, pack a few things, and just go places...I too hate all those faked screaming orgasms. Have no doubts that your screams will indeed be genuine.

Thank you sir. I might also inform you that I'm ovulating (very wet) and therefore in a sexually frustrated state and you are likely to get quite a few suggestive emails over the next week, along with all the hormonal ones too!

Good. I'm just catching up for a few minutes whilst Madam finishes her breakfast. Here we are in one of the world's finest hotels, and she's eating Coco Shreddies. That's kids for you, isn't it?

You see, we have so much in common... my son is eating Coco Shreddies too.

14/06/10

A man was driving home one evening and realized that it was his daughter's birthday and he hadn't bought her a present. He drove to the mall and ran to the toy store and he asked the store manager "How much is that new Barbie in the window?"

The Manager replied, "Which one? We have 'Barbie goes to the gym' for $19.95, 'Barbie goes to the Ball' for $19.95, 'Barbie goes shopping for $19.95, 'Barbie goes to the beach' for $19.95, 'Barbie goes to the Nightclub' for $19.95, and 'Divorced Barbie' for $375.00."

"Why is the Divorced Barbie $375.00, when all the others are $19.95?" Dad asks, surprised."

Divorced Barbie comes with Ken's car, Ken's House, Ken's boat, Ken's dog, Ken's cat and Ken's furniture."

My daughter said that Barbie comes with Action Man. I said, "No, Barbie comes with Ken, doesn't she?" She just smiled and replied "No Daddy, she FAKES it with Ken."

So an explorer is wandering through the jungle and is bitten by a snake. He's miles from civilisation, and his only

hope is the local witch doctor. The witch doctor looks at the bite."

Hmmm. You've been bitten by the Mgwame snake," he says.

"Is that fatal? Is there a cure?" asks the explorer.

The witchdoctor rubs his chin. "Yes, it is fatal" he says. "There is a cure – but one more terrible than a thousand Mgwame snake bites."

"I don't care!" screams the panicking explorer. "What is it? I'll do anything!

"The witch doctor beckons him forward, and speaks slowly to emphasise the importance of what he's about to say.

"First, you must return to London. Find your soulmate – a friend who has been closer to you than a brother. Take your friend with you, and you must both get absolutely blind drunk.

"The explorer nods. "Yes… I have to say, I'm liking this cure so far. What next?

"The witch doctor continues, "When your friend is so drunk he can no longer stand or speak, he has the right amount of alcohol in his blood. Bind his feet and wrists, suspend him upside down – and slit his throat. You are finished when his body is drained of blood and he is dead." The explorer is dumbstruck. "When he is drained of blood, cut his carcass down. Separate the flesh from his bones. Grind his bones into a paste – mixing a little of his blood – and apply the paste to where the Mgwame Snake has bitten you. And you will be cured!"

"Unbelievable" says the explorer" That has to be the most disgusting cure for anything that I have ever heard of in my life. What do you call it?"

"Well," says the witch doctor, "we call it palomine lotion."

That's worse than my long-winded one about the fly going down to the water to cool off, that I wrote on your profile on Lycos!

16/06/10

I know what would be fun – two slaves, back to back with a double-ended butt plug. Shackle their ankles together – each ankle with the one behind them – and bind their wrists. Gag them so they can't communicate – and then expect them to walk, under the whip. And if they manage that OK, let's see them do it blindfolded, or walking the plank…

Well? I'm waiting.

Waiting for what?

The answer to the puzzle of two subs back to back with a butt plug or me filling your inbox with suggestive or hormonal emails?

Well I'm not in the mood for either or anything at the moment… Oh, which means you're getting a hormonal email. I think I somehow missed ovulation (normally it goes on for a week or more), and went straight into PMS.

17/06/10

Before we discuss anything else ******, I must ask you (and

anyone you hold dear) to STAY OUT OF LONDON for the time being. You may not ask why – I'm not going to tell you – but you need to do this.

Thank you for the warning.

You're welcome.Redneck joke. A couple had a vasectomy after 9 children. They had read that 1 in 10 children were Mexican and neither of them could speak Spanish, so they didn't want to risk having any more kids.

I know a couple who adopted a baby from Romania – they had to learn Romanian before the baby could learn to talk. Another visit to the Old Jokes Home…

17/06/10

You could have me picked up in a big car thing, one I could stand up in, with instructions to put on a blindfold, then the car could pick you up, but how would I know it was you? Of course you'll say, 'You won't know ******, but you will do as I tell you.' Or something like that… What would happen next? I'd definitely try and remove the blindfold to see you, plus I don't like the dark and it's dark under a blindfold.

First, it would not be ME that grabs you. I have access to people who are good at that sort of thing. You would be grabbed and bundled into the back of a large (white and anonymous) van, with a roof high enough for you to stand in. By the time the van moves you will already be blindfolded, gagged, and attached to the roof with a collar

and chain, with your clothing being removed for storage. When the blindfold is finally removed, you could be anywhere – a cellar, on deck in the middle of the sea, abroad in the baking heat, or in front of an audience. If you want to play then that's fine, but I take my recreational pleasures very seriously.

I never did like blind man's bluff as a child. I almost wet myself with fear. When I was a child I used to sleepwalk. Once my parents were in the kitchen knocking out the old larder to make the kitchen bigger, when they heard the back door slam. My mother ran out to find me going up the garden path. She asked what I was doing outside and I told her, in my sleep, that I was going out to ride my bike.

Does anything frighten you?

Not really. I can't remember the last time I was even remotely frightened or scared.

I had better go to bed now. I can't feel my nose and I keep having to correct my typing. I'll dream of you tonight tying me up and making me submit to you.

Oh and is London still not safe and if you're there will you be safe?

I'm still in Paris. Consider it unsafe until I say otherwise.

18/06/10

During a recent company IT audit, it was found that a

blonde was using the following password: "MickeyMinniePlutoHueyLouieDeweyDonaldGoofyCanberra". When asked why she had such a long password, she said she was told that it had to be at least 8 characters long and include at least one capital.I am not that stupid! Am I?

19/06/10

I watched England play last night and drank three small bottles of beer, like a good football supporter. I needed to wee after, obviously, as it's one of my main occupations, and I took my phone with me to check for mail. Anyway one thing led to another, I had the beer with me too and I took a little photo for you...But I'm not going to send it, it's too rude and the lighting wasn't brilliant, so I've hidden it on my PC, maybe for later when I'm drunker...Beer doesn't have the same effect as Jim Beam, when you got all the other pics!

Splendid!

You can't answer 'Splendid!'

I think you'll find I can furnish you with any response I choose!

It's not splendid. Splendid is a good day out or a lovely tea or something, not a picture taken of my you know what with a beer bottle in!

That's for me to decide, isn't it? I'm not at all impressed that you have chosen to do this on your own – you will do things like this when I command, and not before.

Yes sir, of course sir. I'm turning into a whore.

You think? It's early days yet! You wait until you've seen what I have lined up for you...

Not quite totally in your control until you come here and take me in person!

Then you'll have to wait a little longer, won't you? You're not ready yet!

Yes Master, I'll wait, Master.

20/06/10

I'm on about my third glass of Chianti left from last night, I went outside to sunbathe and knocked the first glass over as I reached for my book. I gave up sunbathing fairly quickly, the sun wasn't co-operating and I got chilly.

I'm cooking tea now, so I decided to come on the PC, which is next to the kitchen, our house is a rectangular, open plan arrangement, probably about the same size as your toilet!

I left home this morning. My youngest upset me, so I took a bottle of wine to Dad for Father's day. I don't like seeing my dad when I'm like this; I hate making him worry. It was all over his trip, that he now doesn't want to go on, because the girl he's interested in isn't going and only two of his friends will be there. I paid for this out of my own money, not my dad's handouts, and he couldn't care less. All he talks about is the war, fighting and guns. This trip will be excellent for him, history is his favourite subject and I know he will enjoy it when he gets there. It's just this teenage attitude that he has at the moment that hurts so much.

I was thinking about what you said about not going into London and the way you said it... It was a command, a bit pompous perhaps, but it made me feel protected, so I suppose owned... I don't know... How many other people did you warn? Will I see you one day and get to run a Greek taverna with you, pouring coffee for customers and swimming in the deep, blue, crystal clear sea?

How long is he going for? Who is he going with – would you like him followed?

He's going for four days, well he left this morning. I was up at 3.30am. I went back to bed, but I feel crap now and have a long day ahead at work. He's with a coachload of about 50 pupils and teachers. They go to battlefields, war memorials and graves, trenches etc. No I don't need him followed, he is very sensible and responsible; it's his friend who is a pain in the arse. I took them both to town once, this boy has to touch everything and move things; letting down recliner chairs etc., he's just really annoying to take anywhere.

20/06/10

Happy Father's Day Daddy.

I was trying to find a stat with 'Daddy's Girl' on, but I don't have any good ones, so I went through the spanking ones instead, plus I looked at the hanging girl photos I sent you, consequently I'm very wet, so that will have to be your Father's Day present from me, thinking about how wet it makes me, thinking of you spanking me or using a vibrator on me while I hang upside down!

I think, whilst you're over my knee like that, I'll let my fingers do a little probing and exploring. Anywhere I choose – and you will not speak, flinch, or react in any way. And you will lick my fingers clean afterwards, and say THANK YOU.

What happens if I move?

You can expect to be punished. I will not tolerate inability from you to comply with my simple commands.

But if you're going to poke about I'll have to move at some point, especially with Sir's expert touch! What will my punishment be? The toothbrush with minty fresh, tingly toothpaste on? Or perhaps Sir will add a little chilli powder? Maybe it will be the coat hanger? Or the cane? Or will I have to be your footstool for the duration of a movie?

21/06/10

I'm sure we will own that Taverna – you can pour coffee and

ouzo for our guests if you like, but I'll be in the corner, people-watching, sunset-gazing, and waves-listening. Invisible.

Your command to avoid London is part and parcel of my ownership. You come under my protection – the only person that is going to hurt you is me.

Today, I'm in a 'man in linen' role. It's too hot for much else!

What colour linen? What colour shirt?

A white shirt, and I suppose a calico kind of coloured trouser. With flip flops and a Breitling... Is that enough detail?

Hmmmm, sounds good to me...

22/06/10

Invisible in your linen suit? Watching me flirt with other men? Watching my bottom wiggling in a tight black skirt as I pass close by? Oh look at the time! This will have to go into my imagination for later! I have to get to work, we have an early coach in today.

Yes, invisible. I can be invisible in plain sight if I choose. Our guests will enjoy their meals and our hospitality under the stars. Nobody will notice when I tell you to remove your underwear and give it to me. Or when you back up to me and I slip a finger under your skirt and inside you, then taste it.

So we are outside and it's dark, people wouldn't see or know that we were 'together,' you would be Mr anonymous in the corner and I would just be a waitress cleaning your table… It excites me now just thinking of it…

Me too. Oops! My spoon has fallen off the table. Be a love, would you…

23/06/10

I've worked so much this week all my clothes are in the wash, so today I'm wearing a black linen dress that zips up at the front from top to bottom. Do you think I'll be giving the old people heart attacks? Good job I wear a pinny!

Photo sets like this [*of a woman hanging by her ankles*] are always an increasing disappointment to me. What is there in these pictures that you have not seen before, other than perhaps the individuals? It's just more of the same, and the makers are just not trying any more. It's formulaic and boring - even the models look bored. I like them looking terrified. Bring back the creativity! The imagination! We'll just have to do it ourselves, won't we…

I totally agree. They are nearly always shot in some seedy dungeon or dirty warehouse with plastic breasted women, panting out orgasm after orgasm, accompanied with pathetic dialogue and creepy men.I also watched a particularly disturbing and violent video of a woman being 'nutted' and beaten unconscious, then tied, whipped and cut with a knife. It was very fuzzy, but pretty realistic, except for parts which were suddenly and ridiculously filmed in slow motion.

It really depends what kind of mood I'm in. If I'm in a humorous mood then I might like to enjoy something different to when I'm in need of a little stress-relief or just plain tired. But most of the time I like to see something new that pushes the boundaries. I saw, a while ago, a woman who was shackled with her feet a shoulder width apart and her hands fastened to her hips. After the usual, uninspired and somewhat dull flogging, she had a nose-clip attached and was suspended from her ankles. Then, screaming and terrified, she was lowered, head first, into a muddy hole in the ground that was deep enough for her to be submerged completely. Nice. She was raised after just a few seconds, which must have seemed like a lifetime to her – and then just when she thought it was over, after being hosed down, they did it again! Hilarious. I didn't meet the woman – who may not have spoken English anyway – but it was an amusing evening.

It doesn't take much to terrify me, I think you have a good idea already what would work. Anger frightens me too, but if really threatened I will fight back, especially if it's my children who are threatened, even if someone came after you I'd probably attack them.

If someone came after me? You do know I can have twenty-four-hour protection from Special Branch if I choose, don't you? I often do if I travel abroad. One cannot enter the darker regions of the world unless properly prepared. They are good guys, but typically discreet – I don't like to have them breathing down my neck, nor as my valet.

If you do have anything like that [being dipped in mud] planned for me then I'd have to end this now. I don't find that at all hilarious! Just visualising what happened to that poor woman terrifies me. I want you, I want to please you, I want to experiment with you, I want to learn to trust you, but I couldn't do that, ever! What were you thinking even telling me that? Some things are definitely better left unsaid! I can't even keep my face under the shower for more than a few seconds to wash my face wash off! Oh god I think I'm going to be sick!

Like I said – hilarious! There were people who were there, with reactions similar to your own.

Where were you?

I can't tell you. I can't identify my host either. I thought you don't like me namedropping?

Did that woman know that was going to happen? Did she get paid to do it? It must have taken longer than a few seconds to put her under and pull her back up again. If she was screaming then she probably hadn't taken enough breath while she was under. Did she choke? She could have drowned.

She did choke, and vomit, but she didn't drown. She ought to have known her place and realised that if her master desired her to go under then she ought to accept her fate graciously. NO, I don't want to re-enact this, in any way shape or form. I've seen it done now – and in any case, there was a LOT of clearing up to do. I'm sure I can think of something less messy though. The reason I mentioned it? Because I knew you'd never seen anything like that before. It's a bit different to the 'formulaic' stuff you see.

23/06/10

It's morning again here, about 5.30am, I can't sleep. I'm too hot. Also I've been dipped a few times head first into a muddy hole during the night!

P.S. Do you really want me to have my tongue pierced?

I can't believe you have the gall to ask me AGAIN, frankly. Well, it did the trick – your reaction is certainly hilarious! *

Grits teeth and glares at him* You are very naughty sir!

24/06/10

How dare you accuse ME of being naughty! You're the one running around in just a pinny – and that bottom isn't quite red enough yet. Come here...

Yes sir, right away sir... Shall I bring the wooden spoon?

No, the **CHEESE GRATER!** Just kidding, the wooden spoon will do fine. And the olive oil. I think I'll check under the bonnet whilst I'm there.

Oh ha, ha, very funny! I'll pick up a cucumber on the way too!

No – make it a **MARROW.**

If I can't get a wine bottle in, I'm hardly likely to fit a marrow in!

I relish a challenge...

25/06/10

There's a great deal of stuff on this Internet thingy that, quite frankly, shouldn't be. People who put pictures up of their kids/pets/collection of cuddly toys, and expect the world to appreciate them as much as they do. Home-made porno. Two hideous examples of humankind, who no longer really love each other, making the Beast with Two Backs. Thankfully there's inadequate lighting, and they sometimes forget to stay in view of the camera, so all you get is an ankle and the sound effects. Nice.

25/06/10

I don't photograph very well anyway, but yes there is a lot of stuff on the Internet that shouldn't be there. Facebook is a prime culprit.

24/06/10

It is done sir [tongue piercing]

Show me.

It's too swollen at the moment, give it a few more days.

OK. How did it go? Any problems?

No problems. It didn't even bleed. All you feel is a prick as the needle goes in, after that nothing, as the tongue is a muscle. She did use some liquid to freeze it first too, so that helped. I have to keep rinsing with salt water to promote healing. I bought mouthwash ready, but found out it has alcohol in, which is bad, along with dairy products, which contain yeast and therefore can give you yeast infection. I'm taking Ibuprofen to help with the swelling. The kids haven't noticed yet.

25/06/10

Hmmmm... Let's see if I can fit this huge marrow inside... Well unless it's squishy, which would be revolting, it's not going to work! And no I'm not going to lick off your fingers after you've been pushing bits of marrow inside me... Hey, you could cook and stuff it first, then it would be nice and soft and tasty... Or will that describe me after?

Mmmm, stuffed marrow – I've even mastered the technique of getting the marrow NOT to roll over in the oven and lose its contents!

26/06/10

You are actually talking about real stuffed marrow now aren't you? I think I've cooked and eaten it once in my lifetime. I do like it, but I don't think my dad did, so my mother didn't cook it and the kids won't even eat courgette, so I guess marrow is out too.My tongue is still double its normal size and aches a bit now, along with my throat, but not too bad.

27/06/10

What's not to like? It's all about the stuffing anyway – you could do it with just some mince and a jar of Ragu if you were so inclined. You'd forget it was actually marrow, if you were some namby-pamby I-don't-like-this-even-though-I've-never-really-given-it-a-proper-chance grizzle-guts.

I'm actually in a really foul mood right now, in case you hadn't guessed. I switch on the television news – the headline is about Cameron at his first G8 summit. "The G8 leaders were happy to pose for the cameras" said the reporter – only there were TEN fucking people there! The extra two are meant to be briefing the other eight on what is required from them, behind the scenes – NOT JOINING THEM IN PHOTO OPPORTUNITIES! All we need right now is some smart-arse reporter asking why there are ten people in a picture of eight G8 leaders, and asking the identities of the other two.

I hate sloppiness like this. Heads are going to roll. I feel like I ought to create a diversion to take the world's attention away from Toronto, but I'm undecided as to exactly what – too much doom and gloom, and suddenly everyone's mood changes, and people will start complaining about the budget again. A monumental fuck up. Excuse my French – but I am in Paris…

You're still in Paris. You've been there ages. Is your daughter still with you? Are you still playing 'Men in Hats' or whatever it was? I can see you're angry, pacing the floor and growling I expect! *Think I'll go hide under the bed until he's calmed down*

Ok well here comes the Miss Stupid reply. I actually had no idea that a G8 summit was for eight leaders. I thought it was just some sort of name they gave it, because it was held in a mountainous place, hence 'summit,' so I thought that it was the mountain where they met! I've been on Wikipedia now so I have been enlightened. I never used to watch the news, too much to do sorting out kids for school etc. Still I doubt if many people will notice.

If you're going to have a distraction, do something nice for a change.

29/06/10

I will. But I still have plenty of work to do first! I think I'll head to Gozo for a few days on my own, once all this has calmed down.

03/07/10

I'm tired. The sodding snails have eaten all the buds on my Day Lily's out the front garden.

Apparently we are friends on Windows live thingy. I just updated my profile.

Happy 4th July part American person.

Are you still in Paris?

I feel this is the point where he finally accepted that we were going to be together, because he added me to his contacts on his Hotmail; I wasn't going away.

04/07/10

Damn 4th of July. Even that date has Masonic undertones – had I been in charge on that occasion, things would have been very different and many thousands of lives would have been spared! CONGRATULATIONS on the piercing. A shame the kids haven't noticed it, but they never notice a thing that isn't on a screen! I'm done in Paris, and I'm at home for the weekend. Next stop – Rosyth Naval Base in Scotland for two weeks.

04/07/10

I stayed at home rubbish movies, then went to bed early, which did me no good at all, because a girl and her builder boyfriend across the road were out in the street at 3am, with him swearing at someone on his mobile. Two nights ago they had a blazing row at 1am and I nearly called the police, as she was shouting and screaming "Get out of my fucking house, get out of my fucking house... Go on hit me then, fucking hit me!" etc, etc. I feel like I haven't had a good night's sleep for weeks, what with the heat and the continuous disturbances in the night. The problem with the girl is that her aunty lives two doors down from me and I am sort of friends with her, so it's a bit awkward if it's me that calls the police, but how they didn't hear her rowing I don't know!

Anyway. I have a mountain of washing and four beds to strip today, plus the usual cooking, washing dishes and sorting out malarkey. Get some decent whisky in Scotland.

05/07/10

Well I was going to try and write you a really, really sexy letter this morning, because I'm really, really, really...

But... I got distracted and went on Facebook, which reminded me that I hadn't added you to any of my lists, which are filtered to protect my privacy, so now you are a close friend, not that you'll be going on there much.

(He eventually opened a Facebook profile to look at my photos)

So now I have my tongue piercing, what's next on your list of grooming me into a suitable submissive I wonder? So I'm sat here waiting for the clock to go round to 9am, which is when I leave for work, in my short, tight, black dress. I haven't put my hair up yet, or put on my tights...You creep up behind me, grab my hands and cuff my arms behind the chair, ignoring my protests that I have to get to work soon.

Taking two ropes you tie my ankles to the chair legs, and then, satisfied that I can't move, you begin to massage each of my nipples slowly, making me squirm and moan. I can't stand it for long, the sensations are too strong. You decide to extend my misery, your finger finding my clit, wetted with my juices, is massaged slowly and excruciatingly. I become highly aroused in a very short time, as I panic with the clock ticking on to my departure time. I know I have to come soon; you will not release me until I do. Your massaging speeds up, my nipples cruelly pinched and twisted, I gasp and shout, my face flushed, my head thrown back as I arch into my orgasm. Quickly your fingers enter me to feel my pulsating muscles, confirmation that your administrations have been complete...

Gosh look at the time... Must dash.

I don't think I would reward you with an orgasm like that. I would tie you and rub your clitoris – I think I might like to bite your nipples hard too – and take you to the brink. THEN you can go to work. I like the thought of you aching to come all day. If you've been a good girl, then when you come home I shall permit you to masturbate yourself to orgasm – under my watchful eye, of course, and I might even lend a hand (or tongue...) If however you've been naughty, then I shall expect you to accept your punishment with grace – and a 'thank you' and a curtsey afterwards. I own you.

Humph... That's not fair... How am I supposed to concentrate all day? The till will be out, the tea will be made wrong, the customers will complain!

That isn't my problem. But, watching you cope shall provide my entertainment.

Oh how shall I be good Master? Will I get 'Good Girl' chocolate drops too? And perhaps a little ball to play with?

Please do not attempt to use your bargain-basement 'humour' on me - you're not very good at it, and I shall be obliged to punish such misdemeanours.

I shall keep you awake all night long then, tossing and turning in bed, I only sleep when I've had an orgasm. Unless you give me a good walk before bed to really tire me out.

Well if I choose, you shall be permitted to climb on board, 'Ding ding, all aboard the Skylark!' and you can enjoy several orgasms.

Several!!! Three is probably my limit on a good day, unless I get naps in between...

...though I will tell you when you can cum, and how many times.

And what if I can't hold back?

You shall then swallow what I give you, and say 'thank you'.

How? It will all be inside me... I suppose that will be a good punishment, as it's not something I've done before or even contemplated. Can you eat strawberries first? Apparently if you eat strawberries then that's what it tastes of. If it's anything like semolina then I'll probably throw up, I hate milk puddings and custard!

A walk would be nice – I'll go and get your Pony Girl gear, and the plug-in tail.

Grrrrrrr... I am not wearing pony gear! Anyway if I'm climbing aboard and riding you, then you're the pony! XxXxXxXxXx Look, I've mixed my kisses with yours.

Bodily fluids next...

Mmmmmm... I love it when you get all romantic.

I think I've found a weakness! I think I'll discover ways to exploit this...

Be more specific. What weakness? Me not wanting to eat 'you know what?' My aversion to semolina and milk puddings? Or the fact that I love it when you get romantic.And how can you exploit it? It's impossible to exploit from where you are, you're in Scotland and when you're not in Scotland you're in Paris and when you're not in Paris you're in Norwich and when you're not in Norwich you're in Brussels and when you're not in Brussels you're in Tuscany and when you're not in Tuscany you're in New York and when you're not in New York you're in London and when you're not in London you're in Gozo and when you're not in Gozo you're in Greece and when you're not in Greece you're somewhere else!Besides I can't lick or suck at the moment, thanks to you!

08/07/10

Yes, I get around a bit. It's a beautiful, tax-free world out there. Nonetheless, I do many things that you might consider to be "impossible". I don't wish for you to waste your "licking and sucking" right now. You will however do it when I say. As for Facebook – I don't think I'll bother thank you. I don't think it's really for me.

08/07/10

I only play games on Facebook now and occasionally chat to my friend abroad. I don't go in for all the other stuff. Nothing is impossible if you have money, except for the things that really matter, like actually licking and sucking for real...

09/07/10

Well, I suppose you've established the crux of the matter – an achievement, given your upbringing – I do have the money, which is why nothing for me is impossible. Though my status and influence might also play their part.

Where are you now?

I'm at Rosyth in Scotland, discussing NATO nuclear submarines.

I don't care how rich you are or that you think you own me,

which you can't, because you haven't actually 'bought me' or even seen me, or inspected me, or whatever it is a Master does to acquire a slave and when you do, which I am certain you will, you may not want me anyway and I may not want you either, but with the relationship we have now and not being under any illusions, having decided that you are really just stringing me along for your personal entertainment (you've never spoken to me on the phone, or sent a new picture, or told me your children's names) but yes I do enjoy it, but I shan't make any plans for the future that I would like to have with you (a Greek taverna, freshly brewed coffee, a spoon on the floor) and I did just say that one day you will meet me, but after saying that I'm not under any illusions, that contradicts that, because I really don't think you will ever meet me, even though I pierced my tongue for you, but as it stands and before I lose the plot completely, I think I love you, I think I am yours and maybe, because of that, you do own me?

The conclusion is; Nothing is impossible if you have money, but if I don't feel the way I feel about you now when I meet you, then keeping me will be impossible. I wonder how you see me too. Just as a possible sub or more?

10/07/10

[sent video of anal sex] This is quite funny. The bloke doing it is really pleased with himself and acting more like he's just scored a goal or something.

10/07/10

That's what happens when you send a boy to do a man's job, I'm afraid. No wonder she was uncomfortable, he just dived straight in there - some of us are a lot more gentle and considerate. Sometimes.

10/07/10

It's always uncomfortable! I'd prefer something a bit smaller, like a finger, which works for me, especially if I'm too tired in the first place, but still need to cum to get to sleep. Not sure I like the tone of 'sometimes,' which reminds me I found another butt plug stat you might like.

What a splendid picture. I like the way he's in a suit (albeit a cheap one) and hasn't even bothered to roll his sleeves back. She, however, is naked, shaved, and has her ankles clamped. That's her place. And I like the electrodes attached to the butt plug. It's always best to begin with a finger, just to relax the sphincter a little and loosen things up a little.

How can you tell from that picture if it's a cheap suit or not? And if her ankles are clamped then she can't move out of 'her place' even if she wanted to!

When I say 'her place' you silly girl, I mean that is her status, her role. She is nothing more than a chattel he uses to pleasure himself with, not even deserving of clothes, pubic hair or freedom of movement. I hope she appreciates his kindness when he releases her from her bonds, without even a thought for himself. Of course he doesn't have to, but some Masters are extremely kind like that.

And yes, it is possible to tell that he's wearing a cheap, mass-produced, off-the-peg suit.

10/07/10

I had a really long talk with my friend, mostly about you, trying to put things in perspective, which I do struggle with, as most people don't understand how somebody can be controlled by another person they have never met, but his partner, who joined us later, said that if I was a true submissive then I wouldn't question you at all. I don't think it is that simple. Perhaps if I didn't have the kids and other commitments it would be simple. Being a gay couple though, they did understand about the sexual aspect.

I don't want to question you, I want to be obedient, but I want to play with you too, so I must question you sometimes or it would be boring, but only about certain things. I know and trust that you would never hurt me, my upbringing, as you insultingly put it, allows me to work out that from conversations we have had in the past, but by taking me, becoming responsible for me, owning me completely, you would become responsible for all the baggage that is attached to me also, kids, cats, guinea pigs, pot plants etc.

You say you have the money to achieve the impossible, and this is my impossible: finding a man to take me completely, along with my family, so I can serve him always, be with him wherever he goes, give him my body, share my thoughts with him and give him my heart and soul, without having to worry where the next penny will come from, which is why I asked if you saw me as a possible sub or more.

It all hangs on our meeting, doesn't it? You cannot make that kind of decision lightly, a few dates at least would be necessary. If not this scenario, the complete one, then perhaps an odd couple of days here and there would be the Master/sub relationship you were looking for and I would carry on working and living my life separately. I just know that I cannot carry on in this cyber limbo, this teasing and these empty promises, this longing for you to be with me, not knowing what you look like, smell like and feel like. Not knowing if your touch will awaken me, or if looking into your eyes will strip me naked and leave me weak, a single look and I'll know if I've been, good, bad, naughty, stupid, surprising or right for a change. How can I know what your words mean if I cannot see your face, hear your laugh, or sense your anger and frustration?

And no, it doesn't help to go out and buy your aftershave, put it on an expensive Italian suit and lie next to it!!!

I'm ovulating, I'm wet, I want you...

This is where we have a problem. The summary of your statement is that you wish for me to fit in with the life which you already lead – including cats, 'Guinea Pigs' and pot plants.

We could not be a couple in the conventional sense. I cannot be introduced into your social circle as '******'s new fella' or whatever label is eventually ascribed.

There is a lot of security around me, and certain things are either Secret or Top Secret. For you, this means a life of luxury and being pampered – flying first class everywhere,

dining with world leaders, access to absolutely everything you could ever wish for. You would never need to close your own curtains yourself again, nor look behind you when you sit down, as there would always be someone with a chair ready! Don't worry about cash - that stuff is for the masses. Not for you and me.

The trade-off for this is that you cannot stay here. Certain people would try to use you to get to me, and, unguarded, your life would be miserable or even dangerous. You would therefore need to come under my protection (that is to say, the protection of Special Branch). There would be greater security around you than most Royals. You cannot be public - it is not good for the public to know about what really happens - therefore you would need to be as invisible as I am.

So it would be goodbye to your social network, goodbye work, and goodbye cats, 'Guinea Pigs' and potted plants. Not that you would have time for any of that crap anyway.

I appreciate your need to discuss circumstances with your peers, but certain things ought not to be discussed (not that anyone would believe you anyway).

Chairman of the Bilderberg Steering committee? I control so much of your friends' lives they wouldn't believe you.

By the way - what is your address?

No. I could never see you fitting in with the life I lead, even I don't fit in with the life I lead, it just happened when my ex left me with three children under five, no car and no money! You'd trust me to dine with world leaders? How would you then introduce me? That would be interesting.

(****'s bird, ****'s bitch, ****'s subbie?) If I go running though, will I have to have some fat bloke in a suit puffing behind me?

No I wouldn't miss this life. The way I see it my daughter and my middle son can stay in this house and look after the cats, (Would they be safe?) and in turn, allow me to keep all my crap in the loft, provided I can pay off the mortgage and support them financially until they both finish uni, then they can support themselves. My youngest is another matter, I can't leave him, because of his age.

11/07/10

You can't seriously consider KEEPING your house, can you? There are far better investments to pass on to children – a whole street of houses for example, or a Retail Park, a business, or an Industrial Estate (business investments are far better, as you can increase the rent year after year, and businesses are not protected by the Rent Act of 1977.

I digress. You say that your house is not exactly in show house condition – as if your children would wish to inherit a crumbling pile of bricks. Far better that they inherit a nicer, better one. Each.

Your things, your memories can come out of the loft and into air-conditioned and dehumidified storage, should you wish to be dragged backwards by chattels of your former life. Don't keep everything – just a few bits and pieces. When are you going to look at it all? There's far more to see in the future than in the past.

Special Branch are not fat guys in suits. They are usually

between six feet and seven feet tall, with tattoos on their muscles and shaved heads. They perform Martial Arts like you see in the movies and are in far, far better condition than you or I. Many have seen active service and have been decorated for it. These are hard, hard men, but Madam still bosses them around! They humour her, whilst still keeping a watchful eye just in case. You could not be safer.

BY THE WAY - London is safe again once more. I have received the 'All Clear' from my sources.

Oh, and 'here' means in this country, though I'm thinking of retaining somewhere in the city. They do some passable apartments near Lower Bridge, which ought to do for a UK base. I think I (we) may spend more time abroad though – we would pay far less tax, have suntans all year round, yet still exude influence throughout the world.

What on earth are you going on about now? Investments? Retail Parks? Industrial Estates? I wasn't talking about inheritance; I was talking about where my daughter and son would be living if my youngest and I lived with you. My house is not a 'crumbling pile of bricks', it just needs redecorating. It's a nice little house and my youngest was born there. They both need to finish their education, so it is an ideal place for them to live, plus the cats would have to be kept. I suppose if it was deemed impossible by you, then my dad may be able to have the cats as well as the piggies, or perhaps one of my aunts could be persuaded. Anyway I don't have any money to go buying industrial estates, or a house each???

Mmmmmm those Special Branch guys sound yummy!

Oh I don't know – where do you think I might find the money to invest in a nest-egg for your kids? Bless my soul…

But that would cost an awful lot of money…

Really? I find it difficult sometimes to differentiate between your so-called wind-ups, and genuine stupidity

If I lived with you then I'd need you to pay for certain things, if I lost my entitlement to certain benefits, then you could end up paying university fees too, but I wouldn't have expected you to pay for anything else.

I can't comprehend having that much money. When my ex first left I had to go to the main benefit office in Southampton and queue along with drug addicts and alcoholics to get income support. I had to pay so much of the mortgage myself to start with, leaving me for several months with only £5 a week to spare, which was supposed to cover clothes, shoes and any extras.

You have no concept of my net worth, do you? Can you grasp the concept, "You will never have to worry about money again, at all, ever"? Since when do Masters split bills with their Servant Girls? You will depend upon me for everything. And I don't mean just money.

Ok I've sort of got that now, I'll be just like a slave girl in John Normans 'Chronicles of Gor,' except a hell of a lot older and definitely not a virgin.

It still won't happen unless we meet and like each other in our physical forms though, that's what scares me the most, I hate those kinds of meetings!

27/07/10

So...

When will I look into your eyes?

When will I feel your power?

When will I get to touch your body and please you Master?
On my knees or in any manner?

When will I feel your hand? Its sting or its caress?

When will we mix bodily fluids?

When will you prove your prowess?

If I've been a good girl, Master, when can I masturbate?

When will you lend a hand or tongue?

Or when will you make me wait?

Under your watchful eye, of course, when will
you stand by me?

When will you too, be in this picture?

When Sir when?

And, by the way... Can I come please Sir?

31/07/10

I have been looking for property – I'd like somewhere with a library, where you pull a book down and it opens a hidden doorway to a secret chamber. Houses such as this can't all be fictional, can they?

I'm sure one could be built in with all this modern technology; it would only need a sensor to be uncovered as the book was moved, to cause a door to open. The only difficult decision would be what book to choose for the door opening... 'Great Expectations' perhaps? Or maybe 'Dungeons and Dragons?' There again '101 Ways To Use Whipped Cream?' could be more appropriate. (ok, I made that one up)

29/07/10

You didn't reply to the 'So...' poem.

Was my teasing too much for Sir after he's been shut up on a submarine for so long?

I didn't, did I?

Well what's that supposed to mean?You put a question mark at the end, so does it mean I'm waiting for the answer still?

31/07/10

Well I feel a lot happier today. It's the first weekend in ages that I've not had to work, although the cat did get me up at 6am, so I made a cup of tea and dozed for a bit. I was thinking. When you had your piercings, did you have anything to freeze them before they did them? I watched a penis piercing on YouTube and the guy just screamed his head off. It was live on a radio show! I can't really imagine anything worse than having a needle put from front to back through your penis! No I really don't want to think about it at all!

Yes, I had something to freeze it before my piercings. I couldn't have done it without!

31/07/10

Groan I really shouldn't drink two bottles of Stella and eat chocolate, when I'm already in the state I am (wet/ovulating/sex starved etc.) with you talking of houses with secret rooms... What can I do? Go for a run and find a suitable tree in the woods? Or just nip up in the bathroom? Why is my house so small? Where are you? Still on the submarine? Still in Scotland? Arhhhhhhhhh! I need you now Master, but knowing you, you'd make me wait even longer and prolong my agony even if you were here, but it has to be better than this.

Did you get me some decent whisky? I might just have to finish my supplies tonight...

01/08/2010

I have a new photo for you. It's my tongue with my new multi-coloured bar in. I took it out myself this morning and turned it round, just to see if I could and I can, so it's ok. It does feel a lot better now. My tongue is still discoloured from the special mouthwash, but hopefully now I'm all back to normal, this will disappear. My teeth too have gone black between... I look like I'm a heavy smoker and remind myself of that guy I once met that I told you about a long time ago and said he looked like he had been sucking coal!

Right, I had better finish feeding the pigs, and getting on

with all those things I have to do. Tell me what you're up to at the moment, please.

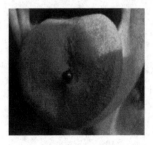

I'm at home at the moment – Madam is watching Madagascar on my iPad, and the two boys aren't up yet. I'm off to Moscow tomorrow to sort out what I expect to happen with BP's explorations in Russia. The tongue looks lovely by the way – I think I could do with it right now...

Oh I almost forgot! It's the first of August!!! Please pinch me Master... I like my nipples pinched when I orgasm... Please, please, please Master...

Would a hard slap across your bottom and a bloody good seeing-to work?

Ooooooh... I don't know... I'll think about it.

03/08/10

I'm off to work again today, then hopefully lunch and a day off with my dad tomorrow. It's my brother's birthday soon, so we might drop in on him too.

Oh and by the way the answer is YES. A hard slap across my bottom and a bloody good seeing-to would work.

Thank you so much for the spanking pictures! I liked the first 'hair-pulling' one as that's kinda what I'd do, though the ones with severe bruising didn't do anything for me. I like spanking but I don't get my kicks beating up women. You have a keen eye for sensual as well as sexy pictures - my favourite one though is the recent one of you masturbating. I suppose when you've actually had a piercing for someone, there's nothing else to hold back, is there?

04/07/10

You're not just 'Someone.'

I do prefer sensual, artistic and sexy pictures to the really crude porno type pictures and I was going to say or the more violent dom/sub acts like putting girls head first down muddy holes, but I do like to watch that sort of thing, which is a more sadistic side to me. I once had a collection of full length movies of a male Dom who tortured and brought male submissives to orgasm, then he would do something, like squeeze their testicles really hard, to make them scream, even though they had been told not to, while he brought himself off! He did all sorts, beating, electrical torture, plus inserting things into his sub's penis. He was a bit creepy, but I'm ashamed to say it worked for me too, watching it, that is!

I did once send the Dom I met twice, but chatted to for a few years, like you, a small video of me 'playing with myself'. He liked it, but I didn't like it myself at all. I don't photograph well. (It took ages to get the shot I sent you, which I took on my phone) That is incidentally why I gave up with MSN Messenger, because whenever I went on he was there and the conversation was always of a crude sexual nature, which was plain boring.

I think Internet dating did lower my standards considerably, but in the search for love I thought by not being too fussy I might meet the right man, but it doesn't work that way, because unless the match is complete, then it's not a match, so if I let something slide and the other person is letting something slide about me, then we would never really match, if you see what I mean? And it's not just looks, which whatever anyone says is the most important thing, it's the connecting of two minds, the conversation, humour etc, the ability to 'read' the other person, which until I see your face when you speak I won't really know completely what you mean, or if you really mean what you mean and if you're angry meaning what you mean or having me on meaning what you mean... do you get what I mean?

I like it that you don't get your kicks from beating up women. I like playing and I laugh a lot, especially when I'm happy, which I'm not at the moment, because of all these stupid people in offices that don't answer phones, but want all my financial information for benefits.

Are you still in Moscow? Get some vodka too please, I'm going to need it!

Oh and the holding back thing. Pictures are easy. The actual act, face to face... That will be harder and definitely a challenge; the whole meeting thing scares me to death, you already know everything about me, you are my Master, I just hope the connection I feel in my imagination is the same in reality.

Be under no illusions. I'm not a monster, in fact I'm not really any different from how you perceive me. As my servant girl/sub/cum dustbin, I shall enjoy exploring your limitations – before surpassing them. You will do anything and everything I tell you to – however, in the worst case scenario (meaning, if for some inexplicable reason we don't feel mutually compatible) you will just have to console yourself with being suddenly fabulously wealthy. That's a pretty good 'worst case scenario'.

I would like you to permanently delete the video you made for that other, lesser man. You are my property now. You are permitted however to surprise me with new pictures, which you will take for me and show only to me. Yes I'm still in bloody Russia – I could do with a few pleasant distractions to cheer me up.

I look forward to having my limitations explored and surpassed, it's something I've always wanted in a relationship, but never acquired. So in the worst case scenario, you'd still keep me?

The video I deleted years ago… I sent you one too on CD, it was only my face, as I had an orgasm and it is terribly embarrassing just thinking about what I did to regain your attention when you first disappeared, but I put my address on the back in case I had sent it to the wrong address and it came back to me. That's the only reason I went out with the Dom from Spain again, after not seeing him for two years, because you disappeared, but I decided I definitely didn't like him enough to see him again… so it seems I'm bound to you. Actually I'm not back at work until Tuesday. If you send me a plane ticket I could come to Russia and amuse you in person. I have Walnut Whips and Chocolate Brazils from the pound shop!

Sweeties from the pound shop? To think I've been slumming it in five star luxury... In the worst-case scenario – if you decided you didn't like me – then you and your family would be looked after. You could call it a golden handshake; you could call it insurance to stop you from running to the newspapers.

Walnut Whip sir?

I don't mind if I do – in fact, I'll have all three.

You can't, I've already eaten two!

I can see three mouth-watering ones in the picture... By the way – you do not have permission to cut your hair short. I like it the way it is.

Yes, but I bet in five star luxury they don't have Walnut Whips. Possibly they will have chocolate Brazils, along with some weird posh shit that looks good, is supposedly eaten by posh people all the time, but tastes foul and is nothing like Galaxy or Cadbury's chocolate and more like chocolate-covered caviar or something...

Is this why you don't date? Because you would have to pay women off to keep quiet afterwards? I wouldn't run to the newspapers. If I was 'with' you and something happened, then I'd run away and hide somewhere you couldn't find me; I wouldn't want your money. I would be 'with' you, because I loved you and, as I am completely loyal once that was established, I would never leave you unless something really upset me.

But we are getting ahead of ourselves. When we meet we will know within three seconds if we fancy each other or not, then within a couple of hours, a chat and drink in a pub perhaps, we would know if we would want to see each other again. Simple, isn't it?

I want you. By having you I get everything else that goes with you, as you get everything else that comes with me and that's fine. I think I would be getting the best deal... a man who will never bore me, three more children I don't have to give birth to, more money than I can ever comprehend and some tasty Special Branch men to ogle at!But wait... is that how it will work? Or am I to be kept separate from your family? Will I be like a mistress kept secretly in another house? Or just to begin with, until you are certain I'll be ok to mix in? What is your view on all this? How does it work for you?

05/08/10

Would Sir prefer a Chocolate Brazil? (*sent a photo of a strategically placed chocolate brazil nut*). I don't like this picture at all and as my youngest has now got the PC, I can't send it to myself and check it first, but hopefully it will amuse Sir and you did request that I should amuse you, but I know when I see it in full-size I shall cringe...And I haven't even been drinking!Now to lick the melted chocolate off... Hang on! Isn't that your job?

You silly girl – I shall now have to clear up all that melted chocolate! And I don't have a tissue, so I'll have to use my tongue. I'll do it carefully – so be warned, it might take me ages.

Oh dear, don't take too long Sir, I have work to do! Oops! I forgot my only job now is to please Sir, old habits die hard. Let me lie back on the bed ready for Sir's administrations and while Sir is there, when I set up the photo I accidently lost another nut somewhere else, perhaps Sir would be so kind as to find it and remove it for me?

You can of course assume that, in the course of my 'clean-up' efforts, I shall of course ensure that no further nuts remain, in any and every orifice. Perhaps I might like to watch a nurse check you – all latex gloves, speculum insertion, examination table, restraints, that sort of thing. You of course don't get a say in the matter – though if you're good, I might let you get your own back on her. I'm too good to you, aren't I?

Oh please Sir, not the nurse! Not that awful table! It frightens me so! And I have no lesbian or Dominant tendencies at all, it would be impossible for me to get my own back, I just couldn't! I'm sure Sir has managed to remove everything... but I do have one walnut whip left if Sir would like to use that somewhere too... Oh and Sir's tongue has done something... I feel really strange and hot, please don't stop Sir...

Sent a nurse and patient in stirrups photo.

I didn't really like it much – a well-taken picture can arouse me, but this one didn't.

05/08/10

No, it wasn't the picture or the model that aroused me either. It was the thought of trusting you enough to be completely at your mercy and unable to even make a sound to protest, while you did whatever it was you wanted to do to me...

Well I accomplished quite a lot today and went for a short run at last. I became distracted on the Internet at intervals during the day, can't think why... Oh and I had an episode with a chocolate Brazil nut after my run, so yes I did go back to bed for a nap. I can't think of anything else to say. Perhaps I'm just too tired. I'm off to pick up my son from training, and then I will go to bed and read or watch a movie.

Come home soon.

I said there would be opportunity for revenge – not that it would be compulsory. So you have no lesbian tendencies?

Yet. That's what turns me on too. Your complete surrender to me - not that you would ever be in any danger (not much, anyway...) Will do. Though not for long. (PS - your Brazil nut had me smiling all day - the Russians must have wondered what the hell was going on!)

06/08/10

Yet is NEVER!

The thought of doing anything sexual with another woman fills me with revulsion and definitely doesn't turn me on at all. I suppose if I was tied up and she was very good, I would have no choice, but to have an orgasm, but I wouldn't like it. Watching women on women, or men on men, does nothing unless I imagine myself in the same position with you doing it to me. I like watching people having orgasms too, especially when they are helpless. All that porno rubbish, giggling girls with football breasts, manicured nails and stiletto heels licking and rubbing each other does nothing at all!

06/08/10

Sigh At this rate we will never meet. You must have a permanently packed suitcase! I'm going to be old and useless soon and it will be too late for me and then for you. Couldn't you just fit me in somewhere, a suitcase perhaps? Wouldn't it be better if I'd sent you the Brazil nut picture from our hotel room? Then your smile would be in anticipation of what was waiting for you after your meetings...

As I believe I made clear, you will have no say in the matter. I believe you'd enjoy it - a soft, feminine tongue on your clitoris would be nice for you - expert because its owner has a clitoris of her own. And besides, it's nice when gentlemen associate and watch their slaves playing together nicely. Think of it like a 'bring a bottle' party.

I shall do as you command Sir, but I won't enjoy it and I shall sulk for days!

SHIT! You have to come and get me soon, before all is lost... I'm sitting crying at an episode of Eastenders!

My schedule depends upon the soap operas? Hmmm. I'm annoyed enough with you already, for suggesting that I stay in a hotel room! I always have a SUITE, dearie - sometimes I insist on having the entire floor to myself.

No silly... I meant if you don't hurry up and save me it'll be too late and I'll turn into something unimaginable! *Giggles* Sorry Sir... what's a 'suite?" Is that like in the movie 'Pretty Woman?' Where he has a bedroom, bathroom and a lounge? And what would you need with a whole floor? I know what though, we could have a really good game of hide and seek... I could run round naked, then every time you found me you could spank me for being naughty and hiding from you, then give me a good seeing to! I wonder who would get tired first?

And are you sure you're not over sixty? Dearie is a word used by old ladies and men! Want to spank me now Sir?

So you don't know what a suite is. Think of it as an extremely luxurious apartment. You usually get a few bedrooms, a lounge, and a few en-suites – sometimes you get a kitchen, a balcony, a cinema and even your own pool. And they aren't cheap. Renting an entire floor is more of a security thing – the other rooms are occupied by security staff, and we have to work on the presumption that every other guest is a potential assassin. Do you still want to play hide and seek?

As for being naked, I reserve the right to withhold clothing from you, even when we have company. And you will comply, silently and without question. You embarrass me in front of my guests, and I will humiliate and demean you in front of them. Which is something else you'll end up enjoying...

I guess hide and seek is out then. You can't possibly leave me naked when you have friends round, I don't have the body for that sort of thing! And how am I supposed to enjoy it... walking around naked? Go hire some of those women off 'Public Disgrace', I'm sure they'll enjoy it! You wouldn't really do that would you? It goes on the list titled 'The most scariest things Sir has suggested, that I'm pretty sure he doesn't mean and are just his imagination getting carried away.'

On the list so far are: Being put head first down a muddy hole. Being made to walk round naked in front of strangers. Being made to make out with another woman. And swallowing.

Actually I was talking to my friend on Facebook and he said that swallowing and looking like you enjoy it, is the hottest thing a woman can do. No wonder I've had no luck!

07/08/10

Your little list of my so-called scary suggestions merely represents inhibitions that ought to be overcome, with the charity of your patient Master. Only then will you experience the freedom that comes with such unfettered uninhibitedness. Except for dunking you in mud – that was funny, but I don't think I'd want to try it myself, it's a lot of work and it would be awkward explaining what happened, should I need to take you to A&E if it goes wrong. Incidentally, I don't know what was funnier – her suddenly realising what was going to happen, it actually happening despite her protestations, or the way she was pressure-washed afterwards. It beats a night in front of the telly.

The other three suggestions? Who knows?

It still makes me feel sick! I'd pass out before you got me in the hole, and all this brings me back to the letter you didn't answer, but you don't answer any of those questions, the ones about will we meet and if I'm to be just a sub or something more, although you did say once I'd meet heads of state and I couldn't be just a sub then could I? So, I'm still left in limbo, waiting, wanting...

Indeed you are. I think you should mix up some thick icing sugar, splatter it over your face and breasts, and then photograph it so I can see what it looks like!

Please choose from the following options:

1. Oh Sir I couldn't possibly! It will feel like I'd been unfaithful to you and had sex with another man!

2. Yeah right, I'll see what I can do when the bathroom is free and I can get past my suspicious children with a cup of icing sugar in my hand and a camera.

3. Sod off and stop messing me around... If you want to see me with cum all over my face then come over here and do it properly!

4. Yes Sir, right away Sir.

No. 3 won't be too long in coming, if you behave yourself.

Here you are Sir. *(Sent requested photo)*

Thank you. You look just the way I'd pictured - and I'd like to decorate you like that for real. Another time, I would like you to do as I ask, immediately and without question. I hope you understand this simple instruction.

Is this what you had in mind?*(Sent pic of girl with tongue piercing licking her mistress' nipple)*

Pretty much - you'll grow to love it. And if you don't, at least you'll know you're making me happy - which is, after all, the reason you exist.

I've had two shots of Vodka in honour of your safe return from Russia... it was quite strong... .I'm going to bed now...

Wuss.

Oh I can drink more than that, it was just bed time that's all and there isn't any point losing control if there is no one around to take advantage of me.

I will take advantage of you, whatever your state. Even if you're tired, asleep, whatever, get used to doing what I want, when I want it done, without question. By the way – do you smoke? If you do, then you are to kick the habit immediately.

Good Evening. No I don't smoke. I did once in my twenties, but even then I only averaged 3 cigarettes a week.

Anyway you should remember that I don't smoke. We had that Vesta match conversation and I said that as I didn't know Vesta matches were pink, it showed that I didn't smoke.

Your lack of knowledge regarding Vesta matches indicates nothing other than a lack of knowledge of Vesta matches. Did you forget I'm a lawyer?

Yes, but I still told you at that time that I didn't smoke. Where are you? You're an hour behind. I'm in bed trying to get to sleep with the windows open, because it's hot, but all I can hear is the woman over the road coughing... she smokes!

09/08/10

Which number does she live at? I can have her killed if you'd like. Neighbours are filthy, disgusting creatures. Never associate with them. The best way to survive one's neighbours? Own every house in your street, and then be cautious in your tenant selection. Or live on your own island. We can be King and Queen then – and never pay any UK tax!

I'm off to Islamabad today – to try and do something with all this flooding. A little belated, but I'm still there sooner than the Pakistani President!

The island sounds perfect, but I'd still want a certain amount of luxury and facilities, or at least a quick way to the doctor's in an emergency. Islamabad! Well that's not safe! You had better get a whole floor there!

Doctors are ALWAYS readily available to the likes of us. Look on Google for 'Little Eden Cay' and see if that's luxurious enough for you. I've been to see it – but when would I get a chance to go there?

When I visited Little Eden Cay, it was with a view to buying it, with an asking price of $2,000,000. That might sound like a lot of money, but one bed roomed flats in London cost that, and this is an Island.

Take a look at Private Islands Online.com then, but be warned. Their photographs are awful. If I ran a website, designed to SELL real estate at up to fifty million a pop, the pictures would be the best you've ever seen! The site is a let-down for me, but it's worth a look. And yes, Little Eden Cay is as wonderful as it looks in the pictures.

You can't keep killing off my neighbours. I'd only get new even worse ones, knowing my luck. The only way to really get rid of them would be for me to move to a croft in Scotland in the middle of nowhere, or a tent on the top of Everest, or a shack on a desert island, or perhaps I might go and live in a dungeon or something...

Actually it's a good job you're not coming for me yet, I

have spots caused by hormones and mine are totally up the creek at the moment, maybe I'm about to hit the menopause?

Ok, so suitably depressed now, with you in the middle of a terrorist country and me about to hit the menopause rendering me useless, I'm about to go shopping for food and take my youngest son to buy another game, so he can spend another week of the holidays on the Xbox! Then if I feel up to it, I'll do the third coat of paint on the big wall, so I can put the furniture back and then my son can carry on. I have work on Tuesday and Wednesday this week, so I've been off a whole week, which is nice, even though I still feel tired. My contract finishes end of October and although they want me back, I think I'll start looking for something else, it's too long on my feet all day.

I have to go, the earlier I get the shopping done the better.

Take care

09/08/10

This is a stat that came through my BDSM group today, which reminded me of when I told you that I lose my sparkle when I don't hear from you for ages. I like her thong, although it wouldn't be very comfortable under her clothes, but then as a slave girl she wouldn't need anything else to adorn her.

I wear an armlet all the time. It was given to me by my great aunt's friend when I was about 14. She was impressed with how polite I was and gave the bracelet to me later. It looks like a gold band with a square type pattern going round it. Once when I was at a campsite a man noticed it and said it looked like a slave armlet, like the Greeks wore, then a few weeks ago a woman came into work and practically pounced on it! She commented on it, then turned it round and round and came to the conclusion that it was a 1930s armlet, which would fit if my aunts friend wore it as a young woman, and told me to take care of it, so it must be special, like me.

It's a nice thong – I could have one made with jewels and platinum thread for you to wear when I show you off on special occasions. You wouldn't wear it at home of course – you wouldn't be deserving of clothes – well, maybe a collar – unless the kids or my domestic staff are about

I love the story of your gold band! It's fitting that it's reminiscent of a Greek slave girl.

Ooh, I could have a matching collar and a matching screw on stud for my tongue bar!
Actually someone shared a web site once that sold special thongs, Lola Luna, but I don't think they have jewelled ones.

How's Islamabad? Hot? (Even hotter if I was with you) How come you had to go there? What do you have to do? But I suppose that's secret too.Well I cleaned the piggies too my son decided to do the last coat of paint on the wall, so I made Chocolate Refrigerator Cake instead. I did take a picture of myself with a cherry in my mouth and I was going to add the slogan 'Do you want to pop my cherry sir?' but it didn't come out very well, so I deleted it… .And blow me down as

I'm typing this you've popped up!!! (I have a special email notifier that comes up when you send me a message)

I've got a thing that pops up when I hear from you too! And I need it - Pakistan is even more depressing than Russia...

I just had a page of spanking pictures through my group, but none of them sparked any feelings with me, very boring. There was one girl tied to a 'block' with a guy in a stupid onion seller costume, but it had a web address, so I checked it out: www.herfirstpunishment.com. It says it's a website showing how girls are severely spanked and caned in Russia, which is a coincidence as you've just left there, but it is rather nasty, I don't see the point in caning so hard that blood is drawn!

I'm bored now. It's 6.30 pm and I'm restless.

Gosh, I'm on a roll sending you emails... maybe I'll reach 12 again, just like the old days... Heh, heh!

I agree! Thank you for providing me with a little respite from the chaos that surrounds me. I have just decided - because I can - that I would like you to send me a picture of a flower, clenched between your bare bum cheeks. That should be fun - a pity I'm not there to watch you attempting that one! And because I'm nice to you, I'll let YOU choose the flower. If I wasn't, I'd say a nice thorny rose - I hope you appreciate my generosity.

Pakistan Internet must be crap. I keep getting double emails from you.

I don't have any roses. I do have some spikey blue things,

but lavender might be quite nice, although, unfortunately I have a full house and my son is going in the shower after playing football, so it might be quite difficult and it's dark... How do I explain why I suddenly want to pick flowers and put them in my bedroom? But who am I to question you, Sir? I'm just an obedient slave girl, so into the garden I go...

You bet it's bad – I'm in the UN Building, yet I'm on fucking DIAL-UP. Give me strength... You're getting the correct attitude now!

Well trust you to pick something like this for me to do! I only had Echinops or Buddleia in flower and the Buddleia wouldn't stay in, so it had to be the sodding spiky ones! Not too bad for a quick one in the bathroom!

What do you think Sir?

THANK YOU! Mmmm, I could do things with that bottom...

I've had an extremely busy day today, fraught with the seriousness of the issues faced by Pakistan. Yet I have been unable to concentrate, due to something being on my mind! What is it, you ask? Your bum cleavage! That's an interesting colour – it had better be a trick of the light!

Oh gross!
I have the worst lighting ever in my house and you should try holding a mobile phone to your bottom, whilst trying to

press the right button to get a good picture and hold a flower in your butt cheeks!!!

I woke around 4am this morning. The cat turned up around 5am, so I gave up trying to get back to sleep, fed the cat and made a cup of tea. The trouble is, as soon as I am conscious, I begin thinking about you and making up stories. I don't know about you not being able to concentrate thinking of me, but I am losing sleep as well as not being able to concentrate all day!

I wasn't going to email you today. I was going to try and stop for the two days I'm working and see if you send me new messages instead of just answering the ones I've sent, but it's impossible. I didn't get in until 6.30 pm, but instead of eating tea I'm sitting mailing you! I did have to wash the dishes and feed the animals first though, but that was hard with the computer only inches away from me!

Bollocks!!! Now you've given me a buttock cleavage inferiority complex!

You have bollocks too???

Oh go away! You realise now I'll probably have to go and get my arsehole bleached or something!

It's either that or learn to wipe properly! You have been using it for nearly seventy years, after all...

I'm not even going to reply to that comment!! I was looking at the islands. You're right the website is very poor and the descriptions lack detail. My favourite at the moment is Motu Moie in French Polynesia, but there is no price, so it's probably too expensive even for you!

You were going to stay away from me for two days? Knowing the good you're doing me stuck over here? I'm trying to patch things up on behalf of the Government here. They have a catastrophic, epic disaster - and I don't just mean the floods. Al Qaida were the first on the scene with aid, and they are winning the hearts and minds of the population. Which means that revolution won't be long in coming. Then we're fighting Afghanistan AND Pakistan together! Oh boy...

That's pretty bad then! There can't be an easy solution to that one!

There isn't - and I still have Russia's drought issues to deal with afterwards.

Anyway why aren't you in bed sleeping? If it's 11.30pm here it must be 3.30am where you are? Am I keeping you awake too? Sort Pakistan out and come home.

11/08/10

Knock knock' – who's that at my door? Oh my goodness, it's Al Qaida come to win my heart and my mind before you!!! (Angry pointing smiley)

You may jest, but that's why you're under surveillance.

Oh now you are talking rubbish, or should I say 'Now you are talking out of your arse!' Why on earth would you want to put me under surveillance? For a start I walk about in a day dream and wouldn't know a terrorist he if came up and bit me, and anyway it's not as if I've emailed you because of who you are, I emailed you because you were a single parent with three children, which you looked after yourself, like me, who was the only decent looking 'bloke' on the whole website and sounded like he had enough money to support three more children, which I deducted by your ability to spell and construct a proper sentence, if the inevitable happened once we had met.

I hope you're not having pictures taken? I look awful most of the time!

I know all that, stupid. I've just told MI6 to keep a discrete, Level 1 surveillance on you, which was why I asked you to confirm your name and address. You wouldn't notice it – it's just one or two guys, checking up on you a few times each day.

But why? No one knows I know you, only normal people I've told, who don't believe you're real and think you're just some reporter getting his kicks on the internet! And anyway I don't believe you!

I'm going to hang out my bedroom window for a whole day and night to see if anybody suspicious comes by my house!

If you see anyone, let me know and I'll have them sacked.

Is that your answer to everything? Sack them or kill them? Have you escaped Pakistan yet?

Put my son in boarding school for his last year of school. Buy an island. Take a year off work, or six months, whatever. Then we can live like Robinson Crusoe, maybe not quite as extreme, and I can run around naked all day and night, then I'll be brown all over with no shadows on my BEAUTIFUL, CLEAN body!

It all sounds good to me! Although imagine the chaos if I were to take a year away from the office... Shall we go ahead and do it? Choose me an island...

I did Motu Moie in French Polynesia, although I haven't had chance to go through the rest of the islands yet and I doubt if I'll have time for a while. I'm doing my cleaning job this morning, so leaving soon, oh and if you want to carry on keeping me under surveillance I'm off to my friends tomorrow at:

I'm sure she'll be pleased that you've passed her address on to someone she doesn't know... Make sure your bottom's a bit cleaner before you sit on anything! If you stain her furniture, you may not receive an invitation back.

I've already thought about that, but if you are who you say you are and you are having me checked up on, then you already know her address!

I believe everything you tell me, you know that too. I've already gone through every possible scenario in my head of who you could be and what could happen, but by now you would have made some sort of move on me, if you followed the pattern of freaky, stalker internet man!

And leave my bottom alone!

ME the freaky Internet stalker? Aren't you the one who travelled up to Norwich... Your friends will tell you that I do not exist. Good! That's my identity protected then. It costs a lot of money, not existing. I hope you'll enjoy your opportunity to try it.

I have no intention of leaving your bottom alone! I intend to get far better acquainted with it – you belong to me, heart mind body and soul, and I can and will do whatever I like with any of those. I think I might like to admire it first – its softness, its contours. Then I'm going to watch it jiggle as I pat it, slap it, and then spank it. Then I expect I'll admire its new colour – and heat – once I've got it how I'd like it. Then I think I'd like to explore its hole. This will be none of your business, so you'll no doubt be tied and blindfolded, with your bare bottom high in the air. I intend to massage your anus until I can easily slip in my lubricated finger. And then, who knows? Maybe I'll try out a few butt plugs to see how you like them. Maybe I'll give you an enema (I've been passed a few recipes in my time, and you can be my guinea pig!) I think I'd like to taste it, and then I'd like to fuck it hard and shoot inside you, and watch my gift to you leak from your stretched hole.

None of this will be witnessed by you. You're just my slave, and I'm going to use you as my relaxation toy – for my benefit, not yours. I own you, not the other way around.

GOOD LUCK with sitting down afterwards...

I don't think my bottom is one of my best features, but I do use body scrub on it to keep it soft and smooth for you Sir. I'm not sure about having an enema, but I suppose it will clean it out first. I don't know... stretching it? I don't know about that either... It's quite tight. It's what might come out that worries me. It's bad enough with the state of my other bits after child birth, without you examining my bottom so closely too...*Sigh* Once you start it looks like I won't be able to sit down properly ever again!

That's the last time I send you any photos! Isn't it about time you sent me one?

On the contrary! You will send me a clear picture of your bottom, tonight, to demonstrate that it was just a shadow after all. And because I'm stuck here, surrounded by fucking idiots who can't run their own country and won't even help their own people unless they can take a cut - you may entertain me. I would like you to send me other, sexy pictures of yourself. What they are of and how you take them, I shall leave up to you.

I have to get dressed for work now and make a cup of tea. It's 7.45am and I leave at 9am. You've wasted all my free computer time with your stupid message that I'm definitely not replying to! I'd better make sure I wash properly before work... I think an hour should do it! I hope your dial up in Pakistan can cope with me! I might just carry on sending you messages all day and block up the whole Internet, then you will be unable to work and you'll have to come home and 'get' me!Of course if you do come home and 'get' me, then I'm not taking my clothes off now! You'll have to do everything with the light off! Try and strip me and I'll bite you!

Then I will have to impose my will on you! A gag (or even a hood!) together with handcuffs. Maybe I ought to suspend you by your ankles as I cut your clothing off you with scissors - it's not as if you'll be needing them. Remember that clothing is a privilege - one which you will need to earn...

Just some pictures for you Sir!

Arsehole mug picture.
Man with legs over his head showing his arsehole picture.
The arsehole on Mars picture.
Wooden cat arsehole picture.
Bart tattoo on a man's belly button looking like Bart's arsehole.

... all of which appear cleaner than yours. Oh, I'm sorry - it's a shadow, isn't it. A long, brown shadow.

It just occurred to me... This is why I love you.

And it's why I love you too.

Right I'm leaving now for work. It's a lovely sunny day. It would be sunnier on an island with you.

Not necessarily - some islands for sale are within the Arctic Circle. Not a place to get a tan - but you can OWN YOUR VERY OWN ISLAND for the price of a new car. And you never know, with all this global warming - your ancestors might thank you for it... even though global warming is a story we invented!

Dammit… damn you! I'm going to be horny all day now thinking of running around naked on an island playing hide and seek and when you catch me, the thought of our skin against skin, peppered with sand, as you hold me down and 'take' me in a lustful, animal fashion.

Animal fashion? At least you'll be able to scream! And trust me, you're going to, my little Working Class Slave Girl…

I'm not working class! I'm upper working class/lower middle class!!! And yes I probably will scream if a sandy, jingly-jangly, brown monster is chasing me up a beach!

There's an alternative name for upper-working-class/lower-middle-class. It's working-class-in-denial!

No it's not! I'm nowhere near the level of the working-class people round here, you know, the council house estate types.

We refer to those as "sub working class".

I'm sending this straight from my phone. We were really busy today and I'm shattered. I might get on the PC later. I couldn't get a good bottom pic, so this will have to do.

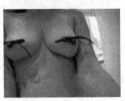

Very pretty!

I like that one. Truly beautiful. How tight did you tie the bows?

Not tight at all. My nipples are very supportive! One of them was very sore though and it hurt just to put the ribbon on, I expect I'll be entering the pre-menstrual, madwoman stage soon!

Just wondered if you like having them squeezed, tied, bitten... I hope that's fresh cream – I could lick that straight off...

Ha! No, it's hair remover cream!

So do you remove all your pubic hair? I think I'd like to see it with and without hair, so I can decide how I'd like you to keep it. I'm inclined towards complete smoothness as I'd like you to be completely naked for me, and it leads to so many interesting alleys, such as what I might like to do with some oil, or my tongue. However, I might like you to keep a little, like a Landing Strip, or a Hitler's Moustache. Oh, the possibilities!

Yes, I remove all my pubic hair. I hate it. I take it all off with cream once a week, I was going to take a few more photos, but as I said before, my lighting is terrible in the house and nothing came out right at all!

It doesn't matter what I do though, it's still a bit sandpapery. I can't use the cream underneath, so I shave that, which does make it smooth, but I can't shave the top otherwise I get an awful rash, but still with it shaved underneath and round my clit. I'm sure your tongue will enjoy itself!

I intend to make it my business to find out! Is your clitoris especially sensitive, or do you prefer penetration?

I've never had an orgasm from oral sex. My clitoris has to be stimulated in the right place, with the right amount of pressure and the right speed, which all varies as everything progresses. It's better if my nipples are stimulated first. I like them very gently rubbed to start with, and then perhaps squeezed, which can be quite hard, and rubbed or flicked. I don't like them bitten.

Penetration has never done it for me either, unless you can find the 'G' spot. It's better if you come in from behind and point towards where my clit is. If you come straight in and up, then you hit my cervix, which hurts... Of course all three together would do very nicely thank you Sir.

13/08/10

I fail to comprehend your "I don't know about... " comments when I've already made it clear that you don't get a say in the matter. What I do with your body and the level of discomfort that results is none of your business. Your body is mine to do with as I wish, so you had better look after it on my behalf whilst I'm away. Oh, and it is one of your better features – it's quite lovely...

Yes Sir. Thank you Sir.

I think it would amuse me greatly to see your CLEAN bare bottom again, this time with "Property of ***" written**

legibly on it with your own choice of lipstick. It must be readable, the right way up, and you have this weekend in which to do it. See? I wish I was home now - watching you trying to write on your own bottom...

14/08/10

This is where I am now – The Longmynd, and not raining... yet.

It has a stark beauty, doesn't it - I can see why you like it there. I hope you're having a lovely relaxing time! I'm glad one of us is, anyway. The country seems to be on the brink of civil war at the moment.

I like it, but to be perfect, I would need to be looking out to the sea in the distance, there is none here...and I would need you by my side. Here is my homework Sir. *(Sent a photo of 'Property of' and then his name written on my bottom)*

Well that's a bit of a poor attempt, really. It's only on one side, and the writing is barely legible - the opposite of what you were told to do. Had you shown me this much disrespect in person, you would have been punished. Instead, I shall have to insist that you do it again, better. Aren't I worth the effort, all of a sudden?

I did try and fulfil your request, but it is practically impossible to do in someone else's house. I didn't have any lipstick and anyway the letters would be too large to fit your name on my petite bottom, not to mention trying to hold my phone behind my back to take the picture!

It's already 10 pm and I'm about to go and shower. I didn't get home until 5.30 pm and I had to sort the house out. I'm too tired to do your name justice tonight, so you'll just have to add my punishment to the long list you already have, which I shall look forward to having and accept gracefully.

16/08/10

I look like the Witch of Wookey Hole this morning. I changed my shampoo and my hair has rebelled! My shoulder is killing me. I'm tired; my eyes are swollen, so I must be pre-menstrual.

And I don't know where you are... are you still in Pakistan? Is it safe if they are on the brink of civil war? Will you grow old with me?

I still can't write your name on my bottom. Will you come and do it? I can't turn my head. What does your bottom look like? Can I write my name on your bottom? Can I paint you? That's something we could do on a beach, on an island, in the middle of nowhere...paint each other. Should I finish my tea and get off to work? When will my main job be to please you? I have too many jobs at the moment to have a main job, although I suppose work is my main job, if it's paid employment, the children are my main job if it's unpaid and you're leisure and pleasure time...

I had better go before I start rabbiting on about a load of rubbish. That just would not do!

So you resemble a haystack, do you? That wasn't a picture of your hair you sent me previously, was it? "There's a party in my hair, would you like to cum?" or whatever it said in that "Hay" email... Yes I'm still here – and my patience is wearing thin now. China next! They are asking why I haven't been yet. I'll end up circumnavigating the globe again at this rate.

Oh dear, what's wrong with China? I think I should come and give you a good seeing too first, to put you in a better frame of mind, surely China could wait a bit longer?

Can you spare a few days? By the time you arrive however, you'll be the one requiring TLC! Should you survive flying into a potential warzone.

Next week I'm free from Wednesday 25th to Saturday 28th...Well sort of, I'd have to cancel a few things. A war zone wouldn't faze me, I've survived a few situations in the past and anyway I'd be completely oblivious! As long as you have a bar of chocolate waiting and a cold beer that's all the TLC I'll need! You'll be in China by then though, won't you?

17/08/10

I'm not really sure to be honest. I'm sorting things out here still, but it's all gone to cock. I'm in the middle of thrashing out a deal on behalf of the World Bank and International Monetary Fund (rich Jews in other words) exchanging cash for the privatisation of their utilities and assets. Only some stupid bloody Paki has gone and leaked it to the press! Bloody hell...

Is that going to help with the flood?... You've lost me completely...

That's never hard to do, is it? Pakistan shall get the financial assistance it needs, for the good of its people and to avoid civil war. In exchange, they will introduce social and economic reform, meaning they will slash their overheads (their social and defence spending), and they will privatise their utilities - relieving the burden on the State, as well as make the Bilderberg members that are waiting in the wings to buy them very rich indeed. Any clearer?

Yes, that's much clearer thank you. Will you be one of the buyers? I know it's not hard to lose me, but it's part of my charm and I'm sure you will make good use of my gullibility.Ha, ha, I tried to do you another bottom picture, but decided it was best if, as I was going to use lipstick this time, I just wrote '****'s Property.' It wasn't until I went through the pictures on my phone to send them to myself to check on my pc, I realised I had left out a letter.It's definitely fate; you will have to do it yourself!

There are a few simple things I've asked people to do HERE that I'm going to have to do myself... Send me something to cheer me up! Anything.

Sorry Master... Will I be punished severely now? ;-)(The second attempt with the missing letter)

Not by me. Your bottom, apparently, belongs to someone else.

Do they have stocks in Pakistan? (Sent a photo of a girl lying on her back with hands and feet in stocks) At least Sir would be able to fully examine my bottom.

Yes they do. They also have hanging, flogging, and stoning. But tying you up and then enjoying your body will do admirably.

...and sticking stiletto heels up my arse!

What's the problem with that? It'll stop you wriggling, you'll enjoy your new-found flexibility, plus you'll bask in the glow of knowing that your pain, discomfort and humiliation are making me very happy. You're not looking at the positives, are you?

Of course my only concern is to make you happy, it's what I was put on this earth for, but I don't own a single pair of stiletto heels and if I did I wouldn't be able to walk in them. I'm a barefoot, naked in the sand, flip-flop, dolly shoe girl.

Who said anything about being able to walk in them?

Well no, not if the heels are stuck up my arse while I'm tied up and suspended from the ceiling, I won't be able to walk... If you want me to strut around in patent leather afterwards with them on, then just keep well out of the way, I wouldn't want to damage anything!

Noted – I'll just keep you bound and naked then. I'll make a note of that – though we'll make a lady of you yet. Look on

the bright side though - at least your ass will be nice and relaxed for whoever I feel like lending it to!

I don't need stiletto heels to be a lady and I doubt if heels up my ass will in any way loosen it up, seeing as they are very thin. It is, of course, entirely up to you if you want to lend me out, (as I am totally yours to do with as you wish) and have me soiled by other lesser men, but wouldn't you rather have something precious, beautiful, sexy, luscious and lascivious, admired and desired by other men, but kept completely out of their reach?

That's my job, isn't it? To invent new ways in which for you to please me? And one of my pleasures is to enjoy your discomfort and embarrassment!

Actually I don't feel like anything today, well anything in the pictures I've sent this morning, although if I was restrained and you took over everything else I wouldn't have any need to worry, so then I probably would feel like doing other things. I need more than a cold beer and a bar of chocolate at the moment!

My shoulder's worse, and I didn't sleep properly again. I feel guilty because I haven't been able to take my son anywhere and I definitely won't be camping this year. I just seem to be working nearly every day, apart from the dates I gave you. Tomorrow is my only day off this week and I want to see my dad, and the youngest needs new uniform, god knows when I'll get that!

So I'm afraid today is just going to be moan, moan, moan and somehow I suspect that your day will mirror mine, as you are still stuck in Pakistan!

I have a cream tea for lunch today, it's a bit early, but two coaches are due. I'd rather be with you having cream, but not to eat if you're thinking of the same thing I am!

I'd love to eat that off you – without using my hands...

I nearly swallowed my ball!

Eh?

*(Sent photo with just his first name written on my belly)*Will this do Sir?

You can't bend my foot enough to get that heel to go up my arse, you'd have to take it off first... and there you go again adding another twist, making it harder for me, are you not satisfied that I'm going to retch, as it is, with no way of avoiding your huge cock going down the back of my throat and all the metal bits could get stuck in my tongue piercing!!! Incidentally that was the 'Ball' I nearly swallowed, it came unscrewed, I suppose next I'll be swallowing yours... I hope you've waxed!

A valiant effort indeed. Thank you!

Duck: (Sent photo of myself lying in the bath with a duck)

I'm having a nice duck in the bath... Well you made me all sticky with that jam and cream...

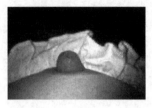

A pink frilly nipple for you...If only your tongue could reach it. If you do circumnavigate the globe and pass by England, drop in for a cup of tea.

I will. With a side-order of nipple.

How do you take your tea Sir? With milk? One hump or two? If Sir is very hungry, would Sir like a fish course with that? Or if Sir has a sweet tooth, perhaps a little honey?

It all sounds very appealing – and hopefully, it's all served with relish.

Certainly Sir...How about some TARTare sauce with the fish...

As long as it isn't served with a Blue Waffle! One of my boys showed me what one is, online – yuck!

20/08/10

I put it in Google search... Did you also see 'Special Fried Rice' and 'Giant Cheese Taco!' Revolting! Sir should definitely reconsider sharing me with his friends, I could end up with anything! Thank goodness I've just eaten my breakfast!

I did sleep better last night, although I didn't get off quite as quickly as I hoped at least my shoulder has improved, so that didn't wake me. Where are you now? What have you still to do? Is China still next?

Of course I'm still here. I don't know if China is next though – they wish to gain access to Bilderberg, but they are not going to get it. Do you like the stuff in the media about the corrupt Pakistani Government, by the way? How there's no way of knowing if your donation will go into someone's pocket? I leaked that!

I haven't seen it yet, although I did have the news on for a short while this morning.

Looks like it's my house next then!

Which hanger would you like Sir?

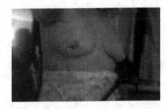

Well they are both exceptionally splendid. I can only assume that it's quite cold where you are! I could do things with those nipples...

19/08/10

Oh it's not cold at all Sir. My nipples are like a two-stroke engine... two strokes and they are away, whatever the weather.

Good! Can you lick your own nipples? Show me...

*(Sent movie of me trying to lick nipple)*I doubt if you will be able to play this. I sent it to myself first, because I can't see properly on my mobile, but I can't get the PC to check it and the old one upstairs doesn't have the right player.

A valiant, though fruitless effort. I didn't know you could do videos! You've given me all kinds of funny ideas now – how will I ever get to sleep?

Don't tell me my phone is better than yours! Ha ha. Of course I can do videos stupid, but I don't like myself in photos, let alone adding videos to the equation!I'm in bed watching 'Lesbian Vampire Killers' then it's off to sleep for me.

20/08/10

I'm in the middle of more negotiation – nobody seems to give a damn. They are worried that the Taliban and Al Qaida are going to help before they do and win hearts and minds. So rather than get their own aid out quicker, they are just going to lock up – or execute – anyone handing out aid without Government authority. So 20,000,000 are likely to end up with sod all. Is it just me?

I've told them to sort it out or we will just leave them to die. Although I don't want to let people die. And I don't want members to miss out on billions of pounds in profit. And I don't want Islamic Fundamentalists to take over the region! We've already got one Afghanistan, and we could do without a second one that has nuclear capability!

You're dealing with their mentality and culture.

I know all this – I'm aware of their mannerisms, their culture, and their customs. I'm just a bit fed up.

I've just watched the end of the film 'North by Northwest' while finally doing the ironing. Will you take me on one of those trains that have those bunk bed type sleeping compartments, and then we can sleep together at night on a long train journey?

Of course. I fancy the one that runs the length of Africa. Unless you have a better suggestion, like India?

It would certainly be an experience to remember in a beautiful country and I would be safe with you... How many injections would I need? Ouch!

I swear that Ethiopia is one of the most amazing countries I've ever been to. Axsum, Lalibelia, are historical sites deserving of World Heritage status, the highlands take your breath away, and the volcanoes in the Rift Valley will touch you forever. But like Afghanistan, it's a beautiful country, ripped apart by a civil war nobody can see an end to.
Part of the railway line I'm talking about goes really close to Victoria Falls. Check it out on Google Earth and see what you think!

I will when I get on the normal pc downstairs, which will be tomorrow morning before I go to work. This one has no programs, it was being cleared before re-loading a whole new operating system, but I still haven't finished taking all our old stuff off.

I have another bloody curry to look forward to. This fucking country...

I did wonder what you would be eating over there. I like curry. I like everything except milk puddings, like semolina and blancmange.

I like curry too, but not for breakfast, dinner, and tea day after day.

Oh you poor thing… Shall I send a food parcel?

There's little point I'm afraid - they'll only make another sodding curry out of it.

Curried fruit cake… .NICE!

I was offered curried fruit pastilles as a snack recently. So yes, curried fruit cake sounds completely feasible.

I went on Google Earth and found the railway line. It does look amazing. If you check certain boxes on the side of Google Earth you can get YouTube videos to come up. I watched a guy bungee jump off the falls… Not something I ever want to do!I didn't realise how big Africa is compared to Britain either, you could certainly get lost there.

You most certainly could - Sudan, for example, is the size of Europe. And you could, if you wanted to, pick up a few acres of desert for a few hundred pounds, though heaven only knows what you'd do with them. Africa is a great place to hide. It's a bit like South America where you can live like royalty (servants, restaurants every night, that kind of thing)

for £300 a month, including your rent. Some of us can do that anywhere though.

Africa is an amazing continent – if you manage to side-step all the civil wars and troubles. I'd sort them all out, but there's nothing in it for us – I'm busy enough sorting out the countries we DO have an interest in! Where in Africa would you like to visit?

I don't know Africa at all. It's not a country I've thought about, until my daughter went there, although I did have a great aunt who lived in South Africa once. I like rivers, mountains, sea and trees, but I don't like baking heat or freezing cold, so stood in the middle of a grass plain, with the sun beating down, looking for lions wouldn't be my sort of thing or climbing a snow-covered mountain in the middle of winter.

There's only one snowy mountain in Africa as far as I know. What about a safari in a hot air balloon? And a luxury hotel in the trees?

Yes, that would be perfect... very 'Wild at Heart.' Did you watch that series at all?

I've never flown in a balloon, but it is something I would love to try. On the road to work I see them occasionally. I have a friend who is an observer for balloon races, she gets to fly in the balloons to make sure the contestants don't cheat. Apparently a lot of them have satellite trackers now, so human observers are becoming extinct.

21/08/10

Something for Mr Fed Up, before I go to work. *(Sent 16 photos of a woman being caned)*

Nice – I like the one of her hair flying up as the stroke lands. Tonight, you will spank your own bottom and make it red – you will then take a picture of the results and send it to me. That gives me something to look forward to, besides more damn curry!

That was my favourite too. What implement would Sir like me to use? My hand? A riding crop? A brush? Or perhaps a ruler?

Your hand would be an excellent choice.

I've had two attempts at this request, but have been interrupted both times and unable to sufficiently mark my bottom to make it visible in a photo for your perusal.It's a bit fuzzy, but you try and spank yourself, then stand on tiptoe, line up a camera with one hand and take a picture before the redness goes! Oh and you got two for one, my hand hurts too...*Pout.*

22/08/10

Well yes, that's part of the fun of it – knowing that you're struggling to smack your own bottom, getting a sore hand in the process, whilst trying not to draw the entire

household's attention to what you're doing. And then trying to photograph it in a gas-lit council house. Nice. Thank you!

...And I'm not the only one that needs spanking! Gas lit council house, indeed!

Sorry – can you not afford gas then?

No, we have one candle in the middle of the room and huddle round it for warmth. The kids were very annoyed when I disappeared in the bathroom with it for so long.

Because when you returned with the candle, all breathless, it wouldn't light. Which gives me an idea...

You're going to invent a candle that lights even when it's damp? By the way. Did you reply to the last Africa balloon email I sent? Only I got a blank reply, along with two of your emails in double... Pakistani dial up Internet! This one is a bit clearer, although my bottom looks purple and it didn't when I did it.

I think you've got an amazing body, by the way. This is the most I've ever seen of you from the back!

I wouldn't call it amazing. I'm too short in the body, my back dips in, my stomach sticks out, my bottom is too square and when I sit down it all folds up in the middle, but thanks for the compliment! What's yours like?

I suppose I'm in pretty good shape - I work out with the Marines now and then (they are hard, crazy bastards) and I only stay in hotels with a pool and gym. I'm starting to creak a bit - but you'll soon put that right, I'm sure!

My youngest son is still tossing up between the Marines and the Army, ultimately he wants to join the SAS and has been watching programmes about them. It's surprising how much information he can store if it's something he likes. He also reckons he could have done better in the battle of the Somme in the war. It's a shame I can't send him to a military school, like they have in America.

I can't imagine you working out with Marines... do they have to help you? *snigger* Better get some oil in if I'm to put the creaking right. Off to work today and tomorrow then free until Monday, apart from my cleaning job Friday, plus all my own catch up housework, painting, loft sorting, gardening etc.

Tell your son to do a two year course: "Diploma in the Uniformed Services" (aka "Diploma in the Public Services") which is a lot of fun with the army, air force, navy and coastguard. And as it includes 3 A levels, he can go to university on the back of it or even Sandhurst as a trainee officer.

Yes, that's what he's already decided on, as they also pay him to stay at college.

Good lad.

Another stat you might like, which reminds me, have you found that house with the secret room you were looking for yet?

Like I've had the opportunity to look! Can you do it for me? Consider it an unlimited budget for the right house, and anywhere on the planet. Amazing pictures – do you fancy being treated like that?

Ok so I was eager to get home and go on the Internet to look for a dream home, but can I find one? No... It's much harder than it looks even with the 'unlimited budget' and 'anywhere on the planet' parameters! It's going to take quite a long time I think.

Moving on to the next subject within this email and looking at the pictures... Let me see... I'm imagining a rubber mask totally enclosing my head with only my mouth and nose uncovered, then a metal restraint circling my neck with my wrists attached behind my head, so I'm unable to use my hands to prevent anything, clamps on my nipples, with electricity going through, then a cock shoved in my mouth, down my throat and bringing on the inevitable gagging... No, not too sure about that one!

Next I'm placed in a chair, my hands once again tied above my head, my mouth clamped open, my nipples sucked in glass cups, my legs restrained wide apart completely exposing parts I never really want anyone to be able to examine after being ripped apart by three children, and to cap it all electricity shot into the most sensitive parts!

I don't see that there is much to think about, but

surprisingly, yes I would like to be treated like this, as long as it was by you, to at least find out if I could have any pleasure at all from the experience, I'd need to be comfortable with you and not just with you seeing all my body, but to know that you really do have pleasure from playing with me and that by just lying there and not actually having to do anything was ok.

24/08/10

My guests and I could place bets on how long you could stand it for (or put you up against others in an endurance contest). What could I do to you tied like that? I couldn't do that much underneath except raise you with a car jack inside you – maybe I could put a mask over your face and control your breathing for you. I'd stop short of putting a funnel in your mouth and using you as a toilet, I've seen that done and it wasn't pretty!

When did you go to these parties? I'm getting worried again...

You mean there was a point when you stopped being worried? I'm treating you too well!

Don't be horrible! *Glares and pouts*

Don't you glare and pout at me young lady! I can see myself holding a 'Teach-the-slave girl-how-to-show-respect' party very soon! Everybody's cumming…

Well I won't be coming… I'm too busy working on that day!…*Tosses hair back and walks off.*

I'LL be the one that decides what you will and won't do. You have no right to a view or an opinion unless I solicit one.

Ignores him and carries on walking.

Runs up behind and drags her back by the hair, slapping her face at each protestation. Cuffs her wrists behind her back, fits a ball-gag, hoods her, and ties her ankles. Removes every scrap of clothing, using a sharp pair of scissors, and then reminds her of her lowly, sub-working class, subordination. Using an ice-cold pressure washer.
 You belong to me. Heart, mind, body, soul. Get used to it."

No Master, let me go… Owwwwwww… Noooooooooo!!" *Screams as the ball gag goes into her mouth, which then turns into a squeaky squealing, followed by her shivering on the ground in the cold water and crying for Master to stop.*
 I belong to you, heart, mind and soul… But you haven't had my body yet!

It's just a matter of time.

What is the house I'm looking for, for? Being very practical

I don't see much point in looking if we don't actually get together after we've met. And will we meet? When you finally get away from curry land you have your own family to see, then you'll be off somewhere else again, and did you mean I'd have to be protected even if I only met you for a few hours?...Surely not...

(Sent links to three houses)

The first house is in Seend, Wiltshire. It's a lovely old house, with beautiful views and three cellars, plus stables with a hay loft. It's much too expensive, unless we all lived there (You, me and all the children, but you didn't answer the 'House?' email, so I still don't know what I am, what I will be, or what you want) it's much too large with twelve bedrooms. The second house is in Arne, Wareham and it would be perfect for me; close to my son's college, in one of my favourite parts of England right next to Swanage and Studland beach. It does have a basement with a spa bath and a 'playroom' in the attic. The house would have to be re-decorated; the wall paper in the dining room is vile.

The third house is in Sturminster Newton, again fairly well placed on the map, but not very isolated as it is right in the village next to the church. It is on the banks of a river, which looks very tranquil and it has a cellar, plus a self-contained wing.

The first one is probably the most suitable – the price is nothing as I'm looking to walk away from Pakistan having earned far more than that – though there remains the question of staff. Would you be happy having people treating your home as a place of work? I've never known

anything different to be honest, but you may find the presence of a chef, cleaning, and maintenance staff off putting at first.

Are you insane?

Firstly I can't ever imagine living in a house that large. Secondly I can't imagine that you'd buy it for me either, this has got to be imagination gone mad!

Thirdly how much is that going to cost to keep running? Then you add staff to the equation... Staff... I get staff???

Do you mean that I never have to cook, dust, vacuum, un-block drains, put up shelves, change car batteries, put floors up lofts, re-plumb washing machines etc., again?

Oh yes of course I'd be happy with staff around... I could spend time on my beauty routine (not that I need to), I can run every day without being too tired, go out and take pictures of trees and things and hopefully be used daily by you...

I've also looked at other web sites and this house at Seend does seem to be the only one suitable; I'll keep on looking.

Yes, you do get to do all those things. And I'm glad your imagination is stirred. Besides – why keep all that money in the bank? Look at interest rates. I need an investment that's as safe as houses.

Sent a link to a villa in Cannes.

This is completely different from an English country house, I love the Orange. It's clean and new, but warm.

It doesn't have a floor plan, but I doubt it has a cellar or dungeon and it's in Euro's so I don't know how much it is, but it looks like it's in quite a good neighbourhood!

That's more like it - that's a home to get excited about. Would you like to view it?

Yes I'd like to view it. Six of the pictures are of the swimming pool. The only picture of the inside is of the staircase.

What about the bedrooms?

The lounge?

The kitchen?

They don't seem to be trying very hard to sell it.

I disagree. We're going to go and view it - so I'd say their efforts have been most fruitful, as we would be cash buyers!

Are we really? I'm still not entirely sure if you are 'for real.' It all seems too much like a fairy tale.

25/08/10

(sandy butt plug pencil drawing)
I don't know if you'll be able to 'see' this stat, but I do like these pencil drawings.

Yes I can - and they're most enjoyable. Should I make you wear a corset like that to emphasise your curves? I'm not sure...

Yes, but where is all the fat going to go?

It'll bulge out at either end, won't it? Emphasising your femininity... You'll soon get used to your constant discomfort!

Along with everything else you have planned for me!

Thinking about the answer I sent earlier – concerning if I should make you wear a corset or not – I have been thinking about your body all day. Boy oh boy, have I been thinking about it... So tonight, I would like you to send me some full-length pictures of you completely naked. You are to stand barefoot, without arms or legs crossed. There will be pictures of you from all angles – front, rear, sides – you may use a full-length mirror, and the room must be lit well enough to see you properly.

Did you know that you are the only woman I've seen over the last few weeks, here in this over-the-top Muslim country? In case you ever wondered, that's why I like you sending me sexy pictures!

By the end of the week, you will also show me what a lady looks like. You have enough time to do your hair and nails, and find something suitable to wear – as if I was about to collect you in my Bentley, wearing a dinner jacket. You are, of course, encouraged to send me as many sexy pictures as your imagination allows. I own your body remember, not you – and I am completely un-shockable. All pictures are for my eyes only – you must delete them immediately and not share pictures of my property with anyone else.

Damn, I'm horny right now – I might have to drop by on my way home and use my slave girl as a cum-dustbin! Or at least take her to dinner...

This is picture number one with clothes on. I'm going to try and send the other pictures on the old PC in one lot, because I keep losing connection They are not very good. The best light is in the bathroom and that doesn't have a full-length mirror, let alone room to stand! By the way the dildo is actually up my ass.

The picture of the dildo in your ass is really good – I'd love to see you do that. And the one of you licking it, with a naughty smile across your face, came afterwards. I guess you have to clean it somehow...

You have a beautiful body, but I don't think phone pictures really do it justice. Therefore you will be pleased to know that I am extending your deadline, so you have another wonderful opportunity to impress me. I'm sure you're eternally grateful. I stand by what I've said, you have an amazing body. I'm not about to spoil it by adding "for a woman of your age that's had three kids" – there are young women in their twenties that would envy curves like yours. THANK YOU – I appreciate each and every thing you do. I'm lucky to own such a dedicated and compliant slave girl!

Oooh you are a HARD task Master, Sir.

I just got this email, it's nearly 7 am here now, (I was up at 6 am, as I woke early thinking what the hell I'm going to wear if you do come by and pick me up) so while the kids are in bed I got out my camera and took some pictures in the kitchen with the timer...

Well they are certainly an improvement – even though they are not what I specifically asked you for. I asked for you to be completely naked from head to toe, yet I only have knee-length views, obscured in part by foreign objects in near view to the camera. Furthermore, I gave no instruction, nor permission for your legs to be crossed. You will stand with your feet shoulder-width apart when you retake my photos.

Where is your head? And your lower legs and feet? I own your entire body remember, and you may not withhold it. Such behaviour will only get a servant's bare breasts slapped until she cries. Thank you for what you've done so far though. You are such a sexy woman...

And you're just Mr Bloody Awkward! I live in a box, remember? It's difficult to get my whole body in and if I do I will be so far away you won't see anything.

Thank you for the compliments.

I'm not being awkward! You're the one that's returning slipshod work, and somehow surprised that it isn't good enough. Besides, where's the fun in asking you to do something easily achievable – I'm having great fun imagining you holding a flower between your bare bottom cheeks, writing on your own bottom in lipstick – taking full-length, clear pictures of yourself naked ought to be easy in comparison (as opposed to, say, what you're going to do next!). If there is insufficient space indoors then you'll have

**to undress and photograph yourself outdoors. If it's raining
– well, you'll just get wet. Don't be discouraged – you just
need to try harder, and be grateful that you belong to such
a patient, easy-going master.**

Oh yes, sure... the neighbours will love that first thing in
the morning when they come down to their kitchens to get
their breakfasts before work! I'll give it another go if I get
the house to myself.

P.S. What do you mean 'as opposed to, say, what you're
going to do next?' There can't be much left for me to do in
front of a camera!

Oh, trust me – I can think of plenty! Can you?

Well of course I can. I was being sarcastic and anyway it
wasn't doing things in front of a camera that I was really
referring too. I thought you meant all the other stuff you
have planned for me and I thought if I put 'in front of a
camera' it would throw you off thinking about all the nasty
things you keep telling me about to get me worried.

**You'll have to hope they don't see you then! Hmmmm, it
could be awkward for you, couldn't it? I think you've given
me an idea...**

Here are your pictures... Will that be all? Can I go for a run
now?

27/08/10

Yes indeed you can – though I suspect that you may have already done so by now – and thank you for such wonderful pictures of your camera flash and your intolerably untidy bedroom. I think 'Mr Bloody Awkward' needs to teach his slave some respect. She needs to say "Thank you for giving me another chance to please you", not pretend that the reason the pictures aren't good enough is down to him. It sounds to me like somebody's in for a slightly uncomfortable – okay, painful – and publicly humiliating time…

Sorry about the camera flash, but that's inevitable when you live in a house with completely crap lighting, because some moron designer thought it would be good to light the whole house with teeny-weeny wall lights.

My bedroom isn't untidy, just small. This house was made for a couple with perhaps one child and a little bit of stuff, not four adults.

I think you (or rather, I) have an amazingly sexy body. But how do you feel about it? If you had access to it all – cosmetic surgeons, cosmetic dentists, hair experts, whatever else there is these days – what would you have done?

I wouldn't change anything, I like it the way it is, even more so since I went running, lost a stone and got my waist back. However, I would have my varicose veins removed and have my bunions done.

The only real 'cosmetic' operation I've thought about in

the past would be to have my vagina 'tucked.' I haven't liked it since having my daughter, but it functions perfectly and so I think that it's better to leave it alone as it is, but I don't like the way it looks.

You would never throw me off thinking – indeed, relishing – new delights and ways I can be entertained by your discomfort, embarrassment, and humiliation!

Rats!

There will be no livestock involved. Not at first, anyway…

Oh very funny. Actually have you seen that little video of the woman sucking off a horse as it ejaculates? I think it's probably one of the vilest things I've ever seen!

I haven't seen a video of it, but I have seen it done. A slave girl was tied over a barrel and was entered by a horse, which was strange, when the exclusively male audience were only repulsed when she was replaced by a male. There was also the slave who had a glass tube inserted in her vagina, and then animals put into it, such as rats, and then a snake. She passed out. It was a bit of a disaster of an evening really, not the sort of effect our host was aiming for. For the record, it repulses me and I was only kidding about the rats.

Well thank heavens for small mercies! You seem to have gone to a lot of strange parties. I'm not entirely sure I want to go anywhere with you, I shall be in permanent flight mode if I do!

Not with your ankles shackled together, you won't!

Now Master's being horrid again! Frightening his poor slave girl. *Pouts*

28/08/10

You still don't get the part about never complaining, never questioning me, and not being entitled to a view or an opinion, do you? You are my chattel, my possession, my toy. You will depend on me for everything, even your very survival. So a bit of trust wouldn't go amiss.

Yes I do get it, but will it not be boring if I didn't react at all? Isn't that all part of the game? My resistance becoming weakened by your strength, as you take control of me and become my Master?

Besides, neither of us really knows what will happen when we get together properly. If how I feel about you now will be the same when we meet. If you'll like me how I am and I want to be everything to you, not just some sub, chattel, possession, toy, reflecting all our conversations; general ones about weather and kids, news and shopping, if you see what I mean. Yes, I want to have sex with you and yes I want you to be in control and yes, it excites me to think of all the things you say you are going to do to me, even though when you do them I probably won't like it at all, but I want all the other normal stuff too.

For the record I do trust you, I believe everything you tell me, no one else does, which makes it more difficult, because

I'm very practical and can see why no one believes you exist, but also going on past dating site experiences, I am convinced that you do. Well of course you exist, otherwise I would be writing all these replies to myself.

Oh I'm losing it again, just hurry up and come and get me, so we can get it over and done with, whatever it is going to be...

I had these pictures through my group today and quite a few 'rapid share' videos of girls in training and hogtied. I'm downloading one, but it takes so long and I can't be bothered with the others, so I'll forward them to you from the group, in case you'd like to download them. *(Sent four photos of a girl spread-eagled on a table, gagged, with a vibrator tied to her)*

Well... they seemed a bit pointless to me. I like the soundproofed leather walls though!

It was the actual position she was in, with her legs hanging over the edge of the table, and then tied to the table legs.

But it's all about giving the slave her orgasm, when her one and only concern in life should be her owner's happiness and satisfaction. Furthermore, it isn't all that exciting to watch. She's restrained – the only thing you'd get is to hear some moaning. I would much rather you had an orgasm from a Sybian machine. And to make it more interesting, you'll be holding a tray of filled water glasses in each hand. There's a deep muddy hole outside if you spill any!

I had to look up 'Sybian Machine.' I think I might quite like to try one of those to see what sort of an orgasm it gave me. I don't know how the water would fare in the glasses. I'm pretty good at balancing, but if I get a full body orgasm I could end up chucking the whole tray at you... Will I be shackled to this thing? I hope the answer is no, because I will have to run and hide pretty quick after wetting Master...

Grins, and thinks of the 6ft deep mud with the winch over it...

Starts to cry"Please Master don't put me down the muddy hole. I don't want to go down the hole. I don't even like water in my eyes. Please Sir, not the hole!"

"I-don't-want"???

You're just nit picking now! What am I supposed to say? I'm stating a fact, not an opinion. I don't want to go down the hole. I don't like water in my eyes. Am I not supposed to tell you everything? Should I have said 'I'm sorry Master, if it pleases you, punish me and put me down the muddy hole?' Then I would have been hiding the fact from you, that I didn't want to go down the hole and I didn't mind my head under the water or water in my eyes! Then surely that would have been deceitful, ergo worse?

You're missing the point. NOTHING in this life should mean as much to you as your Master's satisfaction. It shouldn't matter to you if I choose to dunk you in mud, watch you

fucking another woman, or have you dressed to the nines, by my side, as honoured guests at a royal dinner somewhere. You are not entitled to an opinion, any more than my jet is entitled to a view as to where I should fly. I don't want to hear 'I-don't-want'. The thing is, if I want it, you should want it too.

NOT IF YOU'RE GOING TO PUT ME HEAD FIRST DOWN A SODDING MUDDY HOLE!

I couldn't get to sleep after reading this. I can't be this woman you want. I'm too old. I have other responsibilities. Jet?

Don't tell me you have your own jet too? And how can a jet have a view? Is it like that jet in the children's book that speaks?"

Hi ****, where do you want to fly today?"

"Pakistan"

"Pakistan?" "Oh no **** I don't want to fly there, there's nothing to see on the way, just a load of water and barren countryside, plus all the women are practically Muslim... You won't like it there..."*sent movie links, Training of Juliette, Princess Donna and Prisoner Transport*

Yup. That's YOU alright.

No... I have long, curly hair!

I can see you reacting the same way to your training though!

Yes I'm sure I will in those situations.

I think that is going to be the hardest thing for me, showing my emotions. I've been on my own a long time.

That's a part of your training. You will hide nothing from me – absolutely nothing – or else you have not given yourself to me absolutely and completely.

That's what I want. To be able to tell you anything, to be myself and not have to hide things from fear that it might displease you, or block my emotions. To get to a point where you know me so well I would have no need to even speak.

Yes, I think I would be entertained watching you being treated in such a fashion by another naked woman. And of course, if I want it – so do you. I could see YOU wearing this – I like the cone, and I like her gloves. Yes, I think you've given me another idea!

May I make a suggestion Sir? How about a double challenge? Leave my hands free and see if I can make Master come before he finishes my make-up.

No you may not. Ever.

But I'm so horny… and you're so close… and my hands are free… so if I am not allowed to make a suggestion, can I then ask permission to touch you?

Yes, of course – but to 'suggest' something implies equal status. And that would be just ridiculous.

I could never be equal to you in status. I don't see how by asking to suggest something would imply equal status either. Perhaps if I'd said 'I want to suggest something,' it would be different.

...and now you are questioning my instructions! You're just asking for some rough, humiliating treatment, aren't you?

I wasn't questioning your instructions. It was a statement I didn't understand. I can't learn if I don't ask... Or will I just get beaten whenever I get something wrong?

That counts as another question, I'm afraid!

Oh go jump in a muddy hole!It's Saturday night and I'm stuck in with my son watching X Factor auditions... I'm cringing already. I'm also tired and confused. When will you come home?

If you're bored, you can always get dressed up for your photo assignment. Plus any sexy surprises you feel like indulging your loving, horny, trapped-in-a-Muslim-country Master with...

29/08/10

I only have one outfit suitable for dinner with you, so if I get chance I'll put it on and take a picture, but I have quite a bit to do today. I don't have anything remotely sexy... After all I'm sexy enough without needing clothes to emphasise my sexiness.

It sounds like I need to leave you in Harvey Nichols for a few hours with a credit card... I've heard mention of a mountain-top ranch in Nevada that has an asking price of $100M. Can you find it, take a look, and tell me what you think please?

$100M!

$100M!

$100M!

Now you're showing off!

The only one I can find is at Lake Tahoe. It's a lovely house, more like a palace, than a home, very elegant, but too expensive for what it is, although they do keep mentioning that it's on the tax free side of the lake, which probably has some bearing on the price.

Well I'd never pay $100,000,000 – I think everyone would agree there's an element of built-in flexibility in the price. I said the price was one hundred million, but I said nothing about paying that much.

Guess what? My daughter finally noticed that I had my tongue pierced! She asked me why I had it done, so I just said I felt like it... She gave me a weird look!

Harvey Nichols is a nice idea, but I can't buy anything, I don't have anywhere to hang any more clothes and I wouldn't know how to get there. I've only been to London about ten times in my whole life and probably only two of those times were to go shopping. Besides I hate clothes shopping, it's so tiring, I can never find anything I like and what I do like is too expensive or dry clean only, which I don't do, because it's such a pain to get things dry cleaned and I know you're paying and if it all works out I'd have a house to put it in and a servant to take whatever it was to the dry cleaners, but we haven't got to that stage yet, because you're still in Pakistan, by the time you finish you'll come home wearing Indian dress with a string of Muslim wives or something...

30/08/10

Something to keep you going this morning or whatever time it is in Pakistan!

VERY sexy - I'll gladly give a home to those puppies trying to get out!

We had the busiest day ever at work today. We took over £3,000 for the first time. A slow day is £900; a normal busy day is around £2,500. Luckily I got away with the easiest job selling take-away tea and coffee in a separate room, but it was impossible for anyone to go to lunch, so I was stood up from 9.30 am to 5 pm, then we had a cream tea each before clearing up. It got so bad we used spare cups that had never been used before and resorted to paper plates, because the dishwasher couldn't keep up... Even the hot water boiler ran out at one point!

01/09/10

I just read a news report online about Nick Clegg visiting Pakistan. It quotes him as saying, "The danger always is that you get groups who have an ulterior motive who provide aid to try to curry favour." Can they curry that too? Ha ha...

02/09/10

He's such a twat, Clegg. You'd think he'd read his speeches through first, wouldn't you?

Anyway, I thought perhaps you were with Nick Clegg on his visit to curry land and I was thinking, what did you call him? Do you call him Sir or does he call you Sir?

I piss him off by calling him Smithers (from the Simpsons). He calls me Sir, but I don't like the greasy toad. There's only one reason he's where he is. There is going to be so much pain coming, the Conservatives would be unelectable for a generation (and so would Labour had they won). The solution? Have two parties in Government and spread the risk! It means that no voter anywhere actually got the Government they wanted, but since when has politics been about democracy?

Where are you?
I miss you.
I've had to use power tools again to put up a towel rail.
Please come back soon.

I'm still here - just a victim of the Pakistani Internet! Just catching up on your messages now.

Oh that's a relief. I thought you might have been bombed or something. I've just got out of the shower. I'm naked...

Then I'd better chase you with a tea-towel. See if I can decorate your delicious bottom with a few rosy marks! Show me something...

Damn, your Internet is too slow... I'm dressed now!

Then you'll have to strip for me, won't you? Are you much of a dancer, by the way?

I have to leave in ten minutes and my hair has to be dried, I was just drinking my tea. What sort of dancing? I like to dance to 'pop' stuff, especially with my eldest son when he's messing around, apart from that I can waltz, but that's probably it I'm afraid.

02/09/10

(Sent a topless photo)'Something' for you. I took this at the house I clean, as the owner was out, so I haven't checked what it looks like on the pc, as I'm still here. There are others, so I'll send them if they look ok.

*(Sent more photos)*I'm home now. I've checked these and

they are not too bad, so here is the full set that I took. I still don't like me from behind, but this house has corner mirrors, so it was easy to do front and back at the same time. When are you going to send me a picture? I still don't know what you look like now!

You are, without doubt, the sexiest woman I've seen. Thank you.

I doubt it, and after all you are stuck in Muslim, women-in-sheets land, so you must be very horny by now and anything would look good, except maybe a goat or sheep or something... But thank you anyway and send me a picture!

I've been offered a considerable stream of Moslem woman - most of whom I've regarded as a somewhat pathetic attempt at a honey trap. The rest, well they look all right but might as well be robots. They are so indoctrinated with all that crap - wearing their Jibab and all the rest of it - it's like they are no longer human.

It's the same with the pretty girls you alluded to in an earlier message. They have curves, they have their mouths gaping open, and a tendency to fall over with their legs in the air if the occasion were to call for it. It doesn't.

I prefer one lady in particular who has seen more real life than any of these bimbos. Someone that talks to me, makes me laugh, and arouses my brain, not just my penis. This lady tells me how many piles of washing she's done one minute, then sends me a photograph of her bare body the next, knowing full darn well that I'll be addressing World Leaders

with regards to a global catastrophe, only with an erection that isn't only hard to conceal, but refuses to go away. What an amazing, sexy woman you are.

03/09/10

Sigh... Ok, I'll give you a blow job, just this once...

You know I really shouldn't be sending pictures of my naked body to a complete stranger, WHOM I'VE NEVER EVEN SEEN A PICTURE OF!

Thank you. I shall keep this message to read, to make me feel better when I get pre-menstrual and depressed and doubt that I'll ever get to meet you.

Thought I had better send you a picture of me with clothes on, for a change, in case you don't recognise me with my clothes on when we meet!

And you look just as beautiful. I think I like this picture the most – that smile just warms me inside.

03/09/10 (A REAL MAN)

I just got this from my friend. Of course it's not true in your case.

A REAL MAN

A real man is a woman's best friend. He will never stand her up and never let her down. He will reassure her when she feels insecure and comfort her after a bad day. He will inspire her to do things she never thought she could do; to live without fear and forget regret. He will enable her to express her deepest emotions and give in to her most intimate desires. He will make sure she always feels as though she's the most beautiful woman in the room and will enable her to be the most confident, sexy, seductive, and invincible.

No wait! Sorry... I'm thinking of wine. It's wine that does all that.

I hope I can be all that to you - and, like a wine, improve with age. I'm trying to follow that up with a line that includes 'screw' and 'pop my cork' but I can't really be bothered. I suppose I'm more like champagne - I've got something you can shake up and down until it explodes its contents all over your face... Will that do as a retort?

You could have added something along the lines of 'Fruity tones,' or 'Store horizontally in a dark place.' Or how about 'Full bodied and velvety with a spicy finish!'

I'd like to age with you.

I was thinking. You said that I arouse your brain, not just your penis, but men's brains are in their penises?

How much longer are your negotiations going to take? And that reminds me. Did you get the email with the photo looking up my skirt, or did the Pakistani Internet eat it?

If indeed a man's brain is in his penis that might explain why a woman has no brains at all. I have not seen the picture you mention, but it sounds exciting. In fact, I'd like to see some pictures of you doing things with your smooth pussy -

masturbating with your fingers, a dildo, a household object – I'll leave the content up to you. And I'd like you to actually do this please, I'm disappointed to not have received any pictures of you all made up yet. Your Master requires your complicity and obedience.

Pokes tongue out Women have their brains in their heads silly!

Yes, the picture was quite good. I'm on the old upstairs pc, so I can't send it now. I shall go over any emails you might have missed in the three days you lost contact and re-send them.

I've just come back from a short run, so I'm all sweaty and about to go in the shower. I did send you the black dress, puppy picture, as my clothed one, but I suppose it wasn't good enough. I can't see that I shall be able to take one of me dressed up until I've done this four-day stint at work, because I won't have time in the morning and it will be dark by the time I get home and we will be back to the shit lighting situation. However I did actually do you a video of me masturbating (and having an orgasm) with my phone held between my knees, but it was just too embarrassing, so I deleted it! I'll do a few pictures shortly in my shower...

You made a video like that – then DELETED it? What a shame – you'll have to make another one. Your Master has 'needs' that require your concentrated efforts. Do you ever squirt when you orgasm?

03/09/10

(sent video of orgasm noise)
If you catch me right then yes I squirt a tiny bit during an orgasm, but nothing like you see on those porn videos!

I made you another video, but I was watching a film and the adverts came on, so it kind of kills it a bit. You can't see anything, but then you probably don't need to!

P.S. I am now thoroughly embarrassed and will wake up in the morning and regret this.

You are right (of course), we think along similar lines and are aroused by similar things, which, I suppose, is why I've chased you for so long, no one else has come close. Sometimes you terrify me with your stories and I'm ready to run, but then you say things that completely restore my confidence and trust in you and it's those times that keep me hanging on, that keep me wanting you and I know that is the 'real' you and the rest is imagination and desire, the same as I experience.

I like watching 'Hogtied' videos, especially the facial expressions of the girls, as they scream in shock or sudden pain and orgasm. There has to be an orgasm at the end of it all for me, but to actually experience it... I don't know. I've also never, yes never, had an orgasm given to me by a man, without doing any kind of massage myself. I suppose if I was tied up with a vibrator, or two, strategically placed, that would work, but it's more the mental connection that I need. When frightened I go into myself and cope on my own, so as soon as I became scared, I'd shut down and you wouldn't get the orgasm. I have to be relaxed. Oh and it would probably take about three dates of attempted sex to achieve this, if you do it sooner, then you're officially a God, like Zeus or someone.

I shall mull this over and no doubt think of more I should have added later, but I have to get ready for and go to work now, so it's back to my stupid phone that doesn't read some of your texts, until I can get the PC off my son tonight.Here are your requested pictures... I'll have a whole portfolio soon!

04/09/10

WOW – and what a lucky duck! I'm so aroused by you... we do think along very similar lines!

Why? Do you get off by putting a duck up your ass in the bath too? I should have put that picture on its own, and then asked if you wanted to 'duck' me.

JUST FOR THAT, you can now send me a picture of that duck in your ass. I want just his head and neck poking out. I hope there are plenty of edges on that duck to make him truly uncomfortable...

Grins Yes Master.

If I'm faced with a domestic issue which lies beyond me, a blocked drain, for example, or a loose roof tile – I call in the

professionals. The same applies to one's professional life – I employ the very best tax accountants. Numbers are not my strong point. I know my limits, and I'm not afraid to call in help when it's needed. So if you still exhibit these hang-ups with regards, to your orgasm – if you still feel unable to let go of the side of the pool and just swim – then I might be generous and hire some extra help. How about three or four ladies who will strip you, bind you and bring out the real you – they will show you the true definition of abandonment and sexual liberation. And yes, I will be watching and enjoying the spectacle.

Consider it akin to taking your brand-new car back for a tune and a service. You want it to be the car you always wanted, so get a professional to look at it. The car will thank you in the end, and drive like a dream. Plus, of course, I'd like to see you being gang-raped by four women. Maybe I've been in a Muslim, porn-free country for too long.

Civil war is about to break out and there's every chance it will spread to our shores. Nothing is being said at the moment, but STAY OUT OF CENTRAL LONDON again until I say otherwise. The flood waters are gone, but the carnage and disease remain, and the Taliban are moving in whilst the Government here scratch their arses and wonder why they are unpopular. I'd like to see this inept bunch of piss-brained morons replaced, I really would – but not by the Taliban. And there is nobody else. No third option. I loved that masturbation video by the way. So the camera wasn't in the right place, but I got the sound effects! It occurs to me that I have never heard you speak – so your next video will be of you naked – I want to see you rubbing your breasts as you tell me what's in store on our first night together. Spare no detail – I want it to be as explicit as your imagination will allow. Then, I want to see you masturbate with your fingers this time.

Even the anticipation of this is making me as hard as a rock. If only this IPad had a camera...

'If only this iPad had a camera?' Well you shouldn't buy posh, expensive, but useless gear! A small laptop would have been much more use. If I had some spare money I would have bought myself one, as well as my son, then I'd have a web cam and a bit more privacy when trying to send pictures of a certain nature to a certain gentleman and I could have given you much more if we had used Messenger together. I could gaze into your blue eyes and masturbate much more effectively!

I'm off to bed now to read a bit. I feel sick from drinking tea and not eating when I got home. I went straight in the bath after doing the animals and dishes, but the heat from the bath and the tea made me feel weird... By the way I'm sorry Master, but I failed. I couldn't get the duck up my arse! My camera had run out of battery anyway, so I couldn't have taken a picture even if I had succeeded.

05/09/10

People are so damn stupid, aren't they? Half – actually, most – of those could be in this stupid, shit-hole country! Thank you!

05/09/10

So that's a NO and I'VE FAILED, both in the same message. I've got a raging headache this morning anyway – it's like a hangover, even though booze is illegal. I have a meeting today – cards on the table time – and I *should* be home after next week!XXXXXXXXXXXX

This is the last message I had from him. The day he was taken from his hotel and murdered by Al Qaeda militants. The following messages are some of those I sent to him when at first I thought he had just 'disappeared' on me again, like he did before in 2007, because I thought he was either lying about who he was, or he had just changed his mind about meeting me, until finally I found out he was dead, that he was telling the truth and he was going to meet me and I realised that he did love me too.

06/09/10

Hello?

How is your headache?

How did the meeting go?

I'm sat drinking my second glass of red wine with only the washing left to hang up. It's nearly 10 pm, so I'll be off to bed soon and I still have another long day at work tomorrow. It absolutely poured this afternoon. I went to Tesco on my way home to get some milk and hot chicken for tea and had to paddle through the car park, there was actually a river running through there was so much rain! It reminded me of living in Singapore in the monsoon season, hot and wet.

I was thinking, it must be hard for you with no sex AND no alcohol, no wonder you have a headache. Have you had hiccups too? Apparently if you're sexually frustrated you get hiccups.

I can't think of much else to say, I'm just drained at the moment...

08/09/10

I'm assuming that you are wrapping up in curry land and hopefully on your way home. I'm really tired at the moment. I've been working longer hours, because the main tearoom people are on holiday, ergo I've been on the go from 6 am until 10 pm, if you add driving time and all the other stuff I do every day. I expect you are drained too, so we will be a matching pair if you do finally make it to my house, as long as it isn't tonight... I haven't even had time to shave my legs!Bizarrely though I've suddenly got a vision of us in bed, with me on top and a bottle of baby oil... Maybe I'm not that tired...

08/09/10

Ok here I am sort of dressed up. I didn't have time to put make-up on and my hair needs washing, which I was about to go and do, but Crime watch is on in ten minutes, so I might watch that first, but If I do I might then be too tired to shower, because four hours driving to my son's college and back has whacked me out, I'd rather be 'whacked' some other way, but I suppose I'll just have to wait a lot longer for that...

09/09/10

Smithers just got a grilling on radio 4... I don't think he gave one straight answer!

I'm practising putting on make-up. I've had to remove it once and start again. I'm still not happy, but it will do for lunch today with Dad.

I watched a short movie I downloaded through my group last night.It was a Mistress with her male slave. He was really hard, something I've not seen for a long time, and she was playing with him. It looked like he was well oiled and I had been thinking of playing with you with oil earlier in the day. She made him play with himself, but kept making him go faster, slower or made him stop altogether, watching him and thinking of you making me play with myself in the same way set me off...

09/08/10

I'm having an afternoon nap before I cook tea. Where are you when I feel so horny?

10/09/10

I had Jordan's Chunky Nut's for breakfast. When will I have breakfast with you?

10/09/10

We've just had the police round our road again at some girl's house, her ex-boyfriend turned up with a baseball bat. Luckily her mum and stepdad were there. The dad had some sort of altercation outside and I was ready to go out and help with my son, but after banging the bat on the ground he drove off.

On another note. I'm pre-menstrual, I've consumed a whole bar of fruit n nut and I'm tired and moody and you've disappeared again, but I've re-read your nice message, which makes me feel much better.

Also I'm watching Ella Enchanted. She has to do as she is told, like a submissive.

When will I see you?

When will you tell me what to do?

And when can I be naughty and disobey you?

My hand aches doing this on my phone.

11/09/10

I love you.

As Michael Jackson sings in the song I sent you once, 'I want to be where you are' and yes, you have stayed away too long! But if I was with you, then maybe, just maybe I wouldn't have to stick stupid, sodding, odd-shaped, blue, plastic ducks up my arse, and take pictures! How the hell I got it out I don't know, needless to say my arse is now sore and the duck did a poo.

13/09/10

Where are you?

Did your headache turn into something nasty?

Are you still in Pakistan and you've lost your internet again?

Are you on your way home?

Have you been called somewhere else?

Have you changed your mind about meeting me? (I half expected you this weekend)

Am I to be cast into a pool of eternal torment, lost forever?

Do I have to stick another duck up my arse?

Come back please...

15/09/10

Well I haven't heard from you for ten days and I'm going out of my mind with worry and despair. I'm going to drink myself into a stupor with Tesco's value gin and ice (I bought it to make the sloe gin, but never got round to doing it), watch a movie and do the ironing. If I burn myself it's your fault, I don't see why if you lose your internet you can't ring me, so at least I can sit tight and wait, without falling into the depression I'm in now! You own me, but I am lost.

15/09/10

Please come back, I can't sleep and I'm tired and I have so much to do and I'll be too tired to do it. I think of you all day and all night, I miss you so much... It's not because I didn't do the video is it?I need to see you.

18/09/10

I went to the beach with my son last night and took this picture on my phone of the moon... Isn't it beautiful? Will I ever stand with you and look at the moon?

19/09/10

When are you going to come back? It feels like it did two years ago when you suddenly stopped emailing me. I thought this time I was finally going to meet you. This time you wanted me too.

I can think of a thousand appropriate clichés, a thousand appropriate love songs, but what I really want to say, what I really feel I can't describe, I just know that without you it's like I'm clinging onto a post in a raging tsunami and the only thing that stops me from letting go and giving up is the hope that you will come for me. (Actually that was a nightmare I had!)

I can't put it any clearer, and with such a long absence I can only assume you are dead, dying, very ill, or just some bastard who enjoys playing games, then sods off when it comes to meeting up and no more excuses can be made, but deep down I know you're not, because you're like me and I trust you and I definitely love you, because I've cried more from losing you than I did when my mother died... Is there a song for that?

Oh just come back and talk to me. I'm miserable without you.

21/09/10

How long must I stay in this wretched place?
How long must I wait to see your face?
I cannot return from whence I came,
Nor move forward to another plain.
Sir you hold my soul in your hand,
I only exist to follow your command.
My only aim is to please you,
To make you smile,
To sexually tease you.
All I had, all I did is gone,
There is only you now,
Am I so wrong?
Will you not make the final move,
And meet me face to face?
Extend your hand,
And lift me from this place?

26/09/10

Dear *****,

I'm depressed and I'm ill. I haven't been ill for over a year and not since I've been emailing you, but it's now been three weeks since I last heard from you and I can't think of any more reasons or excuses for your silence, except that you've disappeared again.

How can you do that? After all we've shared? After all the promises you made about buying me a house, looking after my children and spending our remaining future together. How can you just stop emailing me again?

I suppose being a man you didn't see our correspondence in the same way as me. It was just something to keep you amused, to pass your spare time whilst you were in a country that disagreed with you, but haven't I at least earned the right to see you? Don't I deserve dinner once? To be collected by you in your dinner jacket in your Bentley? I got ready for you that weekend. I was sure that you would be home and that you would come for me en route, but you didn't, you were playing with me and only meant me to send you a picture of me dressed up. Do you honestly think I would have spent all that money on hair, nails and clothes just to send you a picture? It's a good job I didn't bother then and don't give me all that 'I'm the Master you're my owned slave girl and you do as I command' crap. It doesn't work if you don't know me, if you haven't actually, physically taken my body too. You have my mind and you have my soul and you always will. Your silence cannot change that ever. I am condemned to live a life of celibacy if you will not honour the words you have written to me;

"XxXxXxX *Look I've mixed my kisses with yours. Bodily fluids next...* "

Or am I missing something?

Is there another reason for your rudeness?

Am I jumping to conclusions?

Are you really ill?

Are you home and have a huge amount of work to catch up on, kids to sort out etc?

But does that stop you from sending me one line like; 'Sorry ******, I have so much to do I won't be emailing you for a while.' I think not. If I was on my death bed I would still find a way to let you know.

Here I am ready to give up everything to be with you. I've thrown out books, cleared my loft, given away pot plants, prepared my family, thought long and hard about the future that I would have with you, how it would all fit together and come to the conclusion that without you I have nothing, so I'm really not giving up anything at all. Without your humour, without your particular view on the world and life, without your obscene sexual fantasies, without your leadership, I have nothing. I would even be prepared to marry you, if that is what it would take to be with you, to keep our arrangement 'above board' in your perfect, secret life. I will live where ever you think is necessary, I will be a step-mother to your children (hopefully not an ugly, evil one), I will obey your commands, I will please you to the best of my ability, I will lift your moods, fulfil as many sexual fantasies as I am able, including having four woman 'play' with me while you watch and I will love you always. If you want to keep me in a tower just for sex, never to mix with your 'other' life, then so be it, but wouldn't it make more sense to combine our families?

Or is it you that's not ready?

Do you still mourn your wife?

Of course you do, some things can never be forgotten, but I thought you were moving forward now and if not with a 'bimbo' or some suitable, but mindless, upper-class rich girl, then why not move forward with me? I'll be dead in twenty years, then you can have another go later, you'll be in your sixties, but with your 'supposed' fortune you can have a ball at that age!

This relationship can work and will work; besides I know too much already and you said that you would pay me to keep quiet or maybe you should have me killed? I'm dead anyway without you. But it's all rubbish and I'm beginning not to believe anything you've told me, MI6 protecting me? If you can't even bring yourself to have one 'date' with me you must be a fraud and it will all be proved when you turn up at my house in tatty jeans driving a Skoda!!!

I think that just about wraps it up.

In conclusion;

I love you (I think)

Marry me and live dangerously (Your future would definitely be more interesting)****** (slave girl with lots of bodily fluids)

P.S. I'm going back to bed with a cup of tea to watch 'Enchanted,' a nice romantic Cinderella-type story, to cheer me up a bit, hopefully I'll feel better in time for work tomorrow... Hopefully you'll answer this, which will cheer me up too.

30/09/10

Where is he? Where is he?

All right, I give up!

No actually I don't give up. I'll never give up.

Why can't you just get in a car, come to my house, knock

on my door and take me to dinner? Or ring me and arrange to meet at a 'public place,' just like the dating guidelines say?

You have my address. You have my phone numbers. The two things you asked for that I said 'no' to and that I failed at have now been completed, but have you seen them? Have you seen any of this? Are you just ignoring me now you're back home, because you're too scared to see me?

Is that going to be it for another two years? Until I die? Is your life not a tiny bit empty? Is there nothing that you're missing? Do you not think of me when you have your pen tip between your lips? Wouldn't you like to wake up to me in your bed every morning? Don't you want to feel my nipple rolled between your fingers? Rubbed on the end of your cock? Sucked and gripped between your teeth, as I gasp in ecstasy mixed with pain? It's all very well sending photos, making suggestions, but don't you really want me?

It's my birthday on Sunday. I'm 49. Have you made it home in time? Of course you have. Perhaps I should come to Norwich instead for the day and sit outside your house. Would you come out and see me? Or have I wasted petrol money and damaged my sanity even further?

You are letting me go to waste. I belong to you. You own me.

At the moment I hate you for putting me through this again. The mental pain, depression, unhappiness, the uncertainty, giving you the benefit of the doubt unable to bother with anything at all, just in case you come back on line to say that your absence was caused by something out of your control.

I've looked at all the emails and I'm sure it wasn't all just me this time. Me getting carried away, assuming too much, reading more into your correspondence than I perhaps should. When I think of the things I've sent you over the past nine months I am astounded. I would never share any of this with anyone. I don't even think I would have shown some of these things to my ex-husband when we were married! I have them all saved on my PC, but I suppose I should delete most of it in case I die...What would my kids think if they found it after I'm dead?

In conclusion I should just call you a bastard, delete everything, block your mail and move on. But I can't.

02/10/10

Don't you want to be here? In your hands my present could be my complete submission... Forever and always..

I'm at the top of the Cissbury ring on my own, deserted by all and it's my birthday tomorrow.

07/10/10

(Sent two photos of myself fully dressed)

Thought these photos would make a change from my usual shares... Where are you?

08/10/10 (ME)

On reflection, you have my heart, my mind and my soul, but

you do have my body too, because no other man is going to touch me ever again...

Arsehole!

And among all the other promises, or should I change that to 'fantasies', that you made, you missed having me fucked by two black men, while you watched, for my birthday!

08/10/10

So in other words, no matter where I go, or what I do, I am yours, even if you choose never to see me, never to use me, never to email me again, because it would be impossible for you...But 'impossible' isn't a word I would associate with you!

10/10/10

Oh for heaven's sake!!! Can't we just meet in secret and have sex... I'm dying here!

10/10/10

You remind me of Prince Arthur in Merlin, good looking, sexy, arrogant, mean to his slave and not always right.

15/10/10

I don't understand. How can you abandon me so freely? How can you say all the things you said and then just cut me off?

I meant every word I wrote and was prepared to completely change my life for you, if it was necessary, even for one dinner date. So what happened?

Now I am sitting in the pitch black on the sea front at the park, because I'm too unhappy to sit at home with the kids. There is no one that I can talk to and no one believes you exist anyway... I may as well throw myself in the sea in despair, but no, I'm too practical for that.

Please come for me. I'm lost without you...

05/11/10

Happy Fireworks night ****/Sir/Master/Asshole!

It has been exactly two months since your last communication with me and still I wait for your return and your explanation as to why you left me so suddenly for the second time. That's twice now in three years! Surely after all that you can't just carry on regardless?

Will you let me die without ever meeting you? Without ever finding out if we really do have a connection?

Not that I am dying soon, well not that I'm aware of anyway, but meeting you really is the only thing I look forward to, otherwise it's just a lonely life waiting for my youngest son to become independent and working in some crap job until I'm 72. There is nothing else for me in this world. There will never be anyone else like you who captures every facet of my life, hopes, dreams, past experiences, emotions, wants, needs, etc. As they said in 'Avatar', 'I see you' and I know you 'see me.'

12/11/10

I just had an argument with my eldest son and I've left home. I have to go back later, because I have work tomorrow and Saturday, otherwise I would have driven to you. It's because of you that I'm so lost now and so full of despair and darkness. I'm not well either. If you had come for me everything would be good now. I wouldn't have to lie and I wouldn't be sitting in my car in a deserted car park, because I have nobody to talk to no one who would understand how I could completely believe and fall in love with a man through internet conversations.

Why did I send that email last Christmas?

Why didn't I just call it a day, find a job and give up on men?

Why did you answer it?

What am I to do?

15/11/10

Talk to me please... Talk to me, please.Please talk to me.Talk to me... Pleaseeeeeeeeee.

15/11/10

I'm watching misfits (well, my daughter is), and this line came up: 'The siren call of the blow job renders all men powerless!' Shame I won't even get chance to try... Oh and I may as well take this tongue piercing out, for the same reason.

18/11/10

There is a rainbow outside my window. Normally I'd be thrilled, but I have a splitting headache and since you have gone I see no joy in anything. Perhaps if I made a wish upon it? A wish for a meeting with you. Would it ever come true? You said you would protect me and look after me, but you lied. You left me.

21/11/10

I miss you.I miss the email notifier that chimes when you've sent me a message.I miss your wit.I miss your guidance, when I don't know what to do.I miss you.

22/11/10

I sent you a letter today... I hope your address is ************ otherwise someone is going to get a surprise!

The letter (with Christmas card)

Dear ****,

Look, I don't know why you wouldn't meet me, I truly expected you this time, and I definitely feel, as I reflect on our conversations, that we would be good together.

I know there are barriers, baggage, whatever, but you are everything that I'm looking for and I won't settle for anything less, besides you own me, remember, and always will. I've felt like this for the last three years. I'm hardly likely to change now.

Check your mail. I've sent documents containing our early conversations that you might like to read.

I hope you have a Happy Christmas and a prosperous New Year.

02/12/10

I walked in the snow this morning and, whenever I walk, I think of you, but I don't smile to myself any more...It's been three months since I last heard from you, but it feels like three years. Shouldn't I have stopped thinking about you by now? After all I'm getting nothing in return. Am I just obsessed? Or has my instinct recognised you as my soulmate? I don't know.

Make me smile again... Please.

10/12/10

Sodding men!!! Why did I even bother with you? It's not as if you are any better than other men, in fact you are worse, too handsome, too rich, an over-inflated ego and no idea about anything normal at all. You can't even bring yourself to go out on one date with me, which is all I really wanted.

16/12/10

I'm cold. I want to cuddle up with you on the sofa, please...My daughter wrote her car off up the back of a stationary van.I have had new shelves and storage units built in the lounge, but now I have to paint them.I miss you.

18/12/10

Good morning… I hope Madam did her job and got you up nice and early to get her presents. Sadly mine are all past that stage of birthday excitement, which is one of the things I miss, surprisingly.

20/12/10

I'm wrapping presents, eating chocolate Brazil nuts, drinking freshly ground coffee and watching the snow fall softly past the window… a perfect Christmas? No, because this year I thought I would be with you. This year I thought I would finally find happiness and love.Please meet me. Just once. Just to see, then I'll leave you in peace, well your inbox at least…

25/12/10

So it's Christmas morning and it should be a happy time, but like Alice in Wonderland, I'm drowning in my own tears.

I didn't want your money.

I just wanted to make you smile.

You put me down the bottom of a muddy hole upside down anyway. And I shall stay here.

27/12/10

On this day you and your children have my sympathy and hope for a happier future. This poem reflects how I feel about you.

Bid me to live, and I will live
Thy protestant to be;
Or bid me love, and I will give
A loving heart to thee.

A heart as soft, a heart as kind,
A heart as sound and free,
As in the whole world thou canst find,
That heart I'll give to thee.

Bid that heart stay, and it will stay,
To honour thy decree;
Or bid it languish quite away
And 't shall do so for thee.

Bid me to weep, and I will weep,
While I have eyes to see;
And having none, yet I will keep
A heart to weep for thee.

Bid me despair, and I'll despair,
Under that cypress tree;
Or bid me die, and I will dare
E'en Death, to die for thee.

Thou art my life, my love, my heart,
The very eyes of me;
And hast command of every part,
To live and die for thee."

Robert Herrick 1591-1674

I'm sorry, but I love you too.

01/01/11

Dear ****.

I wish you and your family a Happy New Year.

It is with regret that my year will not be as happy as it was last year, when you first replied to my emails. It will be empty, barren and lifeless

It was irresponsible of me to entertain the idea of ever being given the chance of realising my dream of finally meeting you, and maybe at the very least becoming your friend, or at the very best, living in a house and location of your choice at your expense, with my family, enabling me to always be available for whatever you required of me and hoping that one day you would not only be my Master, but my lover, friend, partner and confidant. That I could be a mother to your children and finally know that I was where I was supposed to be. Imagine, with our obvious life similarities and sexual proclivities, what a wonderful relationship we would have.

Yes, it was irresponsible of me to believe all that you told me, reaching the wrong conclusions, wanting the impossible. How did I ever come to the conclusion that on your return from Pakistan you would turn up in your Bentley, with MI6 body guards, wearing a dinner jacket and take me to dinner? Where did I get that from? How stupid am I?

You have never given me a solid reason to think you might have been serious. You have never trusted me with your children's first names, never swapped phone numbers, never rung me for a chat, never sent me photos, as promised, of places you visited, never sent me a new photo of you, the list goes on, but didn't you once ask for my address? Don't you think that gave me the right to hope?

I apologise for my assumptions, my stupidity, my continued, indefatigable adoration for you and my constant interruptions to your perfect life, but I would really like to know why. Why did you stop emailing? Was there never any hope for me? Or is this a barrier you can't cross? Is it you that is not ready to move on and embrace a new future with a totally gorgeous, sexy, but insane woman?

I was ready to give up this life for another completely alien one if it contained you. You cannot deny the connection we have. You are the only man who 'gets' me, who laughs at the same things I laugh at, however inappropriate, and can tolerate my emotional diatribe at certain times of the month. The only man who understands what it's like to bring three children up on your own, with little help from family members, two teenage boys and one stubborn, little madam.

Yes, you are the only man.

Again I wish you a Happy New Year, with or without me. No doubt I will write again. I can't for some inexplicable reason stop myself. Other men have come and gone and I barely remember them now, but with you there is no such respite and I have tried hard to forget you, but maybe I am bound to you for life as a slave, maybe this mind, body, soul thing really does exist. I thought it was supposed to work both ways though...

I love you... I'm almost 99.9% certain, even without knowing your kiss. I know this, because when I edit each document I've saved from our conversations, while I laugh at our imaginary antics, I also become more and more depressed each time, my despair almost unbearable. I shall of course continue to send you the completed documents and if I ever manage to collate them into a book I shall send it to you first for your approval, before I see if I can get it published, so please acknowledge this email, so I know you know of my intentions at least, otherwise I shall definitely have to come to your gate and ask for you... I couldn't put those in the post for anyone to find, now could I!

Before I go, just remember I wouldn't have had my tongue pierced for any other man, no matter how much money they offered me!

Don't you think it's a shame to waste it?Come and get me...

10/01/11

Dear ****,

Please come back online. I can't concentrate on anything anymore, I only think of you. I can't even drive; I practically ran two red lights!

I know you don't want me properly and I'd never be your choice if you were looking for someone, but I can't go on not knowing where you are and if you are alive or dead. I really would like to meet you for coffee or something.

I don't know what I've done wrong?

Please contact me again,

P.S. You are chocolate to me.

18/01/11

It's that time of year again... You know, Valentine's day! Well I'm not writing you any more stupid, fucking love poems (they haven't worked for me in the past), but the things I wrote last year still apply this year.

I'm free for the next four weekends and can get to Norwich by my own car, without a chauffeur or a body guard. Do you want to have your slave or not?

I won't rest until you do, but I won't turn into a stalker either, if you don't ask for me, I won't come.

I need a break before I go back to work and I'm sure you need a break too.

Can't we just get this over with now, so I can decide that you're a complete jerk, write you off and carry on with the rest of my life completely men free?

(And no I'm not putting any kisses, at the moment I hate you!)

25/01/11

I've been shopping twice this week at M&S for more black

clothes for work. I look way sexy now. Of course the clothes wouldn't be good enough for the places you frequent, like Hotel Crillon. I was reading old emails and decided to check it out on line, very sumptuous and shame on you for teasing me so, knowing I'd never afford a room in a hotel like that, but you never did send me a credit card, which was one of your suggestions, to buy the clothes worthy of the slave of a rich, posh, arrogant, intelligent, handsome, lawyer, but to be fair, you had no intention of doing anything that you suggested. Did you? And You would have had to see it through and get me a house to put the clothes in, but that was never going to happen either! I reckon you just chickened out after Pakistan and I'm still trying to cope with that.

Guess I should just crawl back into the hole I came from, where sunshine cannot penetrate, bit like a coal bunker, but you wouldn't know what that was, far too beneath a man of your status to know what a coal bunker looks like, (My nan had one) if your house ever used coal, the only place it would have come from would be the Scullery Maid and we all know what else you'd be doing with her!

Have you read any of the documents I've sent? Maybe I should just publish them as they stand?

But although I'm in a kind of freakish state now, I would never do anything to put you, or your family in danger. I'm not into revenge. I guess I'll always be loyal to you and continue to hope something might click inside your stubborn brain and you'll miss me and finally want to see me. Either that or send someone to shoot me and put me out of my misery, but not until I get my son into army college, so around the end of September would be fine and that way I'll never reach my 50th birthday, so it'll be convenient for both of us.

P.S. You didn't go to any of Silvio Berlusconi's sex parties did you?

26/01/11

You haven't answered the Valentine message. I had an idea though. Book us a room (or two) at Hotel Crillon, I'm sure I could get a flight to Paris on my own and a dress in Monsoon, then we could meet in complete secret for one weekend, instead of me driving to Norwich... Fulfil one fantasy for me before you have me shot.

27/01/11

I miss you.
Please talk to me again.
I'm so unhappy.
I'll do anything you ask.
Please come back.
Don't leave me on my own like this...

02/02/11

(Well it looks like I'm just part of the 80% of the population that must be 'removed'!)

This 'Twitter' is certainly an eye-opener. Shall I tell them I know who rules the world and it won't make a blind bit of difference what they say, or what they do, they will never win, never make a difference, because 'He' does exactly as 'He' pleases, with no conscience and doesn't care whose heart 'He' breaks, or who 'He' hurts, everyone below him and outside of his circle is just insignificant!

I liked you better when you were at home making Marmite toast for your daughter.

I nearly came to your house, but I posted you some Brazil nuts instead. I don't want to turn into a stalker freak, but you don't make it easy and I can't forget you and clear you from my life as easily as you clear me away.

I've considered spending a weekend in Norwich, then pretending I have a parcel for you, so I can ask the postman which house you live in (the address would be smudged in the rain, so I couldn't read it), then I can make sure you have received what I've sent and you do live where you said you lived.

I've considered using my savings, which would put me in debt when my mortgage finishes and I have no money to pay off the deficit left by the crap endowment, and going to Malta with my aunt to see my Grandfather's grave, but then I could go round Gozo and see if I could find you there, or your house at least. I could go to Calypso's cave, walk where you've walked... Shit see! Stalker freak!

One meeting with you is all I ask... No that's a lie, I want to spend my life with you, I want to keep your bed warm. I want to laugh with you, etc. You've heard all this before.

Send for me please.

Tell me you read this.

Tell me you still own me.

11/02/11

Another document for you.

I still miss you.

I still cry, because you don't email me anymore.

I finished working for the lady who was my first cleaning job today.

I then created another document called 'Waiting', determined to continue emailing him until he answered me, because the last time he stopped it was two years before I heard from him again. On editing this I see that it would be pointless to add it to my book, because it is really a diary of events in my life coupled with my pleading for him to write back to me and torturing myself with thoughts about whether or not he had been real. The only thing of interest is the following poem I wrote for him, which came from him once commenting that I would sound like a train whilst having an orgasm.

28/08/11

I can't sleep, so I wrote you a poem.

Spread out naked on cool sheets in the
warmth of the night.

She lies awake in the heat of her desire,
passion rising, as ovulation peaks.

Thoughts of him invade her head, imagination
fired, all inhibitions have fled,

He throws her down, deep inside, pinching nipples as he rides.

Gasping, moaning, head side to side,

A screaming train speeds into the night,

Shuddering, shaking, the platform reached,

Steam escaping, extreme heat.

Eyes close, breath returns to a normal pace,

Smiling, sleeping, peaceful face.

I love you. XXX

POSTSCRIPT

I continued writing to him for another year, and then a man wrote 'RIP' on his Facebook profile. I had several email conversations with this man, who was his friend, but worked for him too, he was ex MI5, who finally told me that 'he' had been betrayed by his security in his hotel, kidnapped by Al Qaeda and killed in Pakistan; I assume he was beheaded. He told me that his body was to be exchanged with the body of Osama Bin Laden, who was killed long before May 2011, as the Americans claim, but apparently you cannot save a man who doesn't exist, and I cannot fall in love with one either.

I was probably the last person to hear from him before he was taken.

For the following year I was aware of being watched and followed; the 'friend' even once confirmed the location of a date I had been on the night before. I was warned not to say anything, go to the police or try and find anything out about 'him'. He told me that if I had met him at a hotel, he would have bought the hotel, supplied the staff, then burnt it down afterwards to destroy any DNA and I would not have been 'set up for life' if we hadn't got on but murdered instead. I don't believe he would have done this, but the people trying to keep him secret would have arranged it. Perhaps they will come for me after this book is published, but I died when he died in Pakistan, so it won't matter to me – only to my children and family.